THE KILLING MOON

TO BILL + SADIE

BEST WISHES

"ROBBO"

MICHAEL

About the author

Michael Robinson had a difficult childhood and was diagnosed with schizoaffective disorder at the age of seventeen.

At the age of twenty, Robinson joined the 4th Battalion Parachute Regiment, and later the 3rd Battalion Prince of Wales's Own Regiment. Upon passing out, he was awarded 'most improved recruit'.

Later into his military career, Robinson volunteered for the arduous 'Cambrian Patrol', a type of special forces training, with a view towards joining the SAS. However, during deployment in the Brecon Beacons, Robinson succumbed to hypothermia, and was ultimately sacked from the army on Christmas Eve after they had looked into his medical records.

From here, Robinson ended up in HM Prison Hull and later was locked up indefinitely under Section 37/41. He remained locked up for about three years and on release wrote about his experiences in his autobiography *Sectioned: The Book the NHS Tried to Ban* on Amazon Kindle.

As well as a soldier, other jobs Robinson has done include drummer for two successful groups, carer at a special needs school, chef, bouncer, driver and minder for a Hull escort agency. Also, he has an NVQ in catering, a diploma in Uniform Public Services, and has read law with criminology at university.

Robinson has been married to his long-term partner, Julie, for five years. He continues to support mental health campaigns with help from his local MP and other government agencies. This includes working with the Heads Together campaign, Mind, and other mental health charities.

(YouTube: "heads together campaign michael 'robbo' robinson")

He regularly helps out the homeless in Hull and other persons/groups in need where he can.

The Killing Moon is Robinson's first novel.

Michael Robinson

THE KILLING MOON

Vanguard Press

VANGUARD PAPERBACK

© Copyright 2019
Michael Robinson

The right of Michael Robinson to be identified as author of
this work has been asserted by him in accordance with the
Copyright, Designs and Patents Act 1988.

All Rights Reserved

No reproduction, copy or transmission of this publication
may be made without written permission.
No paragraph of this publication may be reproduced,
copied or transmitted save with the written permission of the
publisher, or in accordance with the provisions
of the Copyright Act 1956 (as amended).

Any person who commits any unauthorised act in relation to
this publication may be liable to criminal
prosecution and civil claims for damages.

A CIP catalogue record for this title is
available from the British Library.

ISBN 978 1 784655 61 7

All characters and events, whilst based upon real life
experiences, are not indicative, nor do they represent, real life
characters and events. All work included in this book is
entirely fictional and any resemblance to real life events or
persons is entirely coincidental.

*Vanguard Press is an imprint of
Pegasus Elliot MacKenzie Publishers Ltd.*
www.pegasuspublishers.com

First Published in 2019

**Vanguard Press
Sheraton House Castle Park
Cambridge England**

Printed & Bound in Great Britain

For Lucy - *in causa excellentiam quaerere*

Acknowledgements

There are several people I need to thank who without their input *The Killing Moon* would not be possible. First and foremost, my typists: Mitch, Laura, Chris and Michael. Had they not typed whilst I dictated, then I can safely say this work would never have been done. Also, I'd like to thank my medical team based at the Humber Centre past and present. In areas their expertise was invaluable, also their encouragement and support have been second to none, for me anyway.

I would like to thank friends and colleagues from Her Majesty's Armed Services, past and present, who have supported me and advised me on certain areas. For obvious reasons, I will not name them, but you know who you are, I know are you are and what you've done to keep me and my family safe over the years. I am grateful for your input and as well, you all know I long for the day to wear the Queen's uniform again, however doubtful. Well done, lads.

Also, I'd like to thank the SAS Authors Andy McNab and Chris Ryan, both of whom I have only met briefly, however, their work has been an inspiration and also made me realise there was a life after leaving the army.

The Jackdaws deserve recognition too for understanding why I had to leave drumming for the group in order to focus on this project. I'm so pleased we're all still mates.

I extend my thanks also to the whole team at the London School of Journalism for your encouragement, expertise and inspiration. The journey to London once a week was worth it.

I am grateful also to one of my neighbours, Anthony, who found the time to read the first drafts of *The Killing Moon*, and advise me accordingly.

I'd like to thank Stan and the team at KCFM, again for their advice and for making everything happen.

Also, I'd like to thank my family, particularly my mother and my grandmother for their endless support since the day I was born.

Anyone else who has not been mentioned, please forgive the omission, and my thoughts and prayers are with you. See you in Harry's. Mine's a Guinness.

Most importantly of all though, I would like to thank my wife Julie. You taught me to take one day at a time, you let me off the leash when I need to run, you cook the best meals in the world and you take care of me better than I do myself. Forever indebted.

Part One

Hull

Chapter One

As the plane taxied toward the bright lights of Oxford where the 747 was approaching Brize Norton, Rob Foster's mind was elsewhere. Most of the regiment had flown home three days before but as always with the infantry, the lads that were effective on the ground were always tasked to stay a bit longer. Rob couldn't get the image out of his mind of the insurgent he had to kill at close range.

He was just a boy, possibly fourteen but totally brainwashed by his manipulators who promised him he would sit at the right hand of Allah if he detonated a bomb near Rob's patrol in the southern Afghan town of Garmsir. Along with the ten other insurgents he killed, Rob had entered a world of pain but it was the fourteen-year-old that scarred his memory. Even though it was a legitimate kill, as with the rest of the kills, the rules of engagement were followed down to the letter, but there was something deeply sickening about killing children.

At the end of the tour the troop returned to Camp Bastion for a ten day debrief, from there it was two weeks R&R in Cyprus. Some of the other lads in the troop were in the same position as Rob, the glazed look in their eyes told you all there was to know. Rob had not slept properly during the two week R&R and talking to some of the younger lads, the medals that they were after at the beginning of the tour became pointless. They just wanted to get home.

As the plane came in to land, a big cheer went up when the wheels touched the tarmac. Most of the families would be there to meet them; wives, parents, children all with tears in their eyes at seeing their loved ones return. Rob didn't know if that was the case for him because he had not spoken with Annie for the best part of three months. Things weren't right between them before he went away and the argument over the sat-phone told him that he knew their marriage was over, despite the fact that she was carrying his child.

Just as he suspected, Annie wasn't at the terminal when he passed through customs and he felt a mixture of anger, remorse and jealousy as his mates got passionate kisses from their loved ones. Rob picked up his belongings and headed for the bus which would take them back to Catterick Garrison where he would be staying for the night until the regiment would be dismissed at eight a.m.

As he stepped onto the bus CSM French collared Rob. "You gonna go for selection then, Rob? If you are, I'll put you forward. You did well out there, mate, eleven confirmed is no mean feat."

Rob didn't feel like talking so just replied, "That's the plan, sir."

Selection had been on Rob's mind since he joined the army five years ago. He was due to start phase one, two weeks before he was told the regiment was going to Afghanistan and as always, the regiment was short on numbers so the CO withdrew his place. He was scheduled to start it in two months where Rob hoped he would be in the SAS.

As he sat in his seat and stared at the rain on the window as the coach weaved its way up the M1, Rob knew things weren't right. Normally he could talk after an operation but that was just a few bursts here and there in Northern Ireland. The can of Carling that the CSM had given him just made him feel sick, whilst at the same time, he had a dry taste in his mouth. He wanted to get off the bus. He wanted to be alone. He didn't want to hear anyone else's voice; but most of all he wanted the image of the fourteen-year-old insurgent out of his head.

The bus arrived in the rain at Catterick at about two in the morning. The CSM was pissed at this point and just said to the remaining troop on the bus, "Square away to your billet, lads! Parade at eight in the morning and then you can all fuck off."

Rob got to his room, dumped his gear and looked at his bed before he turned his eyes to the photograph of him and Annie in happier times on holiday in Wales. He was drained but at the same time wired, he put the photograph back onto his cabinet which had a thin layer of dust then, still in his uniform, he took off his boots, climbed into his bed and tried to sleep.

Thoughts were racing around Rob's mind as he closed his eyes. Most significantly the fourteen-year-old insurgent he had to kill but also there were other issues. The fact he was soon to be a father to an estranged wife played on him dearly, also he knew he would have to start training for selection which would probably start in a couple of months. He questioned himself, whether he was ready for it even though it had been his lifelong ambition ever since he joined the army. He turned over and he tried to sleep.

Chapter Two

While Rob slept, images of his father shouting at him raged through his mind, that was, until he started to stir. Half asleep, half conscious, then all of a sudden, a single bang. It was the unmistakable sound of a discharge from an SA80 assault rifle but this wasn't a dream. As he startled out of bed, Rob looked around the room for the danger. Within a second, he looked for his own SA80 then heard raised voices. "Quick get the medic!" Then again, "Medic, Medic, Medic!"

Rob's mouth was dry as he reached for the door handle to investigate what the commotion was and part of him said to himself, *'Let somebody else deal with it,'* but the curiosity within him was too strong. He opened the door and stepped into the hallway. Two doors down on the right, a bedroom door was open and there was Tony with tears in his eyes as he looked at Rob. Tony was stood outside of Andy's door and Rob quickly worked out what had happened.

As he approached Andy's room, he saw Andy, still in uniform lying on the bed but with a mixture of blood and gore hanging off the walls. His SA80 assault rifle had fallen to the floor and it was a surreal moment seeing one of the regiment, albeit not a close friend, lying down with half the back of his head removed. Rob knew straight away there was nothing he could do for him, even if Andy was still alive, his brain was dead anyway and it wouldn't be long before his body succumbed. Tony turned to Rob and said,

"Can't you do out, mate?"

At the same time, two medics from the guard house were rushing down the corridor. Rob took Tony by the arm to lead him out of the room as the medics came in. He turned to Tony and said, "Let 'em get on with it, mate."

Tony was welled up and said that Andy had got a 'Dear John' letter when he got back to his room.

"That slag Ellen from The Ship Inn, we all warned him about her, apparently she started fucking a sergeant from Signals while he was halfway through his tour!"

Twenty minutes after the suicide, CSM French turned up still drunk from the night before but you could tell it was just as hard on him, losing one of his men. He went to see Andy's body and then placed a private on the door so no one could enter except for the Redcaps (Military Police) who would be on their way to investigate. The CSM turned to Rob and Tony and said, "Lads, get down to the cookhouse, I'll have a chat with you there. Just need to square things out with the OC."

As Rob and Tony made their way across the parade ground, Tony was inconsolable whereas Rob was more numb, almost hardened to death.

The next day, final parade was a sombre affair. Even by Rob's standards, he was completely and utterly shattered. The Redcaps came down to the cookhouse within an hour and proceeded to question him and Tony, as well as the others for the next three hours, as if it had been them who pulled the trigger. He didn't manage to see Tony after that but the way he was talking, it wouldn't be long before he left the army. Andy's family had turned up to meet him at the gate in the morning and were quickly ushered away to be given the news.

At eight a.m., the parade took place with the CO offering a few words of comfort to Andy's mates, with the obligatory words of well done for the work in Afghanistan but even that seemed like a hundred years ago now.

Just before the parade was dismissed, Rob was asked to see the CO immediately after the parade, he assumed it was something to do with Andy. He sat outside his office for five minutes before he was ushered in. The CO sat there and looked up at Rob, "I know you want to get off, Foster, so I'll keep this brief. Special Forces selection starts in three months. Do you still want to be on it?"

Although Rob was surprised how soon this had come about, he knew better than to question. It wasn't the status quo.

"Yes, sir, absolutely."

"OK then," the CO replied. "You'll receive a letter in the post in the next couple of days. Make the most of your time off. Dismissed."

Chapter Three

Within an hour Rob was in a taxi in his civilian clothes and with some of his kit headed for the station at Richmond. Again, he avoided conversation with the taxi driver. Three hours later, having caught the train from Richmond to Hull, Rob stepped off the platform at the Hull Interchange and walked to the taxi rank. It was almost a surreal moment for him watching everyday people going about their everyday lives. All of them were oblivious to what had been going on in the world and what had been done, in their name, to protect their civil rights and civil liberties. Rob didn't know if this was a good or bad thing.

He took a black cab to Hessle where he got out at Hessle Square and decided to walk the short distance to his house where the inevitable argument would happen between him and Annie. As he approached the house, he realised that he didn't have his key and noticed that the curtains were drawn. It was about one o'clock in the afternoon and so this meant Annie was out.

As he approached the front lawn, he noticed the grass had not been cut for some time. He knocked a few times on the door with no answer so he made his way around the back. As he looked through the windows, he saw pots in the sink that looked like they had been left there for weeks. He took out his mobile phone and tried to call Annie but the line went dead.

He was just about to smash the window to gain access round the back when Angie, the woman next door, called him. "Your grass really needs cutting, Rob, it's been like that for weeks."

"Have you still got a key, Angie? I can't get hold of Annie."

"I think she's gone to her mother's," she replied, almost prying for more information that could be used as good gossip later on.

"I wouldn't know, I haven't heard owt from her," Rob replied, starting to get annoyed and added, "I've been away for the last six months fighting for democracy."

Angie disappeared into her house and returned two minutes later with the key. "Well now you're back, you can cut the grass. Also, the windows look like they haven't been cleaned in months."

Rob bit his lip. "I'll get on with it."

The damp smell as he opened the door was an obvious sign that Annie had left him, also the piles of unopened post were the tell tale signs. He looked to see if she had left him a note to let him know where she would be but there was nothing. As he opened the fridge door, the contents were bare except for an open tin of beans which had started to go rusty and a pint of milk which was three months out of date so she must have left him not long after the argument on the sat-phone when he was in Afghanistan.

However, to Rob, it was good to be home in familiar surroundings. He had a month off now in which to do what he liked, although he had no doubt that Annie would have cleaned out his bank account. He made his way upstairs, turned on the heating and saw the empty open drawers where Annie had kept her belongings but he decided he would try and contact her later. He took his shoes off, climbed into the unmade bed and slept.

Rob slept really well in his own bed and although he still had the nightmares, after six hours sleep, he felt recuperated but again the images in his mind woke him. It was still daylight outside and for the first time in about six months, Rob didn't know what to do with himself. He thought about going to Annie's mother's place but Annie's family had never approved of Rob anyway and the last thing he wanted was more confrontation.

Rob took a cold shower. He found some clean underwear, put on his jeans and decided to go for a pint. It was just turning dusk on the spring evening as he locked the door behind him, he could hear the faint bird song. It felt very calming almost like a comfort blanket to hear the birds sing but he still had a lot of pent up aggression inside him of which he did not know the source.

Rob took the short walk into the square to the Admiral pub which was fairly busy with revellers and the landlord, Harry, saw him and rushed over to shake his hand. "Rob! You're back, thank God you're home safe."

It was comforting to Rob to be greeted by a friendly face although again he felt he could not open up to Harry despite his sincerity. Harry turned and said, "What are you having, a Guinness?"

"Aye, spot on, mate, my mouth feels like my throat's been cut."

Rob had drunk in the Admiral since Harry had been the landlord. Basically, because it was the best pint of Guinness you could get, not only in Hessle but possibly in Hull. Rob watched with anticipation as Harry pulled off half a pint of the black stuff and let it settle whilst pulling himself one too. When the drinks were poured, Harry and Rob found a quiet corner. Harry knew what was coming. Rob turned and said,

"Annie's left me you know."

Harry took a swig of his Guinness and said, "I know, she's gone to her mother's on Barrow Lane. She's been out shopping a few times for baby clothes with our Sarah. An' our Sarah's got it coming too cause she's pregnant after a fling on New Year's Eve."

Rob looked surprised and said, "Fuckin' 'ell! That doesn't sound like your Sarah, who's the father?"

Harry looked bitter as he put his pint down and said, "Leave it."

Rob could see the conversation turning cold so he changed the subject. "So have you seen owt of me old man?"

"Yeah he comes in now and again. Apparently, he'd been tappin' up Annie for money just before she left to live with her mother. I don't have a problem with him coming in here but I know he's upset a few people recently."

"Like who?" Rob questioned.

"Big John Squire, he got pissed and spilt his pint all over his wife's new coat. I have warned him but John says he's got it in for him."

Rob replied, "Fuck me, six years after me mum's death, you'd think he'd have grown up a bit by now."

"I know, Rob, but he's still hurtin'."

"It's a pity he didn't realise what he had when Mum was alive."

"I know, mate, but leave the past behind, where it should be. Anyway, speak of the devil, look who's just walked in."

Rob looked over his shoulder to see his dad walk toward the bar ordering a double Grouse. Harry stood up and said, "Well I'd better get back to work then, are you ok then, mate?"

"Get us another one in and one for the ol' fella and we'll leave it at that, mate."

Rob stood up and made his way to the bar when his dad saw him and his face lit up. His dad, Rick, held his hand out and as Rob approached, he could tell his dad had not shaved for some time. He looked scruffy with his four-day old jeans and beer-stained shirt.

"Welcome back to the real world, son," Rick said.

"Now then, Dad, how're you keepin'?"

"So-so," his dad replied. "Getting by on my pension, but that doesn't say a lot."

At the same time, Harry put two Guinness on the bar and Rob handed over a tenner. Harry disappeared, and Rob turned to his dad. "Annie's left me, you know."

"There's plenty more fish in the sea, son." His dad grinned. Rob was annoyed at the comment, but bit his lip.

Rob questioned his dad. "How come you've been tapping up Annie for money?"

"Oh, come on, son, I just needed to square away the bookies," Rick replied.

"Also, you've upset John Squire, and his son Callum's a fucking maniac."

Rick could see Rob was wound up, but played it down. "Oh come on, you know what it's like, we were having a few beers, got a bit carried away, and a few things were said. He'll be all right once he calms down."

A couple of hours into the evening, and Rob was well and truly pissed. He had not drunk in a while, and so he was not used to consuming so much alcohol. Rob was drinking a lot. About half an hour before last orders, his dad Rick tapped him up for £50 and then disappeared.

Rob was just about to go home, when Callum Squire walked in with two of his crew. Rob got another pint from the bar, and sat and watched Callum. From Callum's body language, Rob had seen his type before. The type of person that thinks of himself as a hard man, or certainly gave the persona that he assumed as much. Rob smiled to himself. Callum probably was a hard man, with his crew in the pub on a Friday night. The golden rule was not to underestimate anybody, but by the same token, looking at Callum's body language alone, he wouldn't be able to run more than a hundred metres without collapsing.

To Rob, this said it all. When Rob was on the training wing in the infantry, young lads would make out they were the hardest men in the bar. In the morning, however, when they had to get up and do their work, they became quivering, shivering, pathetic wrecks. Some even cried. The training team would often ask these individuals where the hard man was that was in the bar last night. Usually, these were the recruits that didn't last and quit.

Callum looked up and saw Rob, and continued to give Rob death stares as he turned to his mates. Callum looked back at Rob, in an attempt to intimidate him.

"Thank you," Rob thought to himself, "that's just what I needed."

Rob picked himself up and finished the last of his pint. He made his way over to Callum and his crew. All three looked at Rob with contempt as he approached, and Rob turned to Callum and said, "Here, Cal, can I buy you a drink? Just want to square things away so you won't bother my old man."

Callum continued with the 'hard-man' persona and replied, "Well then, Foster, you'd better tell him to move out of the area. When I see him, he's gonna be squealing like a pig."

"Don't be like that, Cal." Rob smiled. "Come on, mate, let me buy you a drink."

"Get us all a double sambucca and lemonade and fuck off then, soldier boy."

Again, Rob smiled. "It's a bit strong for you that, mate. Wouldn't you rather have a lemonade?"

At this point, the music was booming, and the atmosphere in the pub was light, with the exception of this corner of the room.

Callum took offence "Give us your wallet now, Foster, and fuck off."

Rob turned and said, "Tell you what, I'll get you all a lemonade and lime."

Callum's arm raised to grab Rob by the shirt, at which point, Rob spun his arm out to block. Rob brought his knee up at the same time to Callum's groin. As Callum went down, instinctively, Rob threw his left fist into one of Callum's crew, splitting his lip and breaking one of his teeth. Rob then turned to the other croney, grabbing him by the ears and launching his head against his nose. Callum tried to recover, and smashed a glass on the bar, but Rob was too fast. Rob picked up a barstool and smashed it on Callum's hand which was holding the glass. Rob grabbed Callum by the throat, Rob then placed his leg behind Callum's feet and pushed him to the ground.

As he went down, Callum struggled for his balance, however it was in vain. All he did was push glasses off the bar, sending them crashing like cymbals to the floor. Whilst Callum was down, Rob used the heel of his foot to smash into Callum's face. It was at this point the revellers in the pub moved away from the fight, just as Harry came to sort out the trouble. Harry's first concerns were for Rob, but seeing the three bodies on the floor, he had to make sure that Rob didn't kill anybody.

Harry grabbed Rob. "Come on, they've had enough, and you know better," Harry said. Even by Harry's standards, the look in Rob's eyes told him Rob was full of hate. Harry tried again, shaking Rob by the shoulders. "Come on, mate, look at me. You know better." Harry then got a response, and ushered Rob away from the fight scene. Harry then turned to the three on the floor. "Pick yourselves up, lads, and fuck off. You're all barred."

Chapter Four

Three days after the fight at the Admiral pub, Annie had still not been in touch, although Rob was certain Annie would have heard about Rob being on leave, and almost certainly heard about the fight in the pub.

Rob tried to settle back into a normal routine, but even Rob couldn't remember what normal was. Most of the time, he moped about the house. He tried to read, but could not concentrate. So instead, he went jogging several times and listened to music. The music itself was a great therapy, and it blocked out all the horrors of events he had witnessed. So much so, that he even managed to cut the grass, just to keep Angie off his back. Although he started to clean the windows, he gave up when it started raining.

Within a few days, the letter arrived confirming his place for SAS selection. He didn't have long to prepare, and the letter was short and to the point. He needed to turn up at Sennybridge Training Camp in Wales at eight a.m. in early July, along with the kit which was on the list enclosed in the letter. Also within the letter contained a few short do's and don'ts, the usual stuff: no alcohol, no unauthorised equipment. At the end of the letter in block capitals was the final point, perhaps the most important, that of security. It read:

'FOR OBVIOUS REASONS, YOU SHOULD NOT DISCUSS YOUR APPLICATION OR ANY OF THE DETAILS CONTAINED IN THIS LETTER WITH ANYONE OUTSIDE OF YOUR IMMEDIATE FAMILY.

I LOOK FORWARD TO RECEIVING YOUR DOCUMENTATION, AND GOOD LUCK.'

Rob read the letter again. He had mixed feelings of aspiration, and was more than ready for the challenge of SAS selection. Although he was more-or-less ready physically, he felt mentally almost drained of energy, but at the same time, he knew if he tried hard and worked hard, he was sure he would pass.

That afternoon, he started to prepare his kit that he would use in order to train for selection. He filled his bergen with all of the relevant equipment, and topped it up with things he found around the house. Also, he got a map of the local villages which included the Wolds Way, and started planning various routes along the local hills that he could run in order to get a good head-start on Phase One. Within two hours, he'd mapped his first route and was making his way to Brantingham to start on the notorious Spout Hill. From there, he would make his way over the hills and through the woods towards Welton.

Over the next weeks and months, Rob trained furiously. Occasionally, he would stop and have a pint of Guinness in one of the local pubs, but never more than two. At the same time, he tried to get as much rest in between training as he possibly could. But since coming back from Afghan, sleep was hard, as well as the other domestic issues that were playing on his mind.

All Rob wanted to focus on was passing, it was almost as if nothing else mattered. He wanted to be a part of something that only the privileged few had achieved. A family of brothers whose outlook was not saluting on a parade ground with an armful of medals, but more completing the task at hand, under any circumstances. Almost a band of misfits. Rob felt he'd be at home here.

Chapter Five

THREE MONTHS LATER

Major Alan 'Chalky' White sat behind his desk just as the Adjutant brought him his first cup of coffee at seven a.m. Major White, or 'Chalky', as he was referred to, had been in the SAS since 1974 and was well-known as a good officer, serving in not only the Falklands, but also several tours of Northern Ireland and as a CSM in the First Gulf War.

Although he was known not to mince his words, he was one of the few officers that was approachable. Having worked his way through the ranks, and he was less than a year away for his retirement and this eventuality worried him more than any other operation that he had ever been on. Now his position was in charge of the next selection for twenty-two SAS.

On his desk was the list of every candidate that was to take place that morning for selection. He glanced through the names, but they meant nothing to him. From his experience, he knew it was how an operator conducted himself in the field which counted more than the amount of references he could get from the officers in the bar. The only other person in the room was Sergeant Nott, again, Nott was ten years into his SAS career, but also was not as high up in the ranks as he would have liked to have been, aged forty. However, his drinking habit and early teething problems within the regiment had almost prevented him from going any further up the food chain.

Nott was Chalky's eyes and ears. Not only on the parade ground, but on the whole of selection. As far as Chalky was concerned, if there was any discrepancy with any of the students, it was Nott's job to uncover it, and bring it to light. Both men took this role very seriously.

Chalky turned to Nott and said, "Do any names stand out to you, Sergeant?"

Nott replied in a tough, north-east accent. "Aye, boss, there's several Paras in that have done tours in Iraq and Afghan, also a couple of Marines that I quite fancy to make the grade. There'll be the usual rubbish that won't get past week one, and as you know, boss, there'll be twenty or so that'll turn up late today, or not at all. There is one name however that stands out, boss."

Chalky's ears pricked up.

"There's a guy from Hull, his name's Foster. On his last tour, he got eleven confirmed."

Chalky thought for a moment, then replied, "Eleven confirmed? That's some going. But has he got the tools to handle it, Sergeant?"

"Remains to be seen, boss," replied Nott. "That's what selection's for."

Chapter Six

Rob pulled into Sennybridge car park at seven-thirty. Rob reported at the gatehouse with his documentation, having slept the night before in a bed and breakfast in Brecon, keeping to himself, avoiding conversation and getting an early night. Rob did not want to get there too early, and appear too keen, but by the same token, he did not want to arrive late on the very first day of selection.

Rob had been to Sennybridge before, and knew the layout of the camp. He parked his car, and thought for a second. Again, the image of the fourteen-year-old scarred his memory, but he shook it off, and said to himself, "*I've got a job to do.*" He grabbed his kit and reported to the Mess Hall to await further instructions. When he arrived, he was pleased that other students were there before him, so he wouldn't get noticed as being the first to arrive. A quick glance at his watch told him he did not want to be any later.

The noise in the room was a mixture of nervous laughter and quiet contemplation between the student body. Rob got a cup of tea from the urn and made his way to a quiet corner where he had left his kit. Since all the books about the SAS had been written, Rob had studied these and had a fair idea of what selection was going to entail. The first thing he had drilled into himself was to be the 'grey man', and not get noticed.

Within ten minutes, the Mess Hall was full. There must have been one hundred and seventy guys all thinking they were good enough, some of them had obviously been on the piss the night before, bragging to the local skirt how they were in the SAS. But Rob could tell, at this time in the morning, they were in a shit state. At the end of the Mess Hall was a stage with a microphone on it and a desk for reading off. At exactly one minute to eight, Chalky walked in front of the platform with Sergeant Nott and the rest of the training team behind him. The whole room went eerily quiet.

"Morning, gentlemen," said Chalky as he addressed the student body. "My name is Major White, and I am in charge of phase one and two of the selection procedure for twenty-two SAS Regiment. What you are all about to undertake is the hardest and most taxing Special Forces selection in the world. I hope you have all appreciated the need to prepare for the next six months, because those of you who make it to the end will find it is the most difficult and arduous six months of your life. However, for those that do make the grade, the regiment will accept you with open arms and you'll be among the ranks of not only the finest soldiers in the world, but also a unique band of men. Since I did selection in 1974, some things have changed." But then he added, "But not much. If I could give you any advice, it would be do not try and cheat or answer back the training team. Also, and perhaps the most important, when the chips are down, keep your sense of humour." He added, "Remember, gentlemen, it's harder to keep your beret than to get it. Good luck on selection."

Chalky then turned to Sergeant Nott to invite him to take the microphone. Sergeant Nott approached and introduced himself to the students.

"On the wall behind you, you will see sheets of paper with your name on. This will tell you where your accommodation is and what cadre you belong to. Drop your kit in your barracks and be on the parade ground in PT kit in half an hour. One more thing, you're not here on holiday, lads," he added menacingly. "That's it, square away."

The room went eerily quiet, like a set of rabbits stuck in the headlights. But then, when it sank in, the crowd dispersed.

An hour later, the training team was beasting the recruits. All sorts of expletives were being shouted. Rob knew the score, and he also knew that this was just to clear off the lads that didn't stand a chance. Although no one had quit just yet, an hour into selection, some of the lads were already being sick. This included the lads that had been on the piss the night before. The whole routine was just a beasting, the usual. The Sergeant would shout, "Press up position!" and before the student body had chance to do as they were told, he would shout, "Sit up position!" It was designed to confuse, not to see how physically fit you were.

The next thing, all the men were told to get into three ranks. Most of the cadre managed this no problem. The training team then addressed the selection. "Right then, guys, we're going for a run. Anyone who doesn't want to come, say so now." Although no one said a word, Rob knew some of the bodies on the car park wouldn't keep up and would be back home on tonight's train.

The whole week carried on in the same vein; intense and full-on. Although only two people left on the first day, by the end of the first week, roughly a quarter of the student body which started that morning on the parade ground, had gone. It was after this week the instructors eased off a bit on the shouting, and so began selection.

Rob fought on with the course, and tried his best to keep to himself, avoiding conversation with the other recruits. If truth be told, he was enjoying the process so far, even though he was tired and had sores on his shoulders from the weight of his bergen, as well as the huge blisters like saucers that were appearing on his feet. But to Rob, he felt alive. He'd almost forgotten about Annie, and was enjoying concentrating on the job at hand. If Rob stood out at all, it was probably as a bit of a loner. But with still over one hundred men on phase one of selection, Rob didn't see this as a problem at this stage.

Most of the days were spent running up and down the Brecon Beacons with huge weights on his back and the sun was bakingly hot. Rob combatted this by getting as much fluid as he could inside himself. The routes became more and more difficult, and not only this, Rob noticed the routes were getting longer and longer. However, to Rob, this just meant he was getting closer to the endurance march on the fan dance which would be the final test on the Brecon Beacons.

In between checkpoints, he would get asked a question, and seemingly pointless questions at that, such as, 'What's twelve times thirty-four?' 'Who is the Home Secretary?' 'What colour was the car on the parade ground this morning?' Rob answered these as best as he could, but it was hard when all he could hear inside his mind was his heavy breathing. Some of the instructors would say to Rob, "Remember this number," and then they would reel off six digits and tell them to disclose it at the next checkpoint, which would be four hours march away. Occasionally, the weather would turn, and the rain would come, which was a relief to Rob, when his body temperature was so hot. But also, by the same token, this made the ground underfoot slippery, and Rob had to take more care not to fall over and twist his ankle.

In the evening, when the day was over, Rob would get a shower, get something to eat, make light conversation with the other recruits, and then get an early night. The funny thing was, he slept easier. It was almost as if he was too exhausted to do anything else, but Rob knew he could make the grade.

A week later was test week where all the recruits took part in the notorious fan dance, an extremely taxing endurance march on the Brecon Beacons. Several times on the 'dance', Rob saw other students exhausted on the side of the mountain, but this just spurred Rob on further, giving himself nothing but 100 per cent although, even by Rob's standards, he wasn't sure how much left he had to give. By the end of the exercise, only forty or so recruits had made the grade. Although Rob was proud of himself for achieving such a lot, he was under no illusion that selection was over.

Chapter Seven

Rob, with the rest of the recruits, had a well-earned break of a week. Then, it was back to continuation training. It was here that Rob seemed to come into his own, skills such as fighting in built-up areas, weapons handling, demolition skills, photography, driving skills, parachute training. Also, he learnt some of the black arts, involving various forms of espionage, including how to make fake IDs as well as more basic skills such as medical skills, not just in the field but the regiment sent the remaining cadre to various hospitals in the UK to work in their casualty department.

The regiment even brought in hardened criminals in order to teach the recruits various criminal activities, such as how to break into a car and hotwire it. Also, these misfits gave lectures on how to break into safes, the best way to burgle a house, what tactics you need in order to be a successful shoplifter. All skills that could be useful to an SAS operative. All the time, Rob and the other recruits were constantly being assessed. Not only on what they'd learnt, but what they'd experienced. Again, Rob took to this, lapping up all the information like a kitten with a bowl of cream. Although this month on selection was not as taxing physically, mentally there was a lot of information to absorb in a short space of time. Although two or three of the other recruits saw it as a month to go on the piss, again Rob just kept to one or maybe two pints of Guinness throughout this period, determined to make the grade.

By the end of the second month, there were thirty recruits left. And although Rob made conversations with them, he did not want to get too close to any of the others in case they didn't make it to the end. Again, he felt like he was a loner, and it was around this time that the directing staff picked up on this.

After another week off on leave, the regiment sent the student body to the jungle in Belize. As soon as Rob stepped off the plane, the sweltering heat hit him like a cake being brought out of the oven. All Rob did for the next month was sweat. When he got to the jungle, all he could see was a sea of green and within the first few days, one of the recruits started to come down with claustrophobia. The directing staff soon picked up on this, and the individual was taken from the jungle, never to be seen again. He was not going to make it either.

Rob lost count of the number of insects that were feasting on his skin, and when the rain came, it was like a monsoon. He also lost count of the number of snakes and spiders and other nasties that he had seen whilst painstakingly trying to map read through a constant green enemy. However, one of the good things about being in the jungle was the fact he got a good twelve hours sleep in his hammock, as there was no movement on a night, due to poor navigation.

The regiment lost another ten blokes on this phase of selection. One was bitten, and came down with a chronic fever. One or two others decided selection wasn't for them, and just quit. A fourth, however, received an ultimatum in the post from his wife, a letter which said his marriage was over if he didn't stop this soldiering nonsense and come home. The rest were failed because of poor soldiering skills, lack of discipline, or wrong attitude. The remaining twenty or so recruits headed back to the UK for the final phase of selection.

It was this phase that would ultimately tax Rob more than anything he had ever done before.

Chapter Eight

Major White had a mixture of feelings regarding the student body, some he thought were first class, and this included Foster. However, some still needed to be tested. Most of all, he was relieved that no one had died this year on selection. In previous years, during winter selection, soldiers had frozen on the Brecon Beacons. Also, summer selections had seen guys succumb to heat exhaustion and this was quickly jumped upon by the national press. It then fell upon Major White and the rest of the team to inform the next of kin. No matter how many times he had to contact the families, the job never got any easier.

Behind closed doors, in Major White's office, were the rest of the directing staff. This included Sergeant Nott. Nearly all of the staff had lost or gained money placing bets on who would make the grade. Chalky never encouraged this, but didn't feel it was a disciplinary matter either, as it had been this way for years.

"Right then, guys, of the student body we have remaining, what are the relevant facts and information you can tell me about them?"

Sergeant Nott was the first to speak. "My money's on Burnsey and Foster, boss. Burnsey's showing great leadership skills, and he's not frightened to get a bollocking. Also, Foster has given 100%, and seems to be quite a tough bastard, even though he tends to keep to himself."

Chalky remarked, "Does that mean he doesn't go with the flow, Sergeant, or is he an introvert?"

"I'd say a bit of both, boss, I think he works well on his own, that's where his strengths lie, but, again, I can't say he wouldn't be an effective member of the team."

Chalky turned to the rest of the directing staff. "Has anyone got anything to add?"

Trooper Collins, who was new to the training team added, "I agree wholeheartedly with Sergeant Nott. But I noticed, when we were in the jungle, Foster often had nightmares and talked in his sleep. This may be PTSD, boss, given his previous history."

"I see," said Chalky, and thought for a moment. "Well it's obvious Foster will do okay on escape and evasion, I've no doubt about that. But the screws are gonna have to be turned on the resistance to interrogation phase. If he's of a weak constitution, then the intelligence and psychology team need to pick up on it. I don't want any of the lads that pass to crack in the field."

"We'll get on it, boss," replied Sergeant Nott, and within half an hour, the meeting was concluded.

Chapter Nine

The remaining student body, including Rob, were ushered into a classroom to be given a briefing on the final exercise. At this point, most of the student body had bonded quite well, and again, this was not a priority to Rob, as he just wanted to pass. The training team entered the classroom, followed by Chalky White. Chalky then made his way to the front of the class to address the student body.

"Morning, gentlemen, and congratulations for making it this far into SAS selection. Everyone in this room has proved themselves to be of good caliber and the type of men who we require in Special Forces. However, the job is not over yet, gentlemen. The final phase of selection will last two to three weeks and includes the escape and evasion, followed by the resistance to interrogation. The latter is where you are well and truly tested. When I arrived here today," said Chalky to the remaining recruits, "eighteen of you have made it to this point. However, do not think you have passed selection yet. I expect to lose another five to ten of you at the end of these next few weeks. Follow the rules, and keep to what you've been trained, and you may pass SAS selection. Good luck, gentlemen, and I will see you on the other side."

Chalky then turned to Sergeant Nott. "You can take over from here now, Sergeant."

"Right then, guys, when we leave here in the next hour, you will all be strip-searched, and given ill-fitting clothes to wear. Obviously, these will be army khaki green and may not fit properly, however, you are not to disregard this clothing and change into anything other than what you have been issued. Also, there will be a series of checkpoints where you must make contact with an agent in the field. From there, you will be given another checkpoint in order to rendezvous with another agent accordingly." Nott then added, "Has anyone got any questions at this point, guys?"

Everyone looked like they understood.

"Whilst on escape and evade, you will be given an old tobacco tin filled with a fishing hook and line, waterproof matches, a small penknife, and other things that you would need in the field, if you were on the run. You are to live off the land for the next two weeks, whilst you are pursued by a hunter force who have all the most up to date tracking equipment available to them. Let me make this clear, guys, you are not to use roads, you are not to enter buildings. Do not approach members of the public, should you come across any hill walkers. Also," he added, "no money or personal documents are allowed on this exercise. Anyone who does not understand this, say so now."

Again, the room remained silent.

"The hunter force, I believe, are the Parachute Regiment, and they have all been given a heads-up that if you are caught, the para that catches you, will get three days paid leave. Another thing I should make clear, guys, at the end of escape and evade, we'll proceed immediately with resistance to interrogation. Basically, from the moment you are caught. This is a two-week exercise, guys. If you get caught on day one, then you have thirteen days of stress and interrogation to go through. So, if you're gonna get caught, make sure it's at the end of the exercise. Think of it this way, if you've been in a combat formation and the enemy have taken casualties, they're not gonna be thinking when they catch you, 'we're gonna treat you kindly', or follow the Geneva Convention to the letter. What the enemy will be thinking is, 'These bastards have just done my mates, let's do them'. Also, on the interrogation stage, you must always," and reiterated, "always, keep your mind focused. Square away, lads, get kitted out, and get to the stores. We leave in the next hour."

Two hours later, Rob was sat in the back of a four-ton truck with the other eighteen recruits as the vehicle made its way on a cold December morning through the villages and fields of South Wales along the A40.

Sergeant Nott wasn't wrong about the ill-fitting clothing. The overcoat was too tight, and the trousers were too baggy. In fact, Rob's were held up with a piece of string, and what clothes Rob had on did not keep the biting wind from piercing his torso. Fortunately, Rob had the good sense to get a good breakfast that morning, because he did not know where his next meal would come from, but he was quietly confident he could cope with the demands of this phase of the exercise.

The sleet was pouring down when the truck stopped on a moorland which could have been in the middle of anywhere. The directing staff then ordered the men off the back of the four-tonner, and then paired up the remaining students in twos. Each pair were sent off in a different direction every ten to fifteen minutes. Rob got Burnsey, all the time Rob was thinking he would leave him at the first opportunity, knowing full well, two men together in the hills would stand out more than one. Burnsey pretty much had the same idea. When the last of the teams were dispersed, the directing staff climbed back aboard the four-tonner just as the weather looked like it might snow, and it was obvious the temperature was going to fall to minus degrees. The chase was on.

Chapter Ten

Although it was ten a.m. when Burnsey and Rob set off, the light was dim and grey, and on the mountains that you could just make out, were hard and unforgiving. Both the recruits did their best to stay clear of open ground, both fully aware that they could not deviate from the rules of entering buildings or using roads. Burnsey and Rob made light conversation with each other, which seemed to break the tension between them, and both agreed at the first rendezvous, they would go their separate ways.

Four hours into the march, and the temperature was still just above freezing, and both men did their best to insulate their ill-fitting clothes with some damp straw which they found in an open bale, disregarded by the farmer for the cattle on this bleak and harsh afternoon. As they approached the first checkpoint, both men could clearly see two of the training staff sitting in a Land Rover, and it was obvious they were warm and were enjoying a nice cup of coffee, one of them smoking at the same time as Rob and Burnsey felt like their fingers were about to fall off from the cold.

Burnsey turned to Rob and said, "I'll do this one, mate, you wait here. If it's all clear, I'll give you the nod, and then I'll be off."

"Okay, mate, good luck with the rest of selection."

Both men then shook hands whilst Rob tried to bury himself in the most prickly and unwelcoming bush he could find. Rob watched as Burnsey approached the vehicle but could not hear anything that was said because of the howling winds echoing around the Beacons.

Less than two minutes after the contact, Rob noticed Burnsey put one hand on his head and then half a second later, with the same hand, made the thumbs-up sign. This meant all was clear at the checkpoint. Thirty seconds later, Burnsey disappeared from view. Then Rob continued to go forward to the Land Rover to see what his next RV would be.

"You warm enough then, Foster?" said Collins, as Rob approached.

"Freezing my tits off, thank you, staff," Rob replied.

"We've got coffee and sleeping bags in the back of the vehicle if you wanna quit."

'Smart arse' thought Rob, but he bit his lip, and replied, "I'd sooner continue with the exercise, if it's all the same, staff."

Collins took a drag on his fag, and then answered, "Well done, mate, just keep going,"

Rob then got the following coordinates just as the light was starting to fade, and then pressed on into the night, fully aware that the Parachute Regiment would now be on the Brecons, looking for each individual SAS recruit.

Three days into the exercise, and the cold was no less merciless. Every now and again, Rob would hear dogs barking, and he knew the hunter force was in the area. But he would combat this when the coast was clear by keeping distance between himself and the hungry pack of wolves out to get him. One of the first things he'd learnt whilst on selection was that although bloodhounds could smell you from up to two miles away, the scent would not extend over running water. So therefore, Rob would find a stream and cross it, ignoring the freezing temperature, and then cross again, further upstream, in a U-turn. Every now and again, Rob saw teams of the Parachute Regiment with pick-axe handles, furiously looking through the undergrowth for their prize. But again, Rob would double-back and get out of the vicinity as soon as he sensed his persuers.

With every day and night that passed, Rob was more encouraged. Although he had not had a full meal, he was quite pleased with himself that he had managed to catch at least one wild hare, as well as poaching salmon from the nearby streams and rivers. However, Rob was cold and extremely knackered, but by the same token, at no point did Rob ever think he was going to quit, and he pressed on with sheer bloody-mindedness keeping him warm on a cold winter's night in Wales.

Chapter Eleven

Rob found a copse of trees tucked away on the side of a valley, with the mountain slanting up beside it. He checked the area, and it was clear. So cautiously, he made his way to the side of the copse. It was dark and the only voice in his head was that of the wind blowing against the trees. Rob started to realise how absolutely shattered he was, and knew, that if he was to keep his mind focused for the interrogation stage, he would need to get some sleep. He found a dip along the side of the copse that he felt was not too obvious, and then climbed into the hole, and wrapped his overcoat as much as he could around himself. He shut his eyes, and tried to ignore the cold.

What seemed like fifteen minutes later, Rob heard the sound of a bloodhound howl in the distance. Rob shook himself awake and rubbed his eyes to make himself alert. He looked out over the bushes, but could see nothing. Then he scanned as much of the horizon as he could, and then to his left, less than four hundred metres away, were the sight of flashlights, combing the horizon in single-file.

'Shit,' thought Rob to himself. *'I've got to get out of the area sharpish,'*

Less than a second later, and Rob felt a sharp pain on his leg. He fell to the ground, and looked up, and the silhouette of a menacing-looking para was stood there with a pickaxe handle in his hand. Then the para yelled to his troop. "Got one here, lads! Edge of the copse, to the right." Within the same sentence, the para then hissed, "Three days paid R&R thanks to you, sass boy."

Instinctively, Rob then brought his foot up, and connected it with the para's groin.

'That'll sedate him for a second or two,' thought Rob, but as he tried to charge past him, the para caught Rob's jacket.

"You're fucking having it for that," cried the para, but again, Rob was too fast, and within a split second, Rob punched the para right in the nose, hearing the crack and the cry as this lad went down. At the same time, all the lights were on the copse, and were drawing ever-closer. Rob just ran, thinking his heart would explode, but every second gained was a second without capture. Rob climbed up the ravine of the valley, putting a good distance between him and the para he assaulted.

Then he heard voices. "The bastard's got me, lads, he's gone that way."

Two seconds later, a raised voice shouted "Two section, check the copse, one section, check the valley to see if he's backtracked. Three section, check the ravine to see if he's there."

Rob had to think fast on his feet. He was absolutely exhausted, therefore he doubted he'd be able to out-run the hunter force. The idea came to him. He would slowly make his way back to his original lie-up point, into the heart of where his pursuers were lurking. Only to find the biggest, and most unfriendly tree he could find, and climb up it until the paras dispersed.

Rob couldn't believe his plan had worked, when he looked down from the top of the oak tree to see the paras oblivious to his position. He saw the para that he'd hit, sitting down looking deflated as he used his fist to reshape his nose, all at the same time smoking a fag. Others started to gather round him, when it was obvious their prey had flown. Within an hour, the whole troop had dispersed, and Rob was alone again, with nothing but the dark, the howling of the trees, and his thoughts to keep him company.

Chapter Twelve

Major White sat in the Operations Room at Sennybridge Camp, along with other members of the directing staff. Ten days into escape and evasion, all but one of the recruits had been caught by the Parachute Regiment. The interrogation phase for the recruits that had been caught was well underway. Most of the student body had been captured within the first four days. Even Burnsey had made it to nine days, but no one had any idea where Foster was, other than that he was seen in the copse near Gerard's farm. By all accounts, he'd done a good job on the para that had nearly caught him. Sergeant Nott was particularly pleased with himself that Foster had done so well, as he was going to cash in big time with the bets he'd made with the other directing staff at the beginning of selection.

"Well he certainly knows how to look after himself in the field, Sergeant," said Chalky.

"Aye, he's a good lad, boss. I reckon if he can make it through interrogation, he will make the grade."

Chalky looked worried and reiterated his point to Sergeant Nott that the screws would well and truly have to be turned on interrogation for Foster.

"I understand what you're saying, boss, but by the same token, he's lived off the land for the last ten days, interrogation would be difficult for anyone who's lived wild like that."

Chalky then replied, "I know, Sergeant, and I understand totally what you're saying, but again, I need to know that his mind can handle an interrogation centre."

"Yes, boss," Sergeant Nott replied.

Rob had done well on the escape and evasion side of selection, and two weeks after the start of the exercise, he made his way to the next RV. He had fourteen days growth on his beard, and by all accounts looked like a 1950s tramp as he approached what would be, ultimately, the final RV. Trooper Collins and Sergeant Nott were sitting in the Land Rover as Rob approached.

"Look at the fucking state of him," commented Collins to Sergeant Nott.

Sergeant Nott replied, "You've gotta hand it to him, not that many can last this long, especially not at this time of year."

As Rob approached, Sergeant Nott got out of the vehicle. "Well done, Foster," and he held out his hand to shake.

"Thank you, staff," replied Foster in a weak but determined voice.

Sergeant Nott then replied, "Right, that's the end of escape and evasion, jump into the four tonner, and you'll be given your next orders from there."

Rob looked at Sergeant Nott, knowing full-well he wasn't telling him everything. A few yards down from the Land Rover was the four-ton vehicle, and Rob made his way along the side of the track road and forced himself up the ramp into the back. Within a second, someone had placed a hood over his head and forced him to the ground.

Chapter Thirteen

"Hiya, remember me, sass-boy?" It was the unmistakable voice of the para, whose nose Rob had broken. As the engine revved up, Rob felt a sharp pain between his legs as the para then kicked him in the groin. Then, all he felt was light kickings and punches from the other three paras onboard. Rob tried to be sick, but all he could taste was bile, and he could not see anything. At this point, his arms were then cuffed behind his back, and his feet were shackled together. For the next hour or so, all Rob felt was the odd kick or punch as the four-tonner weaved its way around the Welsh countryside, totally disorienting Rob into which direction he was being taken.

After some time, the four-tonner stopped, then, all of a sudden, the paras started shouting. "Get up, you fucking sack of shit, move forward."

Rob tried to stand, but could not move, so two guards then picked him up and walked him to the end of the truck. It was at this point he then felt a kick in his backside, launching him into the air as he fell five feet to the ground. There were more expletives being shouted, and again the odd punch and kick, but Rob did not feel afraid, he knew it was only an exercise. The shackles on his legs were then removed, and it felt good to Rob to feel the blood flow through his legs again, but he was quickly manhandled across what seemed to be open ground.

All the time in the distance were various shouts and screams, but these were not aimed at Rob, therefore Rob knew he was not alone, and it was other students on the interrogation stage that were bearing the brunt of these expletives. The next thing he knew, his cuffs were being removed from behind his back, and again the circulation in his hands almost returned to normal, but it was only for a split-second as the next thing he knew, a rope was being tied around his wrists, and his arms were being forced up into the air on what felt like a pulley. His ill-fitting waistcoat fell open where the buttons had been forcibly removed, and before Rob had time to digest any information, he felt icy water being poured onto his front.

The shock of the cold was sharp and biting, and Rob could not stop his teeth from chattering as the icy-cold liquid made its way down his body. Just as he had time to recover, there was another icy bucket. This time, it went up his nose, and he struggled to breathe. Then it was as if they'd left him alone. Maybe this is what they wanted him to think, and he stood there, in the dark, with his hands raised above his head.

For what seemed like an eternity, Rob was left there with nothing but the shouts and commands in the background, again, this was aimed at other recruits. The next thing he knew, there was a sharp pain to his kidneys from a punch, and two guards grabbed him by either arm, and started to make him run. As he was still hooded, it felt unnerving to be running somewhere blindfolded. Then he tripped, and fell on his face onto granite stones.

The guards then grabbed him by his feet, and started pulling him along, at the same time as more expletives were being shouted. He then managed to pick himself up, with the help of the guards, and he had the feeling he was entering a building or a farmhouse. Soon, he was being pushed against a wall, and his legs were being prised apart.

"Give me your arm," shouted one of the guards, and he felt his hand against cold damp brickwork as the other guard did the same with his other arm. "Right then boy, keep that position, and don't fucking move," shouted the other guard.

The first two minutes weren't too bad, but then the lactic acid started to build up in his legs and arms, and he could feel his shoulders start to seize up from the awkward position he was placed in. After five minutes, Rob could take no more, so he removed his hand from the wall to make himself more comfortable. Within a second, he felt a boot to the side of his stomach whilst, at the same time, he heard the shouting, "Put your fucking hand back where it was!" and the guards then grabbed Rob by the arm, placing him back in the stressed position. Again, this felt like agony as he tried to combat the thoughts racing round his own mind.

Some time later, Rob was moved from the stressed position, the bag still around his head, and still soaking wet. They came out of the farmhouse. In the distance, he could hear a noise, and as the guards drew in closer, the noise became more prominent. It was similar to that of static on an analogue radio. Rob knew what this was. It was white noise. All of a sudden, a creaking of a door, and the white noise was deafening.

Rob almost thought he couldn't hear himself think as the constant screech in his ears was almost painful to listen to. The two guards on each side of him then kicked his legs out from under him, and he was placed in another stressed position, albeit on his knees. Again, as before, every time Rob tried to make himself comfortable, all he received was a kick to the stomach for his efforts, and, as before, he was replaced right back into the stressed position.

Rob could not gauge how long he had been in the centre for, but he knew at some point he would be taken and interviewed. So, to comfort himself, Rob said over and over in his mind, *'Name, rank and serial number'* and again, *'Name, rank and serial number'* as this was the only information he was allowed to give to his interrogators. Rob could not tell if time was passing quickly or slowly, and he could not tell if he had been in the stressed position for an hour or four. He felt his guards pick him up and remove him from the room which had the deafening white noise in it. As he was dragged along the courtyard, all he could hear was tinnitus running around his ears. All of a sudden, the temperature changed, and he felt he was in a corridor from the echo of the boots on the floor. Rob heard another door open and was pushed aggressively into a chair.

"Guards, take that blind off," boomed a northern voice, and within a second, his hood was removed.

In front of him was a table, and behind it sat a burly man in his fifties who Rob didn't recognise.

"Bit warmer in here, son, isn't it? What's your name?"

"Foster," replied Rob.

"Where do you come from?"

"Sorry, sir, I cannot answer that question," said Rob clearly.

The interrogator looked annoyed. "What, you don't know where you come from?"

Again, Rob replied, "Sorry, sir, I cannot answer that question."

Then the interrogator's tact changed. "Well let's not worry about that for now then, sunshine," and he pulled out some papers that were in a suitcase on the floor. "We just need your family to know that you're here, so can you sign here where there are these Xs, and here, where these other Xs are."

"Sorry, sir, I cannot sign anything,"

The interrogator then turned nasty. "What's the matter, son, can't you fucking write?"

"Sorry, sir, I cannot answer that question."

The interrogator then stamped his hand on the edge of the desk, causing the papers to fall to the floor. "Are you fucking dumb? Sign that fucking form."

Just as Rob was about to reply, the interrogator shouted again. "I said sign it! What's the matter? Didn't you go to school? Can't you fucking write?"

The interrogation carried on like this for another two minutes. All of a sudden, the interrogator then shouted, "Guards! Get in here!" The door burst open and two burly men walked in. "Put his fucking blindfold on, that piece of shit, and get him up against the wall."

The room went dark as the hooded sack was man-handled over Rob's head. As before, he was shoved roughly, pushing his face against the brick wall. The interrogator then shouted in Rob's ear, "You're going back to the compound, man. You need to start telling me who you are and where you're from. If you ever want to see your family again, you need to tell me these details and sign these documents."

The next thing he heard was the interrogator scream, "Get him out of here, guards! He's scum! Fucking scum!"

Rob was taken back down the corridor and back into the courtyard, where the wind and rain were beating down. The sound of white noise and the unwelcome stressed position that he'd been placed in before were once again upon him. Rob could not gauge whether it was day or night, whether he was close to the end, or whether it was just beginning.

Chapter Fourteen

Lieutenant Chelsea Parsons was in her early twenties and was known as a great interrogator, although her colleagues referred to her as the 'Ice Queen'. There were also plenty of rumours about Chelsea, including that she slept her way to her rank as well as other rumours about her sexual preferences and antics. However, Chelsea was a ruthless operator, and knew too well the best way to make gains in her career was to crack as many of the SAS recruits as she could. She had already broken four trainees, three of whom had signed documents and some cried every time they were broken. Every time she saw a recruit cry, a wicked smile, almost a laugh, appeared on her face. It was for this reason she was regarded by her peers as the Ice Queen.

As she looked through Rob Foster's file, she knew she had a good chance of breaking him by playing on the fact that his marriage was over, as well as the horrors which Foster had witnessed overseas and at the end of his tour. Another incentive was that she had been ordered by Major White to turn the screws on this particular student. Again, an evil smile snaked its way across her face the more she read about Foster.

Rob had been in the compound now for three days and three long nights. He had lost count of the amount of interrogations he'd had. Was it five? Was it seven? Each of the interrogators wanted the same thing; for him to leak information verbally, or to sign documents. Various tactics were used; sometimes the interrogators were in pairs, other times it was just one individual. The last interrogator was a fifty-year-old woman who told him that her family had been taken hostage, and that she'd already been raped, and could he help her get her family out by giving her information and signing documents. Even Rob was beginning to think that whoever came up with the ideas for interrogations must be some sick bastards. He tried his best to keep his mind focused, and remember it was just an exercise.

Some time later, the guards removed him from his stressed position and back towards the corridor. *'Here comes another one,'* thought Rob to himself.

This time he was taken to a different room. A room which had a huge mirror on the wall. What Rob did not know at this stage was that behind that mirror stood Sergeant Nott, two interrogators as well as Lieutenant Parsons.

Sergeant Nott turned to Lieutenant Parsons and said, "This is his last one, if he gets through this, I'm gonna pass him. By all accounts, he's the best I've seen in a long time."

This was not what Lieutenant Parsons wanted to hear, she was determined to make Captain before the start of the next selection. "He's not in the SAS yet, Sergeant," she said coldly, as she left the room to interrogate Foster.

Rob's hood was removed and he was left alone in the room, albeit for a few minutes. Then entered Parsons. There was nothing in the room except for the two-way mirror, two chairs and a desk. Parsons had long blonde hair and was wearing a grey powersuit, the type of thing a solicitor or a doctor would wear. In her finely manicured hands, she held a file.

She sat down opposite Rob and introduced herself. "My name is Detective Chief Inspector Karen Day. I'm working on behalf of The Hague and I am investigating war crimes I think you may be involved in. I need you to cooperate with me in this investigation. Do you understand, Rob?"

"Sorry, ma'am, I cannot answer that question."

"Please tell me what happened in Garmsir."

"Sorry, ma'am, I cannot answer that question."

"Look, Rob. Work with me here. You're no longer a member of the army because we think you killed that fourteen-year-old unlawfully."

Rob shifted in his seat. It was the body language Chelsea Parsons was looking for.

Again, Parsons pressed on. "Your patrol informed us that you tried to cover it up. The boy was playing with a football. It was a hot day, and you'd been on patrol for seven hours. You saw him, and then killed him, didn't you, Rob? You knew your wife Annie was going to leave you anyway, and you were so full of hate and anger that you just took it out on that poor little boy, didn't you, Rob?"

Rob could not believe what he was hearing, he knew she was talking shit, but even he thought that was a step too far.

Again, Parsons pressed on with the interrogation. "Why's Annie leaving you, Rob? Do you know why?"

Rob just answered, more aggressively, "Sorry, ma'am, I cannot answer that question."

Again, it was the tone of aggression that she was looking for. She knew she had him in her sights.

"That baby Annie's carrying's not yours, is it Rob? It's somebody else's."

Rob was growing increasingly annoyed. Parsons continued. "It's Andy Smith's baby, isn't it Rob? Not yours. That's why you killed him when you got back to Catterick Garrison," At the same time, Parsons got out a photograph and placed it on the table in front of Rob, which clearly showed Andy, with the back of his head blown off. Parsons continued, "You killed him, didn't you Rob? Because you knew Annie didn't love you any more. You killed him, and that fourteen-year-old boy in Garmsir."

Rob saw red, and within a second, he grabbed the Lieutenant by the throat, pulling her from the chair and knocking her to the ground. Then with his left hand still clinging onto her throat, he punched her right in the nose and she let out a howling scream. Within a second, the door flew open and Sergeant Nott, along with two other interrogators tried to pull Rob off Chelsea Parsons. Rob was like a wild animal. His eyes had nothing but hate for his interrogator. At the same time, Parsons shouted in defiance, "That's it, Foster, you've blown selection now!" Sergeant Nott tried to calm Rob down, and at the same time ordered two of Parsons' colleagues to remove her from the room.

"Calm down, sunshine," bellowed Sergeant Nott to Rob. "It's the end of the exercise, son."

Rob then looked at Sergeant Nott and realised that he'd blown it. The last six months had been for nothing. He was shattered, and emotionally drained. And when the anger left him, he just sat and stared into space on the chair in the interrogation room.

Within an hour, the interrogation phase of selection was over, and Rob knew he had failed without being told.

Sergeant Nott personally escorted him to the debrief room, where all the other students had gathered. At this stage, no one knew who had passed selection and who had failed. All the recruits were shattered, and in the debrief room was food and drink. Rob managed to make himself a brew, but could not stomach eating anything. Part of him was still wired after the last three weeks, part of him was still in SAS mode.

Individually, the recruits were removed from the room and ushered to sleeping quarters. Although Rob was drained, he could not sleep, after all the images flashing through his mind. These included the interrogation centres, Annie, the fight in the Admiral, his father Rick, everything was swirling around Rob's mind at a hundred miles an hour. All Rob could say to himself was, *'I could murder a pint of Guinness'*.

Chapter Fifteen

It was less than a week before Christmas and Rob was back home in Hessle. Although Rob had failed selection, he wouldn't get the letter confirming this until Christmas Eve. From there, he thought it was doubtful he'd be able to remain in the army at all. As a rule, people that left the regiment to join Special Forces selection were not welcome back to their parent units, or even if they were, their career progress would be very slow indeed.

Again, when Rob returned home, he found the usual piles of unopened letters strewn across the doormat. And again, no one had been to his house, including Annie. The thought struck him. *'Jesus, Annie. She must be due to drop anytime soon, I'm gonna have to get in touch with her.'*

Rob dumped what gear he had in the living room and shut the curtains and put the lights on to give the impression someone was in. He shut and locked the door behind him and made his way up to Annie's mother's on Barrow Lane. *'God only knows what welcoming I'll get when they answer the door,'* Rob thought to himself. As he made his way through the square, the Christmas lights were well and truly alight, along with the massive Christmas tree which was usually in pride of place in the centre of the square. There was the normal hub of activity as he made his way through the sleet and snow; last-minute shoppers, kids off school throwing snowballs at each other. Rob just ignored this; he wasn't in the festive mood. If anything, depression had started to sink in.

As he left the square and made his way up towards Annie's mother's house, he dreaded knocking on the door, and almost turned around to go back home. However, he pressed on and on, and when he reached the door, he could see the lights were on. He removed his hands from his pockets as the icy wind blew, and knocked three times on the door.

After a few moments, the door opened, and the one person Rob did not want to see answered. It was Sue, Annie's mother. Sue's face was a picture when she saw Rob. It was almost as if someone had slapped her with a wet kipper.

"She's not in, Rob. And don't come back here again," was the stern greeting that she gave her son-in-law. "She's carrying my grandchild, and I don't want you anywhere near it. She doesn't need any more drama."

"What drama are you referring to, Sue? The only arguments we ever had were because of your meddling."

"That's because I knew my daughter could do better than you. Look at the state of you, you're a mess, Rob. You've never been there for our Annie, always away on exercise or deployment, and as soon as you got home all you did was go to that bloody pub. Annie was never happy with you."

Rob thought about an old Bernard Manning joke, but thought best to keep it to himself. Instead, he just turned and said, "Just tell her I called," and with that, Rob made for the gate as the door was slammed shut behind him.

As he turned into the street, he thought he heard voices. He thought it was Annie's voice asking who was at the door, but either way, he knew Sue would dismiss it, telling Annie it was carol singers.

Defeated, Rob made his way home. As he walked in the night, he toyed with the idea of going for a pint, but thought against it. The last thing he wanted to do now was meet people. When he got home, he dumped himself on the sofa and turned on the telly and did his best to think, rest and come to terms with his lot. Rob's real war was just about to begin.

Chapter Sixteen

Within the space of a month, two significant things had happened. Firstly, Annie gave birth to Rob's child, Noel, weighing a healthy 9lb. At this point, Rob had still not seen his son, and was growing ever more frustrated whenever Annie and her mother would not permit Rob to see him. The other prominent thing that had happened was Rob had been kicked out of the army.

After his post-traumatic stress disorder (PTSD) had come to light, the powers that be did not want a loose cannon amongst their ranks, despite all the loyalty Rob had shown to his regiment and to his country. The way the infantry saw it, Rob had failed SAS selection and was not welcome back anyway, and in their eyes, far too many good, efficient men had been lost when joining the ranks of the SAS.

Rob didn't know what he was more disappointed at, being out of the army, or being unemployed. Both amounted to the same thing, and Rob endured one of the worst Christmases he had ever had, which was saying something considering the way his father Rick had carried on over the years. To combat his dark mood, flashbacks and frustration, Rob drank. In fact, Rob drank a lot.

Even Harry from the Admiral noticed how much Rob was putting away, and felt almost guilty taking his money off him. The fact was, Harry was pleased Rob was in his bar, where Harry could keep an eye on him. But even Harry had noticed Rob had changed. Not so much as a nasty drunk, but more of a lost soul. The more Rob drank, the more it blocked out the demons in his mind. The frustrations with Annie and the baby. Also, the inevitability that soon the money he had saved would be spent.

Chapter Seventeen

THREE MONTHS LATER

The sun was blinding at about two p.m. the heat scorched the baked sand outside of the small village. You could hear the feint laughter of children playing but nothing could escape the sweltering heat. In the distance, the patrol was approaching four or five children. An adult was with them, but you could not make out his features from two hundred metres away. As the patrol approached, the adult patted one of the older children on the head, then quickly made his way back into the compound.

A few moments later, a motorbike engine started, but quickly made his way away from the patrol at speed. In fact, all that could be seen was dust rising up from the road. The boy that received the pat on the head made his way slowly towards the patrol whilst the other children watched from afar, not talking, just staring at them in amazement. It didn't take long to figure out what was going on, the boy, fourteen or so, was mumbling, but you could not hear the words accurately, even if it was in Arabic. The only thing that was clear was the term 'Allahu Akbar'.

The patrol got into fighting formation, which meant two flanks facing the compound. Someone gave the order, "The fucker's coming! Do something!" Someone else shouted, "I'm not fucking slotting him, he's just a kid!" Then, two shots rang out when the boy was fifty metres away. The boy fell to the ground instantly, and at the same time, the other four children ran back into the compound.

Slowly, but deliberately, the patrol made their way towards the boy's body. The Sergeant in the patrol removed the [GARB] from around the boy's torso, which confirmed what the patrol already knew. There was enough C4 explosive to wipe out all of the patrol and some, had it been detonated. Ignoring the gunshot wound to the head and throat, the sergeant disabled the device as best he could. It was basic and primitive. The Sergeant then looked at Rob. "He's dead,"

Rob looked down at the pathetic body on the floor. The forehead had a hole where the 22 round penetrated the skull. However, the back of the head was missing, and all that remained was gore and bits of meat. Also, blood wept out of the neck wound.

Rob knelt down over his victim just as the boy's eyes opened, and the boy screamed, "Allah will avenge me!" In shock, Rob took a step back but could not move. Again, the boy screamed, "Allah will avenge me!" The boy's body reached out to grab Rob.

At that moment, Rob woke up from his sleep, screaming. It was dark. There was no light on. But again, Rob screamed. After realising it was just a dream, Rob took a few moments to get his bearings together to realise he was back at home as the rain cried against the windows of his bedroom. Rob then laid back on the bed, still in the dark, and began to cry utter pain and sadness, as well as anger and fear. He could not stand the nightmares that he was getting. The truth be told, the nightmares had been getting more prolific and more regular.

Rob remembered he had a bottle of Jack Daniels along the side of his bed. With his heart beating, he reached down to find the square bottle. As he placed it around his palm, the lid was removed, and as he held the bottle to his lips to swig what was left, the bottle was dry. He'd already drank it, several hours ago. Rob did not want to stay in bed, it was mid-March, and it was cold, but despite this, Rob got dressed, made his way downstairs, and opened the front door. Just to walk. Maybe get his thoughts together.

The cold was biting with every step Rob took. However, the snow which came in January was starting to disappear. As he walked through the square, one or two cars drove past. Rob did his best to ignore them. He did not know what time it was, but it was dark, and he did not think it was a weekend. He walked through the pedestrian walkway up towards the Weir. Then slowly made his way up Ferriby Road towards the Humber Bridge. Again, cars passed him. It was a red car again. Was it the same one he'd seen in the square? He didn't know, he had not seen the registration number, but even then, he doubted he'd be able to remember it. Rob's mind was elsewhere anyway.

As he approached the entrance to the bridge, this time on Boothferry Road, he could feel the wind howl against his ears. He passed the collection booths, and looked at the guy inside the ticket office, but the guy ignored Rob, and went back to his book. As the wind howled past, Rob wanted to chuck himself off the side. He passed the first pillar that towered above the road, and stopped. Again, Rob thought about his nightmare. Was Rob being punished? Was it not God's will to kill that fourteen-year-old boy? Rob had never cared much for religion, but right now, he thought about praying.

In the howling wind and rain, Rob leaned over the barrier and put his hands together. He prayed to the god he was taught about in school. Over and over again he repeated, "God help me, God help me," and over and over again there was no response. Rob wasn't sure what response he would get, but all he could hear was the wind, and all he could feel was the icy rain burning into his face. Rob stopped praying, and this time started shouting, even though there was no one in earshot. He shouted "God help me, for fuck's sake! Help me!"

More and more frustrated, and with tears rolling down his eyes, he put his first leg up, over the barrier separating the footpath from the drop. Rob took a deep breath and paused. *'A few more seconds and it'll be over, all I have to do is push myself off,'* he cried as he contemplated his own death at his own hands. *'One big push, that's all I need,'* Rob thought to himself. All of a sudden, Rob heard a ruffling of feathers, but paid no attention to it. He was just about to launch himself into the darkness when he heard a cry of a guillemot.

The shriek was directly behind him on the footpath, and it almost frightened Rob, because he thought he was alone. With one leg still on the barrier, he turned his head around to see where the cry had come from. Stood there on the footpath was the bird, just looking at him. It was an ironic moment. Guillemots had been somewhat of a cult bird within Rob's family, when Rob's grandad had died before Rob was born, a guillemot had flown to his relatives inland, miles away from the sea, and tapped on the window all night. It was almost as if they were the Foster's own personal carrier pigeon, but this one, on a cold winter's night, on the Humber Bridge, just stood there and stared at Rob.

Rob stared back for a few minutes. Then, he lowered his leg off the rail, and again, the guillemot did not move. Instead, it just let out another defying squawk. Rob fell to his knees, and leaned back against the railings. Rob then turned to the guillemot and said, "You must think I'm a right silly bastard," and almost on cue, the guillemot squawked, in fact, whenever Rob asked the guillemot a question, there was a squawk. It was a surreal moment for Rob. It was almost as if the bird was telling him, "You've got other things to worry about, other than killing yourself."

Just as Rob picked himself up to make his way back home, the guillemot squawked one last time and then made its way off into the night. As he walked the long, cold walk down Ferriby Road towards his house, the odd car passed. Again, Rob thought the car that had passed him was the same one.

'Fuck me,' Rob thought to himself. *'Am I under surveillance?'* Instead of making his way directly home, he back-tracked across himself to make sure he

wasn't being followed any more. Exhausted, and wet to the bone, when he finally reached home, he let himself in, did himself a brew and put the fire on. As he turned on the telly, he realised it was Friday. He would never get an appointment to see a doctor before Wednesday. Rob knew at this point he needed to get advice. As he nursed his brew, he thought about the guillemot, and almost chuckled to himself at the conversation with the bird on the Humber Bridge.

As the sun started to rise, Rob thought he would get a couple more hours' sleep if he could, and then go to the doctor's as soon as he woke up. *'Maybe they can help me before I do something stupid,'* Rob thought to himself. Rob made his way upstairs, got into bed, turned over, and then tried to sleep.

The alarm went off at eleven a.m., and Rob struggled to get himself out of bed. Once he'd showered and had a brew, he rang the doctor's, and speaking to the receptionist, it felt like one of Chelsea Parson's interrogations. But, eventually, he got an appointment, as he thought, for Wednesday. When he put the phone down, he thought to himself he would only have to get through a few days, then hopefully everything would be rosy. Basically, all he had to do was get through a long weekend.

Chapter Eighteen

Later that night, Rob was in the Admiral. He did toy with the idea whether to go for another pint whilst all of this was going on, but he thought to himself *'Fuck it, I've got nothing better to do.'*

It was about seven p.m., and the weather was cold and damp, but the full moon made the square look electric. Rob felt quite calm as he drank his Guinness and chatted to the regulars, including Harry. Although he did not discuss anything from the night before, he felt like he had turned a page by trying to get himself some help. About an hour or so later, Callum and his crew walked in, and, on seeing Rob, Callum looked like he'd seen a ghost.

Rob turned to Harry and said, "I thought he was barred?"

Harry nodded and said, "Yeah, he has been, but I've got to make a living, brother. He won't start no shit. Especially after the kicking you gave him last time."

As the evening wore on, Callum approached Rob and held out his hand. "Listen, Rob," said Callum, "I'm sorry about all that shit I said, I was out of order."

"Okay, mate, let's put it to bed. Get us a pint of Guinness."

For the next twenty minutes or so, Rob and Callum were chatting like they were old friends. Then, Rob went to relieve himself in the gents. It was at that point Callum turned to his side-kick. "Liam, you still got that spice on you?"

"Yeah, four bags, why?"

"Give us two, then keep an eye out."

Liam then handed Callum two packets of the so-called 'legal high'. Callum then ripped open the two packets and emptied the contents into the half pint of Guiness that Rob had left at the bar. Callum then smiled a wicked smile, and turned to Liam and said, "That's gonna fuck him up for tonight," and then added, "We'll have this, then get off."

A minute or so later, Rob returned, and picked up the conversation that they were having. Within a short time, Callum made his excuses and he and his crony left. Although Rob saw them chuckling as they left, he thought nothing of it, and then ordered another pint.

After about an hour, Rob started to feel funny. He didn't feel like finishing his beer, and it was almost as if he was hearing voices. Other regulars in the pub began looking at Rob, almost staring, even though there was no eye contact. Rob didn't know what he was thinking, so he put his Guinness down, and made his way to the door. As he walked out, Harry noticed him leave, and almost as if Harry could sense something, a shiver ran down his spine.

As Rob left the Admiral, he turned to his right, just as the red car he'd seen earlier went past. Rob wasn't thinking straight, he began to run.

The sky was clearing, and the full moon could easily be seen, along with a peppering of stars. Although the cold did not affect Rob, in his mind, all he could think of was the surveillance he was under. As he ran into the night, he made his way into Boothferry Estate and stopped outside the Sainsbury's Local. Rob knew he couldn't go home, and walked into the store which was quiet. He needed to defend himself. Inside the store, he picked up the right weapon, it was a chef's knife. The shop assistant didn't think twice about taking Rob's money and hardly noticed him leave. Rob thought, *'At least I can defend myself.'*

As he ran into the night, Rob kept looking for whoever was following him. *'It must be something to do with that fourteen-year-old insurgent,'* he thought to himself. *'Maybe it was an ISIS sell, they're looking for me to seek their revenge'.*

Rob ran towards Boothferry Road, at the crossroads to leave Boothferry Estate, towards Costello Park. He would wait in the park, and see if he was followed further.

Chapter Nineteen

Simon Grant was a thirty-two-year-old practicing solicitor with a good reputation within one of the most successful law firms in Hull. He had a close loving family, and lived quite comfortably in his four-bedroom mortgaged house in Anlaby, which was nearly paid off in full. He'd recently come out of a bad relationship, where he was engaged to be married, only to find out his fiancée was sleeping with one of his roommates from uni. For a while, Simon was paralysed with hurt. Until one day, one of his colleagues from the law firm suggested he take up running.

Seven months later, he'd run three marathons, and was hoping to do the New York marathon later on this year. The adrenaline buzz Simon got from running was almost a tonic to the break-up. Plus, he'd met a new circle of friends within the running community. He was due to go on a run Sunday morning, where he hoped Alicia would be there, because she'd jokingly said she would allow him to take her out on a date if he beat her on the next run. Simon was determined to make good on it. Alicia was twenty-eight and a successful accountant, and Simon thought she would get on well with his family, if only he beat her at the next run. Simon changed into his running gear, and then put on his iPod. He turned on his answering machine just before he left to go for his run.

Covertly, Rob had made his way into Costello Park past the stadium. All Rob could see was a dog walker, and no one else. However, Rob was sure he was being followed. In the centre of the park was a row of oak trees adjacent to a small road. Rob made his way behind one of these oak trees, pulled the knife out from his coat, and waited. Rob had never been so scared in his whole life.

Simon Grant was starting to warm up and get his breathing right as he turned into Anlaby Park Road North. As he approached Costello Stadium, he toyed with the idea of going up Boothferry Road towards the Fiveways pub, but just as he approached the entrance to the stadium, Simon changed his mind and made his way towards Costello Park.

The music was pumping, as was the adrenaline, as he knew his timings at this point were the best he'd ever done. He started on the road with the oak trees on either side.

Rob could hear footsteps. In fact, they weren't footsteps, it was somebody running. Whoever it was had to be armed. They must be looking for Rob, as this was his last known location. The steps were getting closer and closer, although Rob daren't look round the side of the tree, for fear of giving his position away. As he gripped the handle of the knife tighter in his palm, he tried to remember what he had been taught.

At the same time, as well as the footsteps, Rob heard the faint crackle of a radio. This confirmed it for Rob. Just as the footsteps got closer, Rob psyched himself up. Rob pulled himself from behind the tree, jumped out behind Simon and grabbed him by the shoulders. At the same time, Rob thrust the knife into Simon's throat, severing the carotid artery.

There was no sound other than the squelch of the blade against Simon's flesh, and at the same time, Simon had no idea what was going on, other than a sharp pain in his neck. Both men fell to the floor, and Simon died within thirty seconds. Another kill for Rob, but this time the kill felt different, with every other kill it was almost as if he felt justified. But with this one, it didn't feel like the others, almost unnecessary.

Rob was in full-on military mode, as well as shock, he quickly did a basic frisk of Simon's body to look for ID and also retrieved the radio Simon was carrying. Although there was no ID, there was a set of keys. Rob looked around to see if there were any other agents, but again, all he could see was a dog walker in the distance. The moonlight shone on Simon's body, and the blood that was pumping onto the road looked black.

As Rob turned Simon's body onto his back, more blood sprayed onto Rob's face. The agent was definitely dead, and as quickly as he could, Rob frisked the body further for a weapon, but found nothing.

Rob was in a dilemma now, either way, he had to ring it in, but also, should he try and move the body? Should he contact the police first? But other questions were nagging at Rob's mind. Why was the agent looking for him in particular? And also, how come he could not find any weapon?

Within the space of a minute, Rob had decided he would leave the body where it was. He ran further through the park towards Pickering Road. As he came out of the park, there was a police station to the left, but that wasn't what Rob was looking for. Outside of the police station was a public phone box. Rob made his way to the phone box and dialed in the number he'd been given to use in case of emergencies when training with the SAS. It was the number for the guard house in Hereford, and it was constantly manned by the military police. As Rob dialed in the number, he saw the blood stains all over his hand, some of it, in patches, still warm.

The phone rang three or four times, and then was quickly answered. "Sterling lines gate house, Corporal Green, sir."

Rob wasted no time, and informed Corporal Green of what had just happened. The fact that he'd been followed for some time, and that he had just assassinated his pursuer. Corporal Green quickly took notes, not knowing whether this guy was just a fruit-loop, or whether some serious shit had just gone down. Everything Rob disclosed was taken down in shorthand by Corporal Green.

When Green had enough information, he told Foster; "Hold the line, I'll put you through to someone."

At this point, Corporal Green put the phone on silent, and then turned to the first officer in the room. The officer then directed the call to the CO's office. And, at the same time, rang Humberside Police. The CO 'Chalky' White took the call from Rob Foster. "Foster, it's Chalky White, explain to me again what's just happened."

Again, Rob reiterated the events that had happened in the park. Chalky quickly realised what had gone on, and it was like a low blow to the pit of his stomach. One of his own had blown a gasket and killed a civilian. Either way, Chalky had to keep Foster on the phone until the police arrived.

Within twenty minutes, Humberside Police had discovered Simon Grant's body, and it soon became obvious there was nothing to be done. Ten minutes after discovering the body, the police turned up at the phone box, where Rob was still on the phone to Chalky White.

Initially, when the police arrived, Rob thought they were there to help deal with the incident, but as soon as he pulled the knife out of his pocket, he was quickly tasered, and six police officers held him to the ground whilst his hands were quickly cuffed behind his back.

All the time, Chalky White heard the scuffle on the other end of the line. As one of the police officers grabbed the handset of the phone to find out who Rob was talking to, Chalky had had enough, and had replaced the receiver where it stood.

Chalky opened his side drawer in his cabinet, and took out his bottle of Bushmill's, which was there for medicinal purposes. A week before his retirement, and this is not how he wanted it to go.

Rob was quickly placed into a police van, all the time Rob was saying, "What're you arresting me for? I'm a Special Forces Operative." He continued, "For Christ's sake, I'm not the enemy."

Within an hour and a half of the incident taking place, Rob was taken to Priory Road Police cell, and placed into police custody. Arrested for murder.

Chapter Twenty

Ken Hunter had been a member of Humberside Police for over twenty years and was now the custody sergeant at Clough Road Police Station. It was his job to ensure the well-being of any prisoner taken into custody. This included any prisoner's mental health. Ken had thought he'd seen it all in his twenty years of experience but he also knew no day was the same in this job and this was certainly the case with the suite's newest arrival, Rob Foster.

It was obvious Foster was either out of his mind or on drugs, possibly both but the computer system told Ken that Rob was a former member of the local infantry unit until recently. This did not marry up. Normally the army lads that came in had been fighting with the locals in Beverley when on leave from Leconfield army barracks. Yes, they were always aggressive and yes it was always alcohol fueled but they were never arrested for murder and rarely substance abuse. This was definitely not the norm.

By all accounts looking at the initial notes on Foster's arrest form, Foster was banged to rights. Even the Detective Chief Inspector took one look at the evidence against Foster and passed it straight over to the Detective Sergeant. In Ken's mind, this usually meant that it was an open and shut case. Foster had refused to answer any questions when he was arrested other than his name and his serial number. Apart from this, Foster had said, "No comment."

Either way, the lad needed to be assessed by the mental health team. He would also need legal representation whether he liked it or not. Ken picked up the phone and dialed the number for the mental health crisis team but as always whenever you needed the crisis team, the line was engaged. Ken replaced the receiver and dialed the number for the duty solicitor.

Chapter Twenty-one

Laura Allison from Gregory and Thomas Solicitors received the call from the custody sergeant and was given a quick brief on the night's events. As it was a murder, she had to go straight away to Clough Road Police Station. She grabbed her keys, put on her long overcoat and kissed her husband as she left. Secretly, she was quite excited, she had not done a murder before. Within an hour she had pulled up in the police station car park.

Walking into the police foyer, Laura gave her name to the reception, and was quickly ushered into the custody suite, where she was met by Ken Hunter. Laura had always respected Ken, as he was one of the few police officers who told it like it was, regardless of what the arresting officer's quota was.

"Hi, Ken," said Laura. "What have we got with Rob Foster, then?"

"Well," replied Ken, "he's been arrested for murder, but personally I think there's more to it than that."

"How so?"

"Well for a start, he's a former squaddie, and by all accounts, he's only just left the army. But the DNA we took from his hair and the mouth swab indicates he's off his head on spice. Also, we cannot find the connection between Foster and the victim, although it's early days yet. My own opinion, is that the lad's probably ill, and doesn't know what he's done."

"Has the CATS team got involved yet?"

Ken sighed. "I've tried ringing them, several times, but the line's permanently engaged." Then he added, "I'm sure they just take the phone off the hook so they can sit on their arses and drink tea."

Laura smiled. "Okay, Ken, if I can have a look at the custody record and get a room where I can have a quick chat with him, then we'll take it from there."

Ken smiled and said, "Yeah, I'll have a man stood by the door."

As Laura took a look at the custody record, she made a note of the time of the arrest and what comments Foster had made, then went to view Foster in his cell. Approaching the cell door, the custody officer opened the hatch and explained to Foster that there was a solicitor here to see him. Laura looked at Foster through the hatch, and he was sitting in a corner in white overalls, where his clothes had been removed, with just a blanket to keep him company.

"Mr Foster, I'm Laura Allison. I'm the duty solicitor here to look after your interests. Can I have a quick word with you?"

Rob just looked up, and then looked down. Laura then paused, and tried again. "Mr Foster, do you know where you are?" she asked. "You're in Clough Road Police Station, and you've been arrested for murder. That's quite a serious charge. I'm here to represent your legal requirements. I do not work for the police, and I'm not trying to put one over on you, but I do need to speak to you. Would you mind if we had a quick chat somewhere quiet?"

Although Rob didn't feel like answering, he mumbled, "Yeah, whatever, love."

Within half an hour, Rob was escorted from his cell to the interview room, where Laura sat. As promised, Ken put a man outside the door.

Rob was still out of his head from the alcohol and the spice he had consumed in the pub. The only thing Rob did know was that he was out of the army, and that he was in a world of shit.

For the next half hour or so, Laura tried engaging in conversation with Rob, but Rob only gave small, short answers.

"I don't know."

"Yes."

"No."

This was about the sum of it. It soon became apparent to Laura that her client was definitely ill. In fact, the DS would not be getting any interview today. Certainly not until Foster had been assessed by a psychiatrist. Laura realised she wouldn't get much more information from Foster so she finished the interview and Rob was directed back to his cell. The solicitor then went to have a word with Ken.

Before Laura could speak, Ken said, "The DS wants to interview Foster in half an hour."

"Sorry, Ken," replied Laura. "My client's not being interviewed by anyone until he's been assessed by the mental health team."

Ken knew this is not what the DS wanted to hear, and sighed. "Great, that's me off his Christmas card list then. I'll try the CATS team again, but I'm not holding my breath. Either way, he's going to be up at the magistrate's court by the morning. Which probably means they'll remand him in Hull Prison."

"If what you say is true, Ken," replied Laura, "the last place he needs to be is Hull Prison. He needs to be in a psychiatric hospital, where he can be assessed."

Ken reiterated the fact that he'd tried the CATS team, but again, with the government cut-backs, it was doubtful anyone was going to turn up to see the lad tonight.

Twenty minutes later, Laura was escorted back to Rob's cell, and again, as she looked through the hatch, she almost felt sorry for him, as she saw him wrapped in a blanket, staring into space.

"Mr Foster," Laura said, "it's Laura Allison, the duty solicitor. Do you remember talking to me a few minutes ago?"

Rob just looked at the solicitor and nodded.

"You're going to be kept in tonight, and will be up at the magistrate's court in the morning. I'm going to try and get you assessed by a psychiatric doctor, however, the court will probably remand you to prison. This will probably be Hull Prison. Do you understand?"

Again, Rob just nodded.

"Mr Foster, I do not want you to give any statement or go on interview without me present. Is that clear? I will see you at court tomorrow morning, and then we'll take it from there."

Just before she left, Laura asked Ken to get Rob a cup of tea.

Chapter Twenty-two

At seven a.m. the next morning, Rob was handcuffed and put in the back of a Group 4 van, along with the other lags who had been arrested the night before. Rob just stared out the window as the van made its way out of town towards Hull Magistrates Court.

Arriving at the court, he was taken from the van and put into a cell, again on his own. Even though this cell was bigger, it had no inside toilet, and nothing but a wooden bench along the back of the wall.

As promised, Laura Allison arrived at the court and took the clerk to the side to explain about Foster. "My client's been arrested for murder, however I do not wish to make a plea at this stage."

The clerk smiled, and said, "Okay I'll let Judge Bainton know."

After being in the cell for a good three hours, Rob was ushered through the secure corridors, up the steps, and into the dock, which was surrounded by secure glass, with nothing there but a seat and a microphone. The public gallery was full, and Rob looked across to the prosecution, and then to the left was his solicitor, Laura Allison. Rob couldn't be arsed to sit down. He was still half-comatose. Then, a voice echoed around the courtroom. "All rise."

Everyone in the court stood to their feet as Judge Bainton entered from his chamber and took his seat in order to start proceedings.

"Please be seated," Judge Bainton said.

The prosecution stood up, and read the charge of murder. Judge Bainton looked at Laura Allison, and asked how her client would be pleading.

As if on cue, Laura stood up. "My client is a former soldier, and we suspect he may have some kind of mental health condition, your honour. We will not be entering a plea at this stage. Also, I would like to ask the court for an assessment at a psychiatric hospital before my client is remanded in to prison."

Judge Bainton rubbed his eyes. "Did he not get assessed when he was at the police station?"

Allison replied, "As far as we're aware, many attempts were made to contact the CATS team, however, they were unresponsive."

"I see," said the judge, and turned to the prosecution. "Does the prosecution have any objections?"

"No, your honour," was the reply.

"Okay," replied Judge Bainton. "I want Foster assessed, however, he will have to be remanded to Hull Prison until the CATS team get their affairs in order." Then he added, "Also, as this is a murder charge, I'm referring this case to Hull Crown Court, and a later date will be confirmed." Judge Bainton then looked at Rob. "Mr Foster, you have been charged with murder. That is one of the gravest of crimes. However, this court is not aware of your mental state at this stage, but given the nature of the offence, I cannot grant any type of bail. Therefore, I'm remanding you into the custody of Hull Prison, where hopefully you will be assessed. Do you understand?"

Rob just stared forward, not even replying. The judge waited for a response, but when he realised he would not get one, he concluded. "Once an assessment has been made into your mental health, then the crown court will start proceedings. Case adjourned."

Again, there was a deathly quiet around the courtroom, until it was broken by the sound of "All rise." The courtroom stood as Judge Bainton made his way back to chambers. A few seconds later, Rob was removed from the dock. His next stop would be Hull prison.

Chapter Twenty-three

Rob had been in Hull prison for less than three hours when he was involved with his first fight. He hadn't even been assigned a wing or a cell at this point, and was still locked up in holding along with the other lags. A short but stocky prisoner came in convicted for supplying Class A cocaine. He wanted to take out his frustrations for being incarcerated out on Rob, although Rob was almost placid initially.

The prisoner initially tried conversation to belittle Rob, which he ignored. This, in turn, frustrated the prisoner more. When he grabbed Rob by the top of his overalls, Rob struck out within a second. Using a karate move, he brought his right hand up to get hold of the prisoner's arm. Then, with full aggression, he threw his left arm towards the prisoner's neck, disabling him within an instant. Rob wasn't done there. When the prisoner was on the floor, Rob grabbed the drug dealer's arm and twisted it to break the humerus. As if that wasn't enough, he then continued to use the heel of his foot to smash into the drug dealer's face.

Although the guards could hear the scuffle from inside the holding cell, they couldn't be bothered to deal with it, and prudence demanded it was best to let them get on with it. It was only three quarters of an hour later when holding was opened up, when they found the drug dealer in a sorry state on the floor. This was Rob's introduction to prison. It wouldn't be the last time Rob had fights either on the wing or along one of the many corridors in Hull Prison.

Over the period of three weeks, Laura Allison was deeply concerned about her client. She heard that Rob had been in several scuffles, and this was not going to do her client any favours when it came to a court appearance. Also, she was increasingly frustrated with the lack of input from the CATS team. Although, when she finally managed to get through, they did promise a referral, however they could not give a date.

All the time, Foster and his mental state was not being addressed. At the same time, Rob had lost count of the amount of times he'd been back-and-forth to appear in front of the Crown Court. Sometimes it was a physical appearance at court, and on other occasions it was just via a video link from within the cells at the bottom of Hull Prison. Rob was tired and weary, but at the same time, angry and aggressive.

Chapter Twenty-four

It was just another day staring at the cell walls when his door was opened. Three guards stood there. "Foster, you've got a visitor."

Rob was escorted through the gothic Victorian prison to a different form of holding and was given an orange bib with the number thirteen on it.

"Who's my visitor?" Rob asked the clerk.

"Annie Foster," was the reply.

Rob almost felt like crying, but held it together. As he walked into the visitor's area, which was a large room with tables and chairs nailed to the floor. He looked around and saw Annie there. His heart was in his mouth. He wanted to run up to her. Annie was as beautiful as she'd always been, but there was no sign of his son, Noel.

When Annie saw Rob, there was almost a look of disappointment on her face. Rob held out his arms to hold Annie and although she accepted his embrace, it was almost a pleasantry, as if it were a handshake.

"How you doing, babe?" Rob asked.

"Me and the baby are okay, what the hell's happened to you? People are saying you killed somebody? What's going on, Rob?"

"I'm not sure myself, Annie. I don't know why I killed that man. I don't even know who he is. At first I thought he was some sort of government agent out to get me."

"So, you did do it?" Annie said, and she began to cry. Rob tried to hold her hand from across the table, but she withdrew it. "Six years of marriage, and this is what we've got?"

Rob replied, "I didn't ask for this."

Annie got angry. "You didn't ask for this? Is that all you've got to say? All you've ever wanted was the next mission, I didn't even come a close second."

Rob protested. "Oh, come on, don't be like this."

"Don't be like this, Rob! I thought if you got your SAS selection out of the way we could be a family, but apparently that's not good enough for you. And now, you're going to be locked up in here for God knows how long, for killing some poor sod who was just jogging through the park. Can you imagine the gossip? And what about Noel? What type of life is he going to have, when he's in the playground, knowing full-well his dad's a murderer? Well I've had enough, Rob, I'm filing for divorce."

Rob felt his heart sink upon hearing Annie's words and tried to say something but Annie continued. "I'm filing for divorce, I can't cope with this life any more. My solicitor will be in touch."

"Annie, wait!" Rob pleaded.

"It's no good, Rob, I can't do this any more." She stood and turned for the exit, tears rolling down her cheeks as she headed towards the door. Rob tried to follow, but the guards quickly realised what was happening, and ushered Rob back to holding.

Chapter Twenty-five

Laura Allison sat at her office and was increasingly frustrated with her workload regarding Rob Foster. The CATS team did little or nothing to support Foster in his darkest hour and to Laura this was a travesty. Not only had this man served his country doing God only knows what in the name of freedom, but the fact was, nothing was in place within the system to support service personnel like Rob.

Laura was frustrated at the response of the CATS team whom, when she did get through, promised to call her back only for these calls never to materialise. So instead, Laura took it upon herself to contact the forensic doctor directly, Dr Charlotte Beaumont. Unsurprisingly to Laura, Dr Beaumont knew nothing of Foster's plight, other than what she'd read in the press, which Dr Beaumont made clear to Laura, she viewed with disdain.

Both lawyer and doctor agreed the way forward was a Section 35. The nature of the section meant

Foster could be assessed initially in prison and then moved to the safer environment of a forensic hospital. It would be here that the true needs of someone suffering from deep mental psychosis would be addressed. Laura had a feeling Dr Beaumont would be ideal in assisting Foster to the best possible outcome he could hope for.

This, in turn, meant she hoped that Foster would be treated in a medium secure hospital with a view to being released after several years. The only other alternative was that Foster would be locked up indefinitely, probably for the rest of his life in a maximum secure hospital. This would probably be Rampton. Even though the lawyer had to remain neutral when it came to her clients, she still felt Rob deserved more than to be locked up for the remainder of his life.

Chapter Twenty-six

By now, the local press were well and truly milking the story for all it was worth. Even the national press had got wind of the deranged killer, murdering someone in cold blood. Some of the headlines included, 'Crazed Killer', 'Madman strikes', but the one headline that stuck out the most was, 'Paranoid Schizophrenic' which then went on to mention Rob's name. It was these headlines which infuriated Doctor Charlotte Beaumont.

Doctor Beaumont was in her mid-thirties and had been married for seven years now although her marriage to Jonathan looked to be drawing to an end very soon due to infidelity on Jonathan's part. Although Charlotte had known Jonathan since her university days, Jonathan who now worked as a senior architect, had always had an eye for the ladies. Initially, when they first met, Charlotte made a point of not listening to the gossip and rumours which seemed to follow Jonathan after every night out.

She knew before she married him that he was a bit of a player, however by now, Jonathan and

Charlotte had a child together, Amelia, who was born just after Charlotte had finished her finals. Although Amelia was not planned, it was the one saving grace of the relationship between Charlotte and Jonathan. However, Jonathan had gone too far when it came to light that he had been sleeping with his PA, Maggie, who had not only befriended Charlotte but also on several occasions been round for meals and even babysat Amelia once. It was a stab in the heart Charlotte did not see coming, and as far as she was concerned, the marriage between her and Jonathan had run its course.

As a result, Jonathan had now moved out and Charlotte consoled herself by throwing herself head-first into her work as a forensic psychiatrist. It was a role she cherished and because of her dedication to her work, Charlotte had risen to a senior position within a short space of time. Her latest client was Rob Foster. She had the file on her lap which told her about the events leading to the death of Simon Grant and given the notes on the autopsy report, it was clear that he had died efficiently at the hands of Rob Foster.

It was Charlotte's job to assess Foster and give this assessment to the crown court. This in turn meant that if Rob was found to be mentally unstable, he may well be locked up indefinitely, possibly for the rest of his life. As far as she was concerned, what the press failed to grasp was the effect this would have on Foster's life as well as the fact the file said that Rob Foster had also just become a father.

Charlotte grabbed the remote in her study and turned off the news, annoyed at the way the press were painting the picture of the story. It was the one part of the job, besides the politics, that she could not stand. She sighed as she picked up the glass of red wine she had poured for herself and continued to study Foster's file. As she turned the pages, she began to realise that Foster was certainly very unique. Most of her clients had serious mental disorders for some time before forensics got involved.

This was not the case for Foster and so automatically she started to think that Foster had Post Traumatic Stress Disorder. Also, she could not understand how someone who had, by all accounts, a successful military career, would test positive for spice. Charlotte had relatives who had served in the military and knew too well, military personnel were subject to regular drug screenings. She was almost looking forward to meeting Foster, simply from an academic point of view. She had to assess whether Foster was either a very bad man, or a very sick individual that needed the best care she could provide.

Foster was currently in Hull Prison and she had scheduled a meeting to see him in the next few days. She knew from experience that her first assessment of Foster would more than likely determine the facts. If she could help him, she would.

Just as Charlotte was drawing to the end of her case file, she turned around and Amelia was stood there in her night clothes. "Mummy, can I have a glass of water?"

"Of course you can, sweetheart," Charlotte replied, "but then you must go straight back to bed because it's very late and you are seeing your daddy tomorrow."

"Can you read me a story please, Mummy?"

"It's a bit late for that now darling, but I will come up and tuck you in."

"Will you tuck Bo-Bo in as well?"

"Tell you what, I'll tuck you and Bo-Bo in and bring you up a glass of water now if you can get into bed straight away and try to go to sleep."

"Ok, Mummy," replied Amelia and quickly disappeared upstairs.

Charlotte put the file on the kitchen table and finished off the rest of her red wine in two sweet swallows. She then filled a plastic beaker with some water and a little juice and went to see to Amelia. As she made her way up the stairs, she knew what was coming. Lately, since Jonathan had gone, Amelia was asking after her father all the time, and the usual innocent grilling's of a little girl as to where Daddy was always ensued around bedtime. Tonight was no different. Charlotte kissed Bo-Bo, the favourite lion teddy, and then Amelia. Just as she was about to switch the bedroom light off, Amelia asked, "Does Daddy not love us any more? Is that why he's gone?"

Charlotte closed her eyes as she heard the words and sighed under her breath. "No, darling, that's not the case at all. Daddy does love us both but Mummy and Daddy just need a little bit of a holiday from each other for a while."

"So is Daddy coming back then?"

These were all questions that Charlotte had to answer. The questions of a curious seven-year-old little girl. But the truth be told, Charlotte did not know what the answer was.

"Daddy will come and see you in the morning and then very soon, he will take you away for a few days sailing on the boat."

"Will we see the dolphins again?"

"I'm sure you will see the dolphins," Charlotte replied.

"Will you come too, Mummy? asked Amelia.

"You must try and get some sleep now, sweetheart, and try not to worry, Mummy and Daddy love you very much."

Dr Beaumont then returned to her file after she opened another bottle of red wine, and tried to assess her own life, with little or no conclusions to answer herself with. Soon she fell asleep on the sofa with Rob Foster's file on her lap.

Chapter Twenty-seven

It was a brisk, cool spring morning when Dr Beaumont pulled into the visitors' parking bay at HMP Hull. She removed her file from the back seat and locked the door before making her way to the entrance. This wasn't the first time Dr Beaumont had been to Hull Prison and she doubted very much that it would be her last. The gothic, Victorian prison almost had a charm of its own, similar to that of an old fashioned museum, or failing this, something out of a Marvel or Batman comic.

As she received her pass and was escorted through the various locked doors, blocks and walkways, Charlotte could almost smell the history on the walls. The deep angst was atmospheric and she felt if these walls could talk, this would be a story in itself. The last person in the UK to be hanged by Pier-Point was hanged within these very walls. She was guided to an interview room deep at the bottom of the prison. As she entered the room, everything she expected to be there, was there.

Both the chairs and the table were securely fastened to the floor and the arrogant looking guard nonchalantly encouraged Dr Beaumont to take a seat, and he shut the door behind her. Charlotte removed the file on Rob from her leather briefcase, and flicked through the pages making one or two mental notes on her subject.

Ten minutes later, the interview room door was opened and a tall almost handsome figure came in. It was Rob Foster. This was obvious from the photograph within the file. However, both his legs and hands were chained together, and Rob had an escort on either side of him. Both escorts systematically put their arms on Rob's shoulders, forcing him onto the bolted chair. Rob's face looked weary and older than his years, and his right eye looked like it was swollen. It was obvious either the prisoners or the guards had taken a dislike to Rob. He just looked at Dr Beaumont, but made no comment.

"Mr Foster, my name is Dr Charlotte Beaumont. I'm a forensic psychiatrist. I'm here to assess your mental health for the Crown Court, would you mind if I had a chat with you?"

There was pause in the room for a moment. It was almost as if Rob was too shy to answer. "Yeah okay love," was Rob's reply, "but can we get rid of these two goons?"

Charlotte almost smiled but instead turned to the guards and asked them to leave the room, and then added that the guards should remove the restraints. Both guards looked at each other, then the senior of the two smirked and replied, "Sorry, darling, he's a bad man this one, do you know what he's done? Don't you read the papers?"

'Typical macho wanker', thought Charlotte instantly but then firmly spoke. "I am a forensic psychiatrist and this is my patient, he deserves respect and dignity whilst I am in charge of his care. Also, anything that is said in this room is confidential and between myself and my patient. If you do not leave this room, I will be taking it up with the governor within the next fifteen minutes. If I am not happy, I will then take it to the board of governors. I want a confidential chat with my patient, and I want his restraints removed immediately."

On hearing this, the guard was on the backfoot and did not want to lose face, especially in front of this lag. "Tell you what, love", he replied, "I'll leave you alone with this killer and I'll even shut the door but I'm keeping his restraints secured."

"Ok that's acceptable," replied Charlotte, "but if you don't mind, I would like to have your name and number."

He cockily replied, "Okay, love, I'll give you it as soon as you're finished." Both men then turned to look at each other and left the room.

Both Rob and Charlotte were fully aware that they were alone together but it was Rob who broke the silence. "His name's Maguire, he's a fucking cock. He's the reason I've got this black eye."

Charlotte questioned Rob's statement. "Are you telling me a prison guard assaulted you?"

"Yeah but it was nothing serious," came Rob's reply. "Maguire likes to think he's a bit of a hard man but to be honest he hits like a girl throwing a ball."

Charlotte smiled at the comment and then continued with the interview. She asked Rob in detail about his history and it soon became apparent that Rob was telling the truth. However, his body language was that of hopelessness, frustration, and she felt she was looking at a broken man. She continued and asked him how the death of Simon Grant came about. All the time, Charlotte was constantly watching Rob's body language.

Her client was obviously in distress, constantly looking at the floor and almost jittery at the doors being slammed within the holding. Rob found it frustrating to answer because, in all honesty, he did not know himself. All he could say was that he thought he was being followed but also, he had been drinking. Charlotte then pressed on. "How long have you been taking spice for?"

"What's spice?" Rob questioned.

"When you were arrested at the police station Rob, samples were taken from your mouth swab, the toxicology report says you were on MCAT. A particularly nasty variation called Spice."

"To be honest, doctor, I don't remember anything."

As Charlotte was writing notes she looked up and smiled. "Please call me Charlotte," and added, "in forensics we try to be less formal."

Rob looked at her for a second and replied, "Okay, thank you, Charlotte."

The interview lasted for a good hour, and the interaction between doctor and patient, Charlotte felt, was positive. This was obviously a hard man, but by no means a bad man. Charlotte was of the view that her patient Rob was in a very bad place, but she would need to assess him again, and she would tell the court as much. It was as important to Charlotte as it was to Rob's lawyer, Laura, that this man would get the care and support he would need. Charlotte remained adamant that she would see to it personally.

Chapter Twenty-eight

After Dr Beaumont left the prison and was sat in her car, she thought it appropriate to contact Foster's solicitor directly. Soon, she was put through to Laura Allison's office. "Laura, it's Charlotte Beaumont here, I've just assessed Rob Foster."

Almost with relief, Laura replied, "Please tell me you can help my client."

"Well," Charlotte replied, "he's definitely suffering from some form of psychosis and I'm more than happy to let the court know my initial assessment is that Mr Foster is extremely ill."

Laura replied, "Thank God for that, that's a relief, that means once he's assessed, we can argue at the court for diminished responsibility, as opposed to a murder charge. This might save him twenty years of his life. Are you still at the prison now? I can meet you somewhere or in my office and we can exchange evidence over a coffee?"

"Yeah, that sounds great. Give me fifteen minutes depending on traffic and I'll meet you at your office."

Laura was starting to feel quite pleased with herself. The doctor had confirmed what she had believed all along. Her client was suffering from deep psychosis and, on top of this, she had managed to get two character references to present to the court. One was from Harry Woolen, the publican of the pub where Rob drank, and although it was a written reference, painted Rob in an extremely positive light.

The second reference was from Rob's old infantry unit Company Sergeant Major Duncan French, who insisted he would come to court to give evidence in person. All in all, Laura started to think that the case would more or less swing in Rob's favour. However, a lot of this would be dictated by further evidence and which judge was sitting at the court when it came to trial.

Twenty minutes later, Dr Beaumont arrived at Allison's office and both professionals discussed the merits of the case for the next hour or so. After a quick lunch break, Laura headed for the court. Soon, Laura Allison was in court and successfully managed to argue for a Section 35 and there was little disagreement from the prosecution. This in itself was a relief to Laura.

Chapter Twenty-nine

Within the space of a week, Rob was being shackled and placed in a Group 4 van and moved to a local medium secure psychiatric hospital. Although Rob was in a world of pain, he took great comfort whilst travelling, looking through the windows watching everyday people go about their everyday lives.

Soon he entered the airlock at the entrance of the hospital and was greeted by three members of staff. The first member of staff was a woman in her late fifties. She looked completely miserable, almost like a bulldog chewing a wasp. The other two were men, however one of them looked like he had eaten too many pork pies. The woman then introduced herself as Janice and that she was the manager of the ward where Rob would be a guest. Rob's shackles were removed as were all of his personal possessions.

Walking through the corridors Rob was conscious that he was looking for some sort of escape route but nothing sprang to mind immediately. Janice and her two sidekicks, Tweedle

Dumb and Tweedle Dee, escorted Rob to his room. She asked Rob to sit on the bed as she asked him several questions and she wrote his answers down on a form. The whole process took about an hour. All the time, Tweedle Dumb and Tweedle Dee were watching Rob's every move. When Janice had finished, she invited Rob to join the other patients on the ward in the TV room. Begrudgingly, Rob accepted the invitation although he just wanted to be alone.

There were three patients in the TV room as Rob entered. Firstly, Rob noticed a dirty old man nursing a coffee cup coughing and spluttering into its contents and, at the same time, making no effort to cover his mouth. Rob noticed the TV in the corner which was covered in reinforced plastic probably to prevent people kicking off and smashing it in. To the right of the room was a young guy in his early twenties wearing a baseball cap and next to him was a scruffy middle-aged man. He held out his hand to Rob and introduced himself as Eddie. Rob shook his hand and sat down as Eddie made conversation. "So, what you in for then mate?"

"Not sure really, pal, being silly I guess," was Rob's short reply, giving nothing away.

Rob then asked, "What's this place like then? Anything like prison?"

"It's nothing like prison but the only downside is they can keep you forever if they want to. I've been here for six months, the ex-wife said I was harassing her. This here is Smudge. He set fire to a hostel he was staying in." The twenty-year-old looked up from the chair and nodded.

Rob turned to Eddie and asked, "There's not many people on this ward, where are they all?"

"Will's down ICU, he kicked off and so they pinned him down and gave him the liquid cosh. He'll be out for a couple of days yet. The rest are out on leave, apart from The Surgeon."

"The Surgeon?" asked Rob.

"Yeah, Jimmy, we call him The Surgeon, he's a complete lunatic."

"Why's that?" Rob questioned.

"He's a clever guy, in fact he was studying medicine at York University. But he started getting carried away. They caught him doing autopsies on different animals."

"So, where's he now?" Rob asked.

"He's down the gym with the nursing staff. Take it from me he's a proper fruit-loop that one. So what consultant do you have then, mate?" asked Eddie.

"Charlotte Beaumont," Rob replied.

Eddie smiled. "You're lucky then, mate, she's the best one to have out of all of them."

At this point Smudge raised his eyebrows and nodded.

"I must admit," Rob said, "that was the impression I got as well, that she was good at her job."

"Whatever you do, don't get Dr Beechtree," Eddie continued. "I've got him, he locks people up and throws away the key, that one."

The conversation carried on for another fifteen minutes or so when the door to the lounge opened, and a different nurse came in and shouted, "Dinner time!"

All the lads in the room were ushered into a straight line along the corridor. All were walked in single file through the various air locks to the dining area. Rob was constantly looking for some sort of exit or escape route but, as before, nothing came to mind.

Within half an hour after a basic meal everyone was lined up in single file again and frog-marched back to the ward. *'So this is what life is like inside the funny farm'*, Rob thought to himself. He then went to his room and tried to sleep.

Chapter Thirty

"What the hell do you think you're doing telling Amelia you're going to take her on safari?" Charlotte was annoyed with Jonathan and made it clear on the phone from the kitchen.

"Charlotte, we said we would take her when she was old enough."

"Things were different then, Jonathan, and it was long before you started shagging Maggie."

"Don't bring that up again for God's sake, Charlotte."

"Jonathan, don't you think I know what you're trying to do? You're trying to win over Amelia so I take you back and it's not going to work."

"If you just listen to me, Charlotte," Jonathan protested "there's plenty of room on the flight, you can come too."

Charlotte cut him off there. "Jonathan, I have a career and a job, not to mention Amelia has school. We can't just take her out on a whim."

"Don't be like that, Charlotte, we could both sort this out if we got together and spent some time alone, all of us as a family."

"Jonathan, I'm filing for a divorce, you'll be getting the papers soon," and without thinking she slammed the phone down on the receiver cutting Jonathan off mid-sentence.

Within the space of five seconds the phone rang again. Charlotte became more annoyed and picked up the receiver. "Jonathan, stop ringing me, the divorce papers will be in the post!"

"Charlotte, it's Laura Allison here. Have I called at a bad time?"

Dr Beaumont bit her lip and cursed herself silently. "I'm sorry," replied Charlotte. "I thought you were the soon-to-be ex-husband." Charlotte began to feel embarrassed.

"I can call you at your office tomorrow if it's more convenient," replied Laura.

"No, it's okay, are you ringing about Rob Foster?"

"Yes, I was just wondering how he was getting on, and if he was settling in okay."

Charlotte went back to her professional mode. "Yes he was admitted on Tuesday but unfortunately I've not had a chance to assess him again. I've had a lot of work to attend to as well as a few personal issues."

"Sounds like you could use a drink," replied Laura.

"Like you wouldn't believe."

"Do you want to talk about it now?"

This caught Dr Beaumont off-guard. She wouldn't normally share her personal life with colleagues or anyone she worked with. After the meeting with Laura Allison in her office, she felt a kind of kindred spirit, especially when it came to the interests of Rob Foster.

For the next hour or so Charlotte filled in Laura on Jonathan's infidelity, the fact that he'd been sleeping with his PA and God knows how many other women since they were married. And as a scam to try and win Charlotte back Jonathan had told Amelia, their seven-year-old daughter, that he was going to take her to Africa on Safari. Laura Allison listened like a good friend would and in doing so felt grateful to be in a happy, loving and stable marriage herself.

Soon it was getting late and Charlotte realised that she would have to put Amelia to bed and explain to the most precious thing in the world that her daddy might have made a mistake by telling her they were all going on Safari.

Charlotte agreed to call Laura the next day as soon as she'd had a chance to interview Foster again.

Chapter Thirty-one

Rob sat in the ward with a mixture of boredom and hopelessness when Dr Charlotte Beaumont appeared at the lounge door. Rob was almost pleased to see Dr Beaumont from the way all the lads on the ward had talked about her, everyone held her in high regard.

Charlotte smiled. "Rob, can I have a quick word with you? We'll go somewhere quiet where we can discuss a few things."

Both patient and doctor entered one of the quiet rooms off the ward. Charlotte then went on to explain. "Rob, I know it must be frustrating for you being here but it is my professional opinion that you are suffering from PTSD and I suspect it has been going on for some time. Also, I suspect your drinking and substance abuse has exacerbated any condition you may have. However, I do not think you intended to kill Simon Grant and I will be telling the court as much. Your solicitor and I have agreed the way forward would be a Section 37/41. Do you know what that is?"

Rob just shook his head.

"It's a Home Office restriction order," continued Charlotte. "It means you will be here at the hospital for an indefinite period until myself and the staff agree you are able to go back into the community."

"What, you mean a life-sentence?" asked Rob.

Charlotte took a deep breath before she replied. "Not exactly, it just means I can keep you here for as long as I need to and you need to realise that you may be here for a few years yet. However, I do not intend for you to be locked up in hospital for the rest of your life. I cannot put a time limit on how long you will need to be in hospital for, Rob. It may be a few years or it may be several. However, I can help you recover from your PTSD and come to terms with the fact you killed someone you didn't mean to."

Rob could feel a tear welling up in his eye. "Okay, I understand," replied Rob.

Charlotte then picked up her file and began to ask Rob some questions. "Rob, would you mind telling me if you've had any nightmares recently?"

On hearing these words Rob burst into tears. Even Charlotte was surprised at how quickly Rob broke down as soon as she mentioned the word nightmares.

Charlotte and Rob talked for a good hour and a half and Rob disclosed everything he knew. The fact that he had killed eleven people and before Simon Grant the last person he had killed must have been a fourteen-year-old insurgent. Despite the fact Charlotte had run over the allocated time, she continued to talk to Rob about his demons. She went on to explain to her patient, with the impact of everything he had been through, it was little wonder that his mind had succumbed to psychosis. At the same time, Rob could not remember the last time he had cried. But he was secure in himself to know that he felt no shame in crying in front of this angel who had been sent to help him.

After an hour and a half, doctor and patient finished up their session and Dr Beaumont added that she was going to try Rob on some medication. It would be this medication that would help relieve any hallucinations he might have been having. Also, it would help him sleep and generally remain calm. Had it have been any other doctor, Rob would have protested immediately but there were some things he just knew, and the fact was this doctor was definitely trying to help him. On top of this in the next few days, Rob would be going to trial where the rest of his life would be determined by the facts given by this consultant.

Chapter Thirty-two

The day of the trial began and although Rob had been escorted to the court first thing in the morning, he was kept in a holding cell along with two nurses and his solicitor until early afternoon.

'All rise', was issued round the court as Judge Fletcher took his seat. For the next hour or so the prosecution and the defense argued the pros and cons of the case. The public gallery was full, not only with the press but also members of Simon Grant's family as well as Ricky, Rob's father and Sue, Rob's estranged mother-in-law.

It soon became apparent to the court that Rob had no history of substance abuse and although Rob's father Ricky was drunk most of the time, he knew exactly where the source of the spice had come from and also how it had got into Rob's system on the night in question. All the time Ricky struggled to keep his mouth shut. The defense then called for Company Sergeant Major Duncan French to take the witness stand. Rob looked up from the dock to see this man, who was once a father figure to him, give evidence.

Duncan French was in full military uniform including several medals that were pinned to his chest. The clerk then added, "Please state your name for the court."

In a big booming voice, the CSM replied, "Company Sergeant Major Duncan French, Fourth Battalion, Yorkshire Regiment."

The defense then began. "Please state to the court how you know the defendant."

"He's one of my lads," replied the CSM defiantly.

"CSM French, please can you be more specific?" added the defense.

"I've known Foster since he was fresh out of basic training and he's one of the most solid, dedicated and loyal members of my regiment."

The defense then continued, "Please can you give an example of when you've seen his character shine?"

"Aye, I can," the CSM replied. "In Basra he saved two of his colleagues by taking out a sniper. In doing so he put himself in a near-death situation. This is just one example. I can give you at least five others where he has done something similar. Like I said he is one of my lads and I'm extremely proud of him."

On hearing this in the public gallery, Ricky felt a lump in his throat. However now it was time for the prosecution's cross-examination of the witness.

"Not including the victim, Simon Grant, how many people has Rob Foster killed, CSM?"

Duncan French was annoyed at the question. "My man has defended himself, defended his country and I don't think it is relevant to these proceedings what Rob Foster has done in the name of democracy."

"That may be true," the prosecution continued, "but he has killed before, hasn't he?"

The CSM then slammed his fist into the side of the witness stand. "Do you want to know what annoys me more than anything? The fact that in this country we teach Foster and lads like Foster to kill in the name of freedom, or in the name of democracy. They lay down their lives and come back from warzones scarred for life, disabled, with serious mental health conditions and nobody in the country in which they are fighting for gives a flying shit."

Judge Fletcher then picked up. "CSM French, please mind your language in my courtroom. We are not in a barracks."

"I apologise to the court, Your Honour, but the fact is this is happening to too many of my men. Far too many of my men have taken their own lives or ended up in prison because there is nothing in place in this country to look after their needs, and I for one am ashamed of that."

After Duncan French had given his evidence, then Dr Beaumont was called to the witness stand. Dr Beaumont then gave her name and title to the court and explained that her patient was suffering from deep psychosis on the night in question. Also, she added that he had suffered terribly from PTSD for several months since leaving the army. Dr Beaumont also added in her statement that Foster had shown nothing but absolute remorse for the events that had taken place.

All the way through the cross-examination from the prosecution and the defense, Judge Fletcher was seen taking notes.

Lastly, the defense read out a statement from Harry Woollen, the pub landlord from the Admiral pub where Rob drank.

Time was against the court and Judge Fletcher adjourned for sentencing to the next day.

Chapter Thirty-three

The rain lashed down in Hull almost as if the heavens were crying at the sorry state of affairs beholding Rob Foster.

Judge Fletcher read a statement out to the court.

'It is the opinion of this court that Rob Foster acted out this grievous crime without the full knowledge of what he was doing. And it is my opinion that had medical help intervened earlier, there would not be a grieving family here today or a man with serious mental health issues in this dock. Therefore, I have no choice but to pass a Section 37/41 Home Office restriction order against Rob Foster. It is also my opinion that Foster should remain hospitalised in a medium-secure hospital, and not a maximum-secure hospital, given the excellent references provided by the military and the publican Harry Woollen. Foster has shown great insight into his actions as well as remorse'.

At this point a member of Simon Grant's family stood up in the public gallery and protested. "Why not take him on a fucking holiday to Ibiza for two weeks, Judge?"

Judge Fletcher then responded. "Clerk, have that man removed from my court."

The judge then continued. "Mr Foster, you are to be locked up indefinitely until Dr Beaumont and the Home Secretary deem you fit for release. You have a serious mental disorder and until it is treated, you are potentially a serious risk to the general public. I suggest you use your time in hospital wisely and work with the medical team who are there to assist you. That is the verdict of this court. Take him down. Call the next case."

After the court proceedings Rob was ushered back into the Group-4 van and Laura Allison managed to see Rob for the last time in order to wish him well. Ricky Foster left court soon after the judge had summed up avoiding the ice-cold glaze from Sue, Rob's ex mother-in-law. Ricky also managed to avoid the press who were camped outside and made his way to the nearest pub.

Simon Grant's family however were keen to talk to the media, with what appeared to be Simon's uncle slamming Rob Foster as a psycho that should never be allowed out, before adding that he was scum and would go to a nice warm hospital for a few years and he protested that justice had not been done, again reiterating the word scum when referring to Rob.

For the rest of the day, the rain continued to hammer down crying like tears from heaven. And it was almost like the rest of the world was crying with it.

Chapter Thirty-four

Dr Beaumont had tried to explain to Amelia that it was doubtful she would be going with her father on Safari. However, despite all her rationale and reasoning against her decision, the tears of Amelia pulled on Dr Beaumont's heartstrings and in the end, she succumbed to Jonathan's ploy. Charlotte even tried to convince herself that maybe some time alone with Jonathan would do Amelia the world of good, also it was a once in a lifetime experience for a little girl. Despite this, she made it clear to Jonathan that she would not be going on the trip and so reluctantly agreed to take Amelia out of school for educational purposes.

Even as she phoned the school and explained to them what was happening, she could feel herself questioning why she had agreed to such a venture. However, she also felt it was important for her to maybe spend some time alone to think generally about what she wanted from life and what was best for Amelia. In the meantime, Charlotte just hoped that Jonathan would take the best care of the little girl who was her whole world.

"How do you do? My name's James but some people call me Jimmy."

Rob looked up, half comatose from the medication to see a tall, Asian figure in his late thirties with a shaved head. Rob held out his hand to receive and replied, "Yeah I've heard about you, mate, they say you've got a thing for animals," Rob said with a smile.

"I was hoping to train as a doctor and I just wanted to get a head start. I still hope to train in the future. I am very knowledgeable on medical matters hence I tried early autopsies." He continued, "The human mammal is very complex however if you can master smaller mammals then this, in turn, may help with surgeries on a wider scale."

Rob started to chuckle to himself, the guys on the ward were right. Jimmy was a complete fruit-loop despite his manners and pleasantries.

Jimmy went on to ask Rob, "Now tell me, do you play chess?" He then added, "I often like to play and try to find adversaries of an intelligent nature, in fact, I have a local National Master of the Hull Chess Society visiting me this afternoon, however I find it so difficult to lose without making it too obvious." Jimmy continued, "If I defeated him every game, he might not want to come back and play against me."

Rob could see the intelligence in this psycho stood in front of him. Jimmy had a very humanistic appeal but then, by all accounts, what type of madman does autopsies on cats and dogs. Rob exchanged pleasantries with Jimmy and tried to keep the conversation light, he did not want Jimmy to decide that Rob needed any type of reconstructive surgery in the middle of the night.

Chapter Thirty-five

Life on the ward had not changed much for Rob since he had arrived. In fact, for someone that had led such a full life, it was almost torture to be locked up almost comatose by medication with nothing to do except watch daytime television. He reflected on his life and toyed with the idea of calling Annie from the ward phone but, given how their last meeting had gone at Hull Prison, he doubted that she would be very responsive. Not to mention that the court had granted Annie a restraining order, probably on the back of Sue's interfering.

As for the staff on the ward, they seemed a mixture of overworked anxiety, along with contempt for all the patients that were incarcerated. Two stuck out in particular, Sally Cooper constantly went on about how she was under pressure all the time and that the lads on the ward had it easy because they had no responsibilities. When she wasn't moaning about how difficult her life was, she was boasting about her award winning five-year-old Corgi.

Not only had it won best dog in show during the local finals but Sally would also brag that it was a rare breed and the only other people in the country to own one were the royals. As a cruel dig at the patients, she would often remark that her prize-winning Corgi had more brains, manners and social skills than the patients on the ward. Sally Cooper was the senior manager on the ward and it was almost a license to make the patients' lives a misery.

The other nursing staff member that stood out was Chris Daniels. He was a lad in his early thirties, just a bit younger than Rob but liked to carry himself, on the wards, as a bit of a hard man. He often liked to wear clothes that were far too tight on him and it was no surprise the clothes were ill fitting given the amount of food he constantly had in his hands. Daniels had even been known to eat the food that patients had disregarded.

Another sore point for Rob was the fact that Daniels had been in the Territorial Army and Rob regarded this as a bit of a weekend drinking club. Both Sally and Chris made the lives of the patients miserable. Both had superiority complexes and both were arrogant, self-serving and intimidating toward all who were on the ward, including staff.

Chris was telling Rob, for the third time, about all the things he'd done within the TA. Chris was almost intimidated by Rob because Rob was the real deal. Chris went on about how he'd done a forty-eight-hour exercise and that he was the only one in his platoon still awake. As if by magic, with the perfect timing, Dr Beaumont arrived on the ward to see Rob. Chris Daniels was surprised when he saw Dr Beaumont and then tried to make out he was busy with work matters whilst at the same time salivating like a sweating dog around Dr Beaumont.

"Rob, how about a quick walk in the garden to get you off the ward and then maybe we can talk some more," said Charlotte.

This was like music to Rob's ears, especially as he'd received a letter from Annie's solicitor filing for divorce and felt he could confide in Charlotte. The last thing he wanted to do was talk to Sally Cooper or Chris Daniels about it. "Great, I could do with some fresh air," Rob replied.

Chris Daniels looked almost jealous as he opened the security airlock in order to allow Rob and Charlotte to roam free in the garden.

Chapter Thirty-six

It wasn't the first time Rob had been allowed access to the garden although these small treats were few and far between as there were only three patients allowed in the hospital garden at the same time, and this was the rule for all the hospital wards. Even so, the garden was quite large. A grassed area with views of the city of Hull which was spoiled by the secure, ten metre, steel mesh fence.

As with the very first meeting in Hull prison, there was a pause between Charlotte and Rob. However, this time it was Charlotte who broke the silence. "How are you finding life on the wards, Rob?"

Rob sighed. "To be honest, I find it mind numbingly boring however some of the lads are all right, I just wish I had more access to the outside world or more in the way of leave at least."

Charlotte smiled. "Don't worry about that, Rob, I'm going to put you forward to have ground leave within the hospital grounds within the next few days, however I have to get the Home Secretary's approval first."

"OK, give him my regards," Rob said cheekily.

Again, Charlotte smiled. It was obvious, the connection between doctor and patient was there and despite Charlotte only knowing Rob for a short period of time, she felt he was unique and that she could trust him. Both characteristics were rare from an academic point of view. Both doctor and patient continued to walk then Rob mentioned, "My wife has written to me via her solicitor, she's filed for divorce." Rob showed Charlotte the letter.

"There's not a lot I can say, Rob, to be honest, it happens to the best of us." As soon as Charlotte said that remark, she regretted it. It was unprofessional.

"Sounds like you're getting divorced too then," Rob replied.

"Not that it's any business of yours," Charlotte joked, "but yes I might not be Dr Beaumont for much longer."

Rob made light of the subject. "Well then give your soon to be ex-husband my number, we'll go out for a beer together and drown our sorrows."

Charlotte smiled, then Rob added, "Once we've painted the town red and drank away all the maintenance money, then we'll go to a lap-dancing club together, hopefully, waking up in a ditch."

Charlotte wanted to change the subject. "Okay, so how are you finding the medication, any side effects, Rob?"

"I must admit, I've been sleeping a lot better but I do feel a bit like a zombie but I don't know if that's just from being on the ward all day."

Charlotte was happy with the response and it confirmed to her that the medication was working. Then she replied, "You may feel a bit drowsy at first but that will wear off. Also, and this is really important, Rob, you must remember to keep taking this medication as it will make all the difference to your wellbeing."

Both doctor and patient continued their stroll in the garden and both enjoyed the late spring sunshine and continued to talk for the next half an hour or so. Rob almost felt like a child walking in the park with his mother but again Rob knew that this was strictly a doctor-patient relationship. For all he was recovering from deep psychosis, he knew full well he would not be walking off into the sunset with Dr Beaumont like in the movies.

Chapter Thirty-seven

Ricky had been drinking all afternoon in the Admiral pub. By all accounts, he was a bitter man. Although nobody said anything to him about what had happened to Rob, his son. Even his cronies that he'd known for years seemed to snub him and avoid conversation. Ricky could take that, he'd been through worse. What stuck in Ricky's throat was the fact that Rob had given so much for his country and got so little in return. In fact, it was less than nothing. It was almost as if his son had been disregarded by the country for which he served. Ricky was angry with the world. It was getting near eight o' clock when Callum walked in. Ricky couldn't even look him in the eye and Callum made a point of walking up to the bar and standing right next to Ricky in order to intimidate him and belittle him in front of his crew.

"Here, lads, anyone got a spare straight jacket," Callum muttered. "Don't want to get stabbed on the way home." All within Ricky's earshot. At the same time, there was a nervous laughter around Callum's crew, almost as if they felt Callum was going too far. Harry was watching the events unfold in his pub inbetween serving his punters. Callum then went on, "I hear that Annie's single now, bet her dress'll be on my bedroom floor tonight, as for the bastard son, I'll just leave him outside while I give her a good seeing to."

Again, the nervous laughter ensued until one of the crew turned around and said, "Come on, Cal, leave it out."

Ricky finished off his Low Flyer in one quick shot and slammed the tumbler down on the bar. He then turned to Callum and his crew and said, "You don't have to defend me, son, you're scum just like him."

Callum started to get annoyed. "Watch your mouth, old man, or you might get hurt."

Ricky was too intoxicated by anger and whisky to care. "Callum!" Ricky slurred. "You may be the big 'I-am' in here tonight with your crew when you've had a sniff of the barmaid's apron but you've done fuck all with your life. My son's gone out and worn the queen's uniform and fought for the freedoms that you enjoy." He then went on, "What have you ever done with your life."

Callum just stood there, it was as if even he didn't know what to say. Ricky still continued.

"Everyone knows what you did, Callum, and what shit you peddle. The fact is, you're responsible for that man's murder but you're not man enough to own up to it being the grubby little parasite that you are. You're just a fucking drug dealer, scourge to society but you mark my words, sunshine, your day will come."

The Admiral pub had gone quiet at this point. Everybody was staring at Callum whose face was turning red with embarrassment. "Fucking leave this pub now, old man," Callum muttered menacingly.

"What's the matter?" Ricky added. "Does the truth upset your stomach. You want to take on an old man, I'll fuckin' fight you now, you bastard."

And with the dexterity of a lame bird, Ricky struck out, in vain, at the man who was really responsible for Rob's predicament. Callum could see the punch coming from a mile away and stepped back, all the time, smiling. Harry came over within an instant and, for the second time, barred Callum from the Admiral.

Callum did not like to be outdone and while his crew had all made their way home, Callum waited in the doorway in the dark opposite the Admiral for Rob's father to leave the pub.

Chapter Thirty-eight

Charlotte and Amelia stood at the airport reception waiting for Jonathan. In spite of the fact that Jonathan knew Charlotte had other engagements that day, not least of all work, Jonathan still managed to arrive nearly an hour late. Amelia was just starting to get restless when Jonathan appeared wearing his light brown chinos, checked pink shirt and carrying his holdall.

"Charlotte, darling, how are you?" he said, almost ignoring Amelia.

At the same time, the curious seven-year-old girl ran up to her father shouting, "Daddy, Daddy!"

Jonathan picked up Amelia and walked to Charlotte, bending his head to try to kiss his soon to be ex-wife. Charlotte withdrew her face, offering only her cheek.

"You're late, Jonathan," Charlotte protested. "I told you I've got to be at work for a meeting."

"Meeting, shmeeting," Jonathan mimicked, "you know you can still get a flight today if you wanted to come."

"Not now," Charlotte deflected, "and not in front of Amelia."

"But, baby," Jonathan continued.

Charlotte stopped him there. "Jonathan, I've got to go," then added, "Amelia, give Mummy a kiss before I go, I'll see you really soon."

Innocently, the little girl kissed her mother while Charlotte held Amelia for all she was worth. "See you soon, Amelia, I love you very much."

"I love you too, Mummy."

Jonathan held out for a hug too, but Charlotte just gave him an ice-cold stare before making her way across the airport toward the exit. Just before the exit gate, Charlotte stopped to wave but Jonathan and Amelia were gone and at the same time, Charlotte had a cold shiver up her spine. Being a doctor, she quickly dismissed this and under her breath said, "It's only for a few weeks." She left the airport and hurried back to her car.

Chapter Thirty-nine

Ricky Foster woke up in the short stay ward at Hull Royal Infirmary attached to various machines that were beeping intermittently. Initially, Ricky didn't know where he was, but the drummer in his head was banging furiously. It was at this point Ricky realised it wasn't the whisky that was responsible for his pounding head. He looked over to his left to see an intravenous drip in his arm, and various implements placed around his body. As he started to awake, he felt the screeching pain within his stomach but Ricky already knew what the source of this pain was.

The previous evening, Callum had watched Ricky leave the Admiral and followed him down the pedestrian walkway. Callum then attacked Ricky from behind with an old police truncheon that he had kept for just such a purpose. Ricky was powerless to fight as the blows rained down one after the other. Not only had Callum fractured some of Ricky's ribs, but also had managed to knock a couple of Ricky's teeth out with his steel toecaps.

Even after Ricky remained unconscious, Callum continued to kick various parts of Ricky's body, high on aggression and amphetamine. Soon after, Callum had heard revellers approaching and so thought his work was done, and hid in the dark until the potential witnesses were out of sight. Callum looked at the old man on the ground, but decided to make good on his escape.

It was several hours later that Ricky was found at around four a.m. by a passing truck driver on his way to work. Initially, the truck driver thought Ricky was dead but it was only when the ambulance arrived the paramedics discovered Ricky was still breathing. Of course, at this point, Callum had already rang his crew in order to maintain his alibi that they were all together in Callum's flat.

The doctors at Hull Royal Infirmary could recognise a savage attack when they saw one. However, Dr Partridge knew the majority of the wounds were superficial and would heal in time. The routine blood test which the medical staff took initially showed a much more sinister diagnosis. Ricky Foster had cancer. In fact, the cancer was well advanced but Dr Partridge knew, like most men of Ricky Foster's generation, it had not been dealt with when symptoms appeared. Dr Partridge stood at the foot of Ricky's bed, psyching herself up to give Ricky the unfortunate news.

"Mr Foster, do you know where you are?" she said with a caring tone.

"Yes, love, I'm in hospital," was the weakened reply.

"Do you know how you got here, sir?" she asked.

"Ambulance I suppose," was Ricky's response.

"You were brought in at four thirty this morning, unconscious with slight hypothermia. We think you've been assaulted, Mr Foster, so we've called the police and an officer is on the way to see you soon."

Ricky just shrugged. "I don't need to talk to any coppers, love." Then Ricky tried to get out of bed.

Dr Partridge moved closer to her patient placing her hand lightly on his shoulder. "Please, Mr Foster, you need to rest."

Reluctantly, Ricky laid back into the bed.

"We've done some blood tests and I'm afraid we've got some bad news."

"I know, darling, it's cancer," said Ricky defiantly.

The doctor looked up quizzically. "You've been told this already?"

Ricky replied, "I've had it for a few months now, love, but you just get on with it don't ya."

The doctor looked even more concerned. "But you've not been prescribed anything according to your medical records."

"I turned it down, love," Ricky replied. "I want to live my life the way I want to live it not the way I'm told to live it."

"Mr Foster, there are medicines available that can help manage your condition. Also, I fear your cancer is in the late stages therefore it's important to take some medication even if it's just to relieve the pain if nothing else."

Then Dr Partridge continued, "Is there anyone we can contact on your behalf to let them know you're here, possibly your wife or children?"

On hearing this, Ricky just felt disappointed and it showed. With a glazed look in his eyes he said, "My wife's dead, love, there's no one else. If it's all the same, I'll just rest here for a bit and then I'll make my way home."

Dr Partridge took pity on her patient and was almost close to tears thinking about Ricky Foster's predicament. This man was probably going to die very soon, alone, with nobody in the world. At this point, she whispered to herself, "The government doesn't pay me enough to do this."

"Okay, Mr Foster, I'd like to keep you here for a few more hours and then I'll discharge you however I have two conditions. Firstly, you have something to eat before you leave. Secondly, I'm going to prescribe you some pain killers, I want you to promise me that you'll take them."

"Aye, Okay, love, I promise. Also, I'll be no bother."

Ricky then closed his eyes and went to sleep, Dr Partridge returned to her work station.

Chapter Forty

Amelia and Jonathan started their adventure, pleased to be in each other's company. Amelia sat in between her father and the window on the KLM flight, constantly looking through the clouds in amazement and wonder. The last time Amelia had flown, she was still a young toddler and so it was a fantastic new experience. Jonathan, on the other hand, enjoyed all the attention his little girl was showing him and it wasn't long before the bond between the pair grew. At the same time, Jonathan was still checking out the female air hostesses as they saw to the passengers' needs. All the time, the little girl was oblivious to Jonathan's inappropriate innuendos with the air hostess who just smiled artificially.

The plane landed at Schiphol International Amsterdam roughly an hour after they left the UK. At this point, the majority of the passengers disembarked and were quickly replaced by new passengers en route to Jomo Kenyatta International in Kenya. It was from here Jonathan had arranged for a concierge flight to Mandera Airport. Jonathan knew full well the price for his ticket to Mandera Airport was extremely cheap and as such he could not pass up the opportunity to save the few hundred pounds that he would have paid had he gone through a professional travel agent.

The way Jonathan saw it, he lived in a capitalist world and he knew he was doing quite well so therefore if he could save money, he would build up his own coffers. Had Charlotte known, there would be no way the trip would be taking place and this seemed to amuse Jonathan even more.

Both Amelia and Jonathan enjoyed small pockets of sleep on the eight-hour journey. When Amelia did awake, again with all the enthusiasm of a little girl, she looked through the window at the stars and was totally enchanted. Occasionally, she nudged her father to share her enthusiasm but all Jonathan could muster was, "That's lovely, sweetheart, now try and get some sleep."

The plane taxied at Jomo Kenyatta which appeared to be a conventional airport similar to that anywhere in the UK. Both father and daughter were tired however both were excited, even if Jonathan was a little weary. Jonathan soon found the terminal where he would get his connecting flight to Mandera Airport and on seeing the small plane, Jonathan realised it could probably hold no more than six passengers plus the pilot. Again, this did not faze Jonathan and once he and Amelia were in the air towards their final destination, Jonathan was pleased that he and Amelia had the plane to themselves. Jonathan mused to himself by thinking, 'Soon we'll be on Safari in Kenya, Amelia will have a fantastic time and Charlotte will see what a wonderful father I am'.

Three and a half hours later, the plane taxied into Mandera Airport and as the small, light craft came into land, Jonathan saw how basic Mandera Airport was. There seemed to be little in the way of security. In fact, there was hardly a fence from the surrounding airport and there appeared to be various forms of wildlife grazing around the runway. In the distance, Jonathan could see some sort of military com.pound, not that he paid much attention.

As he and Amelia walked into the terminal, in this most basic of airports, once through the arrivals lounge his next job was to get hold of some accommodation. Again, Jonathan wanted to spend as little money as possible and at the same time, get the best on his return. He held Amelia's hand as he looked for the sign he wanted. In the corner of the airport was a kiosk and above the kiosk, read 'Safari'. Behind the desk sat a middle-aged African in a white shirt that was seeped in sweat. At the same time, the worker smoked, constantly looking around to sell his wares to the latest westerner looking for adventure.

Jonathan smiled to himself as he approached the kiosk. "Hello, do you speak English?" Jonathan said patronisingly.

"Yes, sir, very much so, yes, sir!" came the keen reply. "Would you like to go on safari, sir?"

Again, Jonathan knew how to barter. "That depends," came Jonathan's reply. "I'm looking for a good deal."

"Go through me, very good deal. Yes, sir! Very good deal." he smiled and then added, "Best deal in all Kenya".

Jonathan, at this point, thought he was on a winner. The man was obviously very poor which meant in turn, Jonathan felt he could pay what he wanted to pay and get the best deal on a cabin as well as excursions.

The man behind the kiosk then looked down at the little girl who was still holding her favourite lion teddy. "You'd like to go see the lions?"

Amelia just looked up and smiled, she had never seen a black man in person before. Jonathan and the agent bartered over several minutes on what one party thought they should pay and what the other party said they were going to pay. He man at the kiosk looked really disappointed in Jonathan and every now and again would say, "No deal, sir." At which point, Jonathan gave the impression that he would walk away. After a few more minutes, a deal was finally agreed and Jonathan removed his wallet from inside his coat pocket and removed a few notes. At the same time, the man on the kiosk looked at all the notes in Jonathan's pocket and pretended not to notice the huge bundle which remained in US dollars.

Jonathan and Amelia were ushered outside of the airport, to what looked like a local taxi, by the man on the counter. Jonathan felt like he was on a roll. He had paid the equivalent of fifty US dollars for two weeks with accommodation, and excursions to various places and Jonathan knew full well he'd paid way under the odds. All the time the agent pretended not to look offended at what he had just sold to this westerner. Jonathan and Amelia then climbed into the taxi as the agent spoke some words to the taxi driver in a foreign tongue. He turned to Jonathan and said, "Enjoy your safari, sir, enjoy your safari."

The taxi pulled away from Mandera Airport leaving the agent stood watching the vehicle leave. The agent then looked around over his shoulder as he removed a mobile phone from the inside of his trouser pocket. He dialled a number, the line rang several times before it was answered. "Mousa, it's Abass, I've got one. A white westerner is with her, girl about six or seven-years-old, yeah, with her father, got money too. They're both on the way to the farm. Okay, will ring you later." As Abass cut the line dead, he smiled to himself as he thought, 'Young white girls are a good prize in Somalia'.

Chapter Forty-one

Dr Beaumont was sat at her desk, in her office, going through the usual reports for the Home Office when her phone rang, initially annoyed at the ringing tone on her desk which broke Charlotte's train of thought. She quickly shrugged this off and answered the receiver.

"Hello, Dr Beaumont, Psychiatry."

On the other end of the phone was Dr Partridge who, in turn, verified herself as the GP from the casualty department at Hull Royal Infirmary. "Dr Beamont, one of my patients here is in casualty and I believe he is the father of one of your clients."

Dr Beaumont responded, "I'm afraid I cannot give you any details on the phone regarding any of my patients, Dr Partridge, as you will appreciate, occasionally members of the public and the press do call in order to gain information about a certain subject.

"Yes, I understand that fully," replied Dr Partridge. "However, I am reliably informed that my patient, Mr Ricky Foster, is connected to your patient, Rob Foster."

"OK, please continue and I'll see what I can do," replied Dr Beaumont.

Over the next fifteen minutes, both doctors discussed Ricky Foster's predicament. The fact that he'd been subject to a brutal attack and also that he was riddled with terminal cancer. Dr Beaumont, giving nothing away, received this information and almost bit her lip as she realised she would have to tell Rob once she had confirmed the accuracy of the information she had been told.

Dr Partridge highlighted that had it not been for the fact that Ricky had received a visit on the ward from a publican called Harry, she would not know how to contact any of Mr Foster's next of kin. Both doctors exchanged pleasantries before they ended the call and it was now up to Charlotte to inform Rob immediately.

Rob and James were sat in the quiet room debating the pros and cons and what the difference was between a great leader and a dictator. It was a discussion that lead to nothing other than both patients getting to know more about each other. James was pleasantly surprised at Rob's intellect and almost saw him in the same vein as when he was a student doctor studying one of his patients. A few seconds later, both patients saw Dr Beaumont walk past into the staff room only to return, five minutes later, in the middle of their debate. Charlotte then turned to James and politely asked him to leave the room. James obliged and shut the door behind him. Rob looked up at Charlotte and asked, "Do we have a session today? I didn't think we were meeting until next week."

Charlotte sat down next to Rob and swallowed hard before she continued. "Rob, I'm afraid I have some bad news. It's about your father."

Rob had hardly thought about Ricky since he had been moved to the psychiatric hospital. Rob looked straight at Charlotte and asked, "What's happened?"

"He's in hospital, Rob, I'm afraid he was attacked last night and taken to Hull Royal Infirmary."

"Who's attacked him, was it Callum Squire?" Rob questioned.

"The police are still investigating, Rob, however although he's conscious, he's refusing to say anything. It was only because he had a visitor that the hospital managed to contact me."

Rob knew straight away it was Harry who had visited his dad.

Charlotte continued, "I'm afraid there's more, Rob."

"Go on," Rob replied.

"The hospital did some tests and they've found that your dad has terminal cancer." All the time, Charlotte studied her subject to see how he would react at the unwelcome news but Rob remained calm, almost defiant. She saw fire in Rob's eyes as they talked.

"So, what happens now?" Rob asked. "Will I get to visit him in hospital?"

Charlotte replied, "I've spoken to your case worker at the Home Office and they will only agree to a short visit, maximum of half an hour, with three escorts. Also, this will be a one off given the early stage of your arrival here in hospital. The other thing they ask for before I can let you go to visit your father, is that you're tested on ground leave within the hospital grounds."

Rob sighed and looked to the right then Charlotte continued, "I'm sorry, Rob, there's no other way around it however I am putting you forward for ground leave immediately but this may take a few days to come through. Just be patient and I promise you I'll get you to see your father.

It was at this point Charlotte talked to Rob some more about his father and Rob disclosed that his father had been violent in drink in the past. This was one of the main reasons Rob had joined the army, to get away from it all. Rob added that when his mother had died, his father began drinking almost every night however at this point, Rob was already serving in the infantry. Although Rob and his father weren't in contact, it wasn't that they had fallen out. Rob turned to Charlotte and said, "God I could murder a Guinness right now."

"Guinness?" questioned Charlotte. "Is that what you drink?"

"Is it ever?" replied Rob. "Dad and I would often get together to talk politics, religion and culture over a pint of the black stuff."

Charlotte smiled and said jokingly, "If I could get it for you on prescription here, Rob, I would, trust me."

Both doctor and patient chatted for another thirty minutes before Charlotte returned to her desk. She was confident that Rob had taken the news well or as well as could be expected and, at the same time, wished she could buy Rob that pint of Guinness.

Rob was looking out of the window when James returned, hoping to re-engage their debate. Then James sat down and asked, "Is everything all right?"

Rob explained his predicament about his father then James asked, "Who could have done this to your father? Do you have enemies?"

"Not really," Rob replied. "With the exception of the family of the man I killed however there is another small-time drug dealer that I filled in a few months ago."

"How so?" James asked. Rob went on to explain how his father, Ricky, had upset Callum Squire's parents and when he tried to sort it out, Callum, his crew and Rob had ended up fighting with Rob getting the better of all of them.

James asked, "Did Callum say he would take any revenge on you?"

"Not really," Rob replied. "In fact, the last time I saw him was the night I killed that poor bastard in the park. In fact, Callum and I had a drink together on the same night."

At this point, James sat back in his chair with his fingers together and thought. He began to question Rob. "Didn't they say you were on spice when you were arrested?"

"Yeah why?" replied Rob.

James ignored the question and continued, "When you and Callum were having a drink together, did you leave your drink unattended with Callum?"

Rob thought for a moment and replied, "Yeah, I suppose I did, I had to go for a slash."

James then continued, "This Callum seems a very devious character indeed, you said yourself you did not know how the spice got into your system."

The wheels in Rob's mind began to turn as James spoke then James concluded, "When you went to relieve yourself, I suspect Callum has put the cocktail in your drink. This, in turn, has caused you to suffer from deep psychosis. It seems plausible that Callum has spiked your drink and is ultimately responsible for your being here."

Rob sighed under his breath and then whispered, "Fucking hell, I think you're right." Then added, "Fuck me you've got to be right, the bastard."

James remained seated, deep in thought. "It would be interesting to meet this Callum," James remarked.

Two minutes later, the door to the quiet room opened and ward manager Sally Cooper came in. "James, Rob, it's time for your medications," she said with disdain.

James immediately protested. "Sally, I'm not due any more medication today!"

"Yes, you are, it's been written up."

"Nobody informed me," James replied.

"I'm telling you now," was Sally's curt answer.

At this point, Rob left the room and headed for the nursing station to be given his medication but could hear the argument which ensued between James and Nurse Cooper. Ultimately, Nurse Cooper was not going to be told how to do her job by someone she viewed as a simpleton. The last words

Rob heard was Nurse Cooper informing James that if he did not take the medication immediately, he would be written up in the doctor's notes, sent to isolation and would have all of his privileges removed. Rob thought to himself, *'just do as you're fucking told mate.'* At the same time, he looked at the small paper cup he had been handed with the large pink tablet at the bottom. He threw it down his neck as if he was having a low flyer with Ricky in the Admiral.

Chapter Forty-two

Amelia and Jonathan had enjoyed a fantastic few days on Safari even if their accommodation was fairly basic for Jonathan's standards. Amelia had enjoyed seeing the various delights that Africa had to offer. She particularly enjoyed seeing the tower of giraffes, especially when Jonathan said the reason giraffes have long necks was because they have smelly feet. This made the little girl chuckle. There were very few tourists on the same Safari other than an elderly German couple and one or two Chinese tourists. All of whom kept to themselves by the end of each day. The one thing that Jonathan had failed to grasp, was how much danger they were in as the whole group was being watched. Also, the guides were in on what was about to happen.

Mousa was the leader of the gang that had been stalking Jonathan and Amelia for the past three days. Every inch the African warrior, Mousa was constantly armed and constantly paranoid. His paranoia was partially down to the Ganja that he chewed daily. When he wasn't high on Ganja, he was drunk on Juju, which made him particularly aggressive. Even his men feared him when he had too much to drink and Mousa used this as a tool to guarantee his men's loyalty. Even as a young man, Mousa had shown no compassion for anyone who dared to challenge his authority. He once even killed his partner's mother in order to punish his partner for giving birth to a daughter instead of a son. All Mousa cared about was power and money and gave little consideration to anyone who stood in his way.

As night began to fall, Mousa and his men began to approach the small, self-contained cabin where Jonathan and Amelia were housed. All five men were armed. Slowly, without sound, they approached the front door. Mousa gave instructions for two to go around the back whilst he peered through the window. Mousa saw Jonathan asleep on the settee with Amelia cuddled up beside him. Mousa turned the handle on the door he knew would be unlocked. Soon, all five men were in the living quarters. Mousa smiled, showing his gold teeth as he looked at the rest of his men. Then he barked, "Grab the girl."

The first time Jonathan knew anyone was in the room was when Amelia screamed. Jonathan was shocked and tried to grab his daughter. Two of Mousa's men held Jonathan down. Jonathan was no fighter and this soon became evident to Mousa. At the same time, Amelia screamed, "Daddy! Daddy!"

Jonathan, in shock, shouted, "Take what you want, just leave me and the girl!"

Mousa replied, "We will take what we want, white man, which includes the girl and your money, white man."

Despite being held down, Jonathan managed to break free and tried punching Mousa in the face. Mousa was hardened to this type of attack and found it nothing more than an irritation. At the same time, two of Mousa's men managed to regain control of Jonathan.

Mousa barked at the two men that held Amelia and both men disappeared with Amelia kicking and screaming. All the time, Jonathan's eyes widened in terror and he began shouting for help. Mousa barked some more orders at the men holding Jonathan and one released his grip to put some sort of implement or belt around Jonathan's hand. Jonathan didn't know what was happening until his arm was placed over the table. At which point, Mousa removed a bloodstained machete from his side. Then, in a deep, menacing tone said, "No white man ever hits me and keeps his hand."

Mousa's men cheered and laughed as Mousa raised the machete in the air over Jonathan's arm and then brought it down firmly on his victim's wrist. A cheer went up from Mousa's men at the barbarism of what Mousa had done to Jonathan. Within a second of his hand being severed from his arm, Jonathan passed out on the floor. Mousa then turned to the two men holding Jonathan and barked, "Cover his wrist with a towel to stop the bleeding and put him in the car. Take him to the doctor, we will see what we can get for his kidneys."

Both men quickly responded to their leader's orders. Mousa then looked around the room to see where the white man's wallet was and quickly found it. He also looked for a passport but to no avail. He then quickly scanned the room and saw the white man's hand on the table and the blood that had flowed onto the floor. He felt a certain satisfaction with his work. He then turned off the light and discreetly closed the door behind him before quickly making his way into the night. Soon he would take the young white child deep into Somalia and sell her to one of the warlords. Mousa knew a warlord would pay handsomely, especially for a young, white virgin. The warlords believed having sex with white virgins cured HIV. Either way, Mousa didn't care. All he was interested in was the prize.

Chapter Forty-three

Charlotte wasn't surprised that she had not heard from Jonathan since she had last seen him at the airport. She knew it wasn't that Jonathan didn't care, it was more that Jonathan just didn't think. However, it would have been nice to speak to Amelia when she and Jonathan had arrived in Africa. Especially since she had not anticipated how quiet it would be without her little girl at home keeping Charlotte busy.

Even though Charlotte had managed to declutter most of the house, there was a certain sense of emptiness in Charlotte's home without her little girl. The solitude was nice but Charlotte missed Amelia and hoped the two weeks would pass quickly. In the meantime, Charlotte threw herself into her work.

During the MDT (Multi-Disciplinary Team) meeting, Charlotte had only just managed to convince the rest of the senior doctors and management that Rob Foster should be given ground leave with the utmost urgency. Charlotte knew she could trust Rob and made the case, quite articulately, that despite Rob's offence and early admission, Rob was not a threat.

Even so, various members of the MDT held strong objections, but Charlotte's skill as a negotiator shone and she reiterated the fact that Rob's father did not have long to live. When final approval was given, Charlotte went down to Rob's ward to tell him about the progress that had been made.

Rob was sat on his bed, in his room, reading when Charlotte knocked on his door. Both Charlotte and Rob smiled at each other as the door opened. "Good news, Rob," said Charlotte. "I've managed to secure your ground leave. Hopefully you can get out today or tomorrow, certainly in the next few days."

Rob sighed and was pleased to hear the news and replied, "That's great, hopefully I'll get to see the old man at least one more time."

Charlotte responded, "OK, I just need to have a quick chat with you so I know you understand how important this leave is."

Both doctor and patient made their way into the quiet room and closed the door behind them.

"Okay," said Charlotte, "I need you to understand, because of your index offence, that you appreciate it is very rare for you to get ground leave so quickly."

"Okay, I understand."

"Also," continued Charlotte, "you must follow the rules of ground leave, I'm trusting you not to abscond. If you do, you will not get ground leave again for at least five years." But then, Charlotte added, "However, I would not have put you forward for this if I didn't think you were ready and your circumstances were not as they are. Believe me, Rob, there's patients here that have done less than you and are nowhere near ready for ground leave."

"OK, I appreciate all you've done, I'll make sure I don't let you down."

Then Charlotte asked, "So with everything that's gone on Rob, how do you feel?"

"Okay I suppose,", replied Rob. "I just didn't realise how much I took my freedom for granted until now."

"That's common, Rob," replied Charlotte. "And what about with what's happening to your father?"

Rob thought for a second and then sighed, "With everything that's going on, if I can just reassure my dad that I love him, even if it's for the last time. It will probably do us both some good."

Again, both doctor and patient chatted for a good hour. Some of the conversation was clinical, some of it more informal. Rob even disclosed thoughts about his child that he still had not seen and Charlotte agreed how difficult it was to be away from your child and, at the same time, casually mentioned that her daughter was in Kenya on Safari with her father. Neither doctor nor patient felt it was inappropriate for such discussions to take place. Soon however, both would realise how significant this was.

Chapter Forty-four

Jonathan woke up in the back of what felt like some sort of Jeep or Land Rover. He felt dizzy and sick and the pain in his right arm was excruciating. He was alone in the back as he saw his two captors in the front of the vehicle, through the window, smoking weed and laughing. The vehicle he was in couldn't have been going more than thirty miles per hour although Jonathan had no idea where he was other than that he was in Kenya and his little girl was missing.

As he looked again through the window at the front of the vehicle, he saw they were approaching lights in the distance. The vehicle began to slow as if approaching some sort of junction. Jonathan saw his chance. As the vehicle slowed, just before it turned to the right, Jonathan threw himself out over the tail lift, hitting the dirt and dust of the road. Again, the pain was excruciating as Jonathan fell to the ground but he quickly looked up to see the vehicle drive off into the distance, all the time his captors oblivious that Jonathan had escaped.

It was dark but quiet on the unassuming road in Africa. Wearily, Jonathan picked himself up and looked for some sort of indication as to where he was. Across from where he escaped, he saw a sign which read, 'Mandera Army Barracks'. Jonathan made his way in the direction of the barracks, trying to run but it was barely a jog. All Jonathan could taste in his mouth was bile but he had to get help, he had to get his little girl back.

Dawn was just beginning to break when Jonathan reached the barracks. There were two armed guards on the gatehouse, who looked at Jonathan with suspicion as he approached. It was only when Jonathan was a hundred yards away that they realised he had no hand on one of his arms. Both soldiers approached the man who was talking fast and trying to explain what had happened. It was only when one of the guards frisked Jonathan, they found he had a British passport. Both soldiers quickly realised what had happened and ushered Jonathan through.

Jonathan was treated by the army doctor on site and the British Embassy in Nairobi was contacted. It was evident to all parties what had happened. Jonathan would need further treatment, not least to stop the spread of infection in his right arm but in the meantime, the British Embassy had made arrangements for an ambulance to bring Jonathan to Nairobi.

It was at that point, next of kin would need to be informed. At the same time, a search party would need to be deployed. The British Consulate, based in Nairobi, left strict instructions that he was to be contacted as soon as the British citizen was taken to Kenyatta National Hospital. It would be from here that the information would be collected and all the relevant parties would be informed.

Chapter Forty-five

It was roughly six forty-five in the morning when Charlotte heard knocking at her front door. This was no great tax on Charlotte as she would normally be rising about this time anyway to go to work but she did wonder who would be knocking at this hour. She put on her dressing gown and made her way downstairs to the front door. As she answered the door, stood in front of her was a policeman in full uniform along with a tall blonde-haired woman in a formal suit.

It was the woman who spoke first. "Dr. Charlotte Beaumont?" said the woman.

"Yes," replied Charlotte. "Can I help you?"

"My name is Detective Inspector Denman from the Metropolitan Police." As she spoke, she held up her credentials.

"What's happened?" asked Charlotte.

"Do you mind if we come in so we can have a word?"

Quickly, Charlotte ushered both police officers into her kitchen. All the time, Charlotte did not know what to think.

"Please take a seat, I'm afraid I've got some bad news."

"Go on," replied Charlotte as she sat down and braced herself.

"We've received word from the British Consulate in Kenya and it is my duty to inform you that your husband is in hospital. I'm afraid he's been attacked."

"Oh my God!" cried Charlotte.

"Also," Inspector Denman continued, "your daughter Amelia has been taken."

"Oh God no!" screamed Charlotte "Taken by whom?" she asked.

Denman responded, "Enquiries are still ongoing but unfortunately information is very sketchy at this stage. However, the British Consulate is doing everything possible to try to identify the whereabouts of your daughter."

Charlotte was visibly shaken by what the officer had just told her and soon she rose from the chair, ran to the sink and started to throw up. Denman then turned to the other officer and asked her to wait outside, as she sought to comfort Charlotte by rubbing her back and filling a glass of water. It was obvious for DI Denman that Charlotte was just as much a victim as the father and daughter who were somewhere in Africa.

Traumatic as it was, DI Denman had to ask Charlotte several questions in order to proceed with the investigation. After about twenty minutes or so, Charlotte regained composure and then asked to be excused whilst she got dressed, returning a few minutes later wearing a t-shirt and some tracksuit bottoms. DI Denman continued to question Charlotte on everything she knew about Jonathan's trip to Kenya with Amelia.

Charlotte tried desperately to remember any ounce of information she could think of however it felt to Charlotte like her world had just caved in and she was almost lost for words. A mixture of emotions ran through Charlotte's mind as Denman tried to piece together the events leading up to Amelia's disappearance. Once Denman had questioned Charlotte for a good hour and a half, she asked if there was anyone she could call. Friends, family, anyone who could sit with Charlotte in her darkest hour.

Charlotte declined the offer. At this stage, she did not want anyone to be with her. She had to be alone to process what had happened. Soon, DI Denman felt she had enough information to pass on to the Kenyan authorities and then explained to Charlotte that there would be a police officer assigned to the front door of Charlotte's house. Also, at the same time, the Detective Inspector removed a card from her wallet with her contact details. Should Charlotte think of anything, she would be able to contact her all hours. Also, she mentioned a family liaison officer would be in touch soon.

Charlotte tried to compose herself as best she could as she escorted the Detective Inspector to the door but as the door closed behind Inspector Denman, Charlotte fell to her knees, with her arms around her legs, and began to cry uncontrollably. At the same time, Charlotte whispered, "God help me, I need to get my daughter back."

Chapter Forty-six

Soon, the press had got wind of the abduction and as such, were sensationalising the story for all it was worth. It wasn't long before Charlotte started to receive phone calls. One tabloid newspaper even offered her a large sum of money in order to tell her story to the world in a Sunday newspaper. For Charlotte in particular, this felt like a breach of any amount of human decency. Fortunately, by now, the police liaison officer had contacted all of Charlotte's family to save Dr Beaumont from reliving every detail time and again.

It was just another day for Rob. Staring at the four walls whilst trying to remain inconspicuous to any attention from the staff. Although he had noticed there had been no newspaper that day, he thought nothing of it as it was the norm for the hospital to withhold the papers whenever there was a story relating to the hospital or one of its patients. However, as much as they would have wanted to, the hospital could not control what was being broadcast on the television.

The One O'clock News came on as normal. It was the one thing in the day that Rob made a point of viewing, simply to keep abreast of current affairs. Another patient was asleep on the sofa when the newsreader read out the headlines. "British father attacked and child abducted in Kenya," announced the newsreader.

On hearing this, Rob sat up immediately. He moved closer to the television in order to hear the audio, listening intently for the story of the missing child, knowing full well, that Charlotte Beaumont's daughter was in that part of the world. Rob's fears became apparent as not only had the press given Amelia's name and photograph, they also showed Dr Beaumont leaving court on the day of Rob's trial.

Rob drank in as much information as he could. The news story itself was more sensationalised than informative. It highlighted that men with guns had snatched the child in the middle of the night however the child's father had managed to escape, somehow losing a hand in the process. The news story gave nothing away about which organisation had taken Amelia. It also failed to mention whether a ransom demand had been made for the child. The only thing the news did say was that Kenyan soldiers had been deployed in the area to look for Amelia.

This meant nothing to Rob as he knew full well how ineffective the Kenyan military were. From experience, he knew how undisciplined the soldiers acted. Also, given the nature of the location, Rob knew of the corruption amongst the military ranks and those soldiers who were not taking bribes, were out of their heads on drugs. After the story had finished, Rob returned to his room, mainly to think about what assistance he could give to Charlotte Beaumont. He felt he had to, it was a matter of honour.

Rob sat on his bed, occasionally looking out of his window but mainly thinking who he could contact. Over and over again, he ran through various scenarios in his mind which he thought could assist the authorities but every time, he drew a blank. Ultimately, he could not ring the regiment and he was not high enough up the British Army food chain to call in any favours. Even if he had been, given his situation, nobody would have taken him seriously anyway. Rob knew full well, the only way to gather information about the abduction was to be on the ground.

To add insult to injury, the only people that could be deployed effectively on the ground, were members of the SAS. Rob thought long and hard for the next half an hour. Would it be possible for him to get into Kenya? Not only would he need a contact but he would need financial support too, not to mention the medication he would need in order to function. Rob began to devise a plan. It was a plan, not without risk. It was a plan, he figured, that only had a ten percent chance of success.

It was at this point Rob said to himself, "For fuck's sake, Robbo, I'm in enough shit as it is, I can't go." But then he quickly dismissed this thought. "Fuck it I'm going," he muttered under his breath and then he added, "I've got fuck all else to do for the next ten years."

Whilst sat in his room, he began to devise a plan in his mind about how to escape the hospital. With each plan, analysing how to escape effectively. The hospital had a number of airlocks which were only accessible through electric card keys. Also, he would need several cards to open different airlocks.

Another option, Rob thought about briefly, would be to create a diversion. Perhaps he could start a fire somewhere or possibly set off a fire alarm. Would he be able to escape under the confusion? Again, he doubted it. If he got caught trying to escape, not only would he be put in isolation but the hospital would also put into place additional procedures to monitor Rob. "How the fuck am I going to get out of here?" Rob muttered to himself.

Just then, there was a knock at the door. The door opened and Chris Daniels stood there. "Now then, my fellow squaddie, you ready to take your first ground leave? You can get off the ward for a bit."

Within a second, Rob was on his feet. Rob knew this was his chance to get away. "Sounds like a nice idea," said Rob, "I could do with some fresh air."

"OK then, be ready to go in half an hour."

Rob just smiled. "I'll be ready all right."

Chapter Forty-seven

Rob was going to make a break for it. He quickly looked around his bedroom to see if there was anything in there that would be useful to him on the run. All he could find was an old red sweater. He put this on underneath his jacket. Also, he found some loose change on the side. There was one more thing he needed to do before he left the Humber Centre. He quickly took one last glance around his room and shut the door behind him.

Rob then made his way up the corridor to use the phone outside of the staff room. He picked up the receiver and dialled in the number for Annie, hoping that only Annie would answer the phone. The tone rang three or four times before it was picked up. Rob recognised Annie's voice straight away as she said hello, then he quickly dispensed the loose change into the phone. "Annie, it's Rob, don't hang up."

"Rob, what are you doing? You know you're not supposed to contact me," was the response.

"I know," replied Rob, "but just listen. I want you to know that I'm sorry I fucked up everything."

Annie remained silent.

"Also, I'm going to sign over the house to you and sign the papers for the divorce as soon as I can."

Annie knew something was wrong but she could not put her finger on it.

Rob continued, "Annie, I want you to know that you were the best thing that happened to me and I wish so much that I could change things so we could raise Noel together as a family. I don't have a lot of time now, babe."

"A lot of time for what?" replied Annie.

"Look, listen, I just want you to know I love you and Noel very much," then Rob paused. "I had a good thing and I blew it."

At that point, Rob looked up to see Chris Daniels coming out of the office with a form in his hand.

"I've got to go now," Rob said. "I'll see ya, babe."

Rob could hear Annie's voice on the line as he replaced the receiver.

Chris Daniels approached Rob and told him to fill in the form before they went on ground leave as he gave Rob a pen. It was a simple questionnaire. Before any patient went on ground leave, they had to fill in a form detailing how much money the patient had on them, what clothes they were wearing, whether they had a lighter or not. Rob just filled this in as quick as he could; he wanted to be making tracks. Once the paperwork was done, both patient and staff nurse made their way through the airlock.

At the same time as Annie was on the phone to Rob in the hallway, Sue was stood, listening, in the kitchen. As Annie replaced the receiver, Sue began to go to work on Annie. "Who was that?" demanded Sue.

"Nobody," replied Annie sheepishly.

"Who was it?" questioned Sue again.

"Mum, just leave it."

"It was *him* wasn't it?" said Sue spitefully.

"Mum, he was just ringing to say he would give me my divorce that's all," then Annie added, "He's also going to let me have the house."

"And so he bloody well should!" cried Sue. "After all he's put you and this family through and anyway, he shouldn't be ringing here at all, the court demanded it."

"Mum, can you just leave it!" protested Annie.

"No, I cannot just leave it! He's a sick bastard that should be locked away for the rest of his life, in fact, hanging is too good for him. How on earth has he got access to a telephone in order to bother us?"

Annie knew she was not going to win and so picked up Noel from the high-chair in the kitchen and retreated toward the living room. At the same time, Sue shouted to her husband Norman, "What's the number of that inspector you know from the Conservative Club?"

"It's in the book, why?" he replied.

Within a second, Sue was on the phone protesting to the inspector that her family were all in fear because of a vicious, psycho killer that was bothering them from a mental hospital. Sue made a point of adding that Rob was already breaching a zero-contact restraining order. The inspector took all the details and quickly tried to reassure Sue that he would make a phone call straight away.

Chapter Forty-eight

Rob breathed in the fresh air when he left the airlock at the medium secure hospital. For the first time in about six months, Rob's lungs felt alive as he breathed in the sweet smell of summer. Both Rob and Chris headed toward the field behind the hospital via the car park however, Rob knew time was of the essence as he only had half an hour before the hospital staff reported him missing.

As both patient and staff member crossed the car park, the lights flashed on the Subaru that was parked in the car park. It was Chris's Subaru and he made a point of showing it off to Rob as he opened the car door and retrieved his cigarettes.

"Good little runner this," bragged Chris. "I overtook this bird the other day on the inside lane on the motorway and I could tell by the way she looked at me that she was gagging for it."

Rob just ignored the comment but at the same time, made a mental note of where Chris put the key in his pocket.

PC Holland and WPC Emary received a call to visit the Psychiatric Hospital. Whoever had made the call, was pretty adamant that Rob Foster was bothering people. Having just finished a routine patrol of Cottingham, the local village, they made their way towards Willerby. WPC Emary could not stand working with PC Holland. For a start, he was constantly making lewd comments about the women police staff. Not only were they derogatory, they were sometimes aimed at her. However, having only been in the police service for two years, WPC Emary knew better than to rock the boat and make a complaint against her superior. As both officers travelled to their next appointment, PC Holland began preaching about their next assignment. This was the norm and the WPC just remained silent.

"The trouble with these fruit-loops, is that we can lock them up but the hospitals just let them out again." He added, "What they should do, is give 'em a minimum of ten years without parole. That would free us up to do our jobs without these sickos bothering the public."

As he spoke, bits of pastry flew out of his mouth whilst he was eating a sausage roll he got from Greggs. As WPC Emary looked at him, she felt more repulsed by her colleague than ever.

PC Holland continued, "The fact is, all these psycho 'ead cases are all sexual deviants."

WPC Emary stopped him there. "You don't know anything about him." she protested.

"I know how to do my job love, trust me, I've been a copper now for seven years, I'll be going up the ranks soon, love. You might want to remember that cause there's a good chance you'll be taking more of your orders from me. In fact," he added, "I could show you a thing or two," and at the same time, he removed his hand from the steering wheel and placed it, unwelcomely, on WPC Emary's thigh. WPC Emary felt almost sick.

Making their way across the open field, Chris Daniels began to brag again about everything that he had done in the military. In fact, from the way he talked, it was almost as if he had won any war by himself. At the same time, Rob just made little conversation and nodded. It was only when Chris started talking about the SAS, Rob started to get annoyed, Daniels bragged, "Yeah, after I'd done a two-week course in Catterick, they asked me if I wanted to join the SAS."

Rob stopped walking just there. Rob replied, "The SAS is a volunteer force, nobody ever gets asked to join."

Chris blew smoke out of his mouth as he answered, "Yeah but not with me it wasn't, someone from the SAS saw me when I was on exercise and they saw how good I was. He came up to me at the end of the weekend and said, 'I think you'd be good for us, I want you to join'." Then he continued, "I turned it down though, weren't for me that."

"You know something," Rob replied, "you're talking a load of shit. In fact, you talk so much shit, that if you opened your mouth, all I could smell would be a dog's arse."

"Right then, Foster," said Chris annoyed, his pride damaged. "I'm cancelling your leave and I'm writing you up, you're aggressive and you're not playing ball. You wanted it the hard way and you've got it, things are going to get very difficult for you from now on, sunshine, forget about seeing deathbed daddy."

Before Chris had chance to say anything more, Rob punched him squarely in the forehead, totally disorienting him, with Daniels falling to the ground. As he was on the floor, Rob stuck his hands around his antagonist's throat and began to squeeze. He wasn't trying to kill him, he just wanted to stop the flow of blood to Daniels's brain until he fainted. Chris's eyes widened in terror as he struggled against an adversary for whom he was no match. At the same time, Chris struggled to free Rob's hands from his throat but it wasn't long before he succumbed to asphyxiation and fainted.

When Rob knew Daniels was no longer a threat, he quickly frisked his body and removed the radio and the car key from Daniels's trousers. He then checked Daniels's neck for a pulse and when he found one, was quite pleased that he did not kill this prick. Within a second, he looked around the field. There was nobody in sight and he doubted very much that anyone would have noticed anything from the hospital windows.

Soon, Rob had crossed the field leaving Daniels where he lay and was crossing the car park. Rob had always fancied taking a Subaru for a spin. As Rob was getting in the car, he looked up to see a police vehicle approaching. Rob knew he had to play this one very carefully. He watched the police car stop outside the entrance to the hospital as a WPC and a fat male PC, made their way to the entrance.

Rob turned the key to start the engine which revved like a wild cat and within a second, loud hip-hop music blasted from the radio. At the same time, both police officers looked to see where the noise was coming from. Rob wasn't prepared to make his escape listening to gangster rap and as the African-American rapper sang about all the guns, money, bitches and drugs he had, Rob retuned the radio.

Running across the car park was Chris Daniels, as the police looked up, just about to enter the airlock, Daniels was shouting, "Stop him! Stop him! He's got my car!"

WPC Emary was the first to notice Foster sat in the vehicle at which point, both officers tried to run to apprehend the culprit. Rob remained calm throughout, soon he found 'Planet Rock' on the radio, he heard the welcoming sound of an A-flat power chord. Rob suddenly felt the hairs on the back of his neck stand up as the song 'Wheels of Steel' by Saxon kicked into life.

Rob put the car in first gear, aggressively pressing the accelerator and quickly drove past his pursuers, looking in the rear-view mirror, Rob could see Daniels, waving his arms and stamping his feet. At the same time, both officers made their way back to their vehicle in order to pursue Rob. Rob quickly made his way out of the hospital site, reaching a roundabout on Beverley Road and took a quick right turn. Chris Daniels was telling the truth, this car could move and it was more than enough to get Rob away. At the same time, WPC Emary and PC Holland were in pursuit with the blue lights flashing and the sirens screaming.

"Are we gonna ring it in?" questioned the WPC to her colleague.

"No way," replied PC Holland arrogantly. "I don't like anyone getting away from me."

Further up the road, Rob spotted queuing traffic ahead. At the same time, Rob felt alive, aggressive and dangerous. Within a second, he'd reached another roundabout but instead of slowing down, he overtook the cars on the outside lane before using the handbrake to slow him down, whilst at the same time, changing the direction of the vehicle in a doughnut. Rob then accelerated as hard as he could whilst other vehicles beeped and flashed.

All the time, Rob was thoroughly engrossed in the music. Both police officers saw Rob's manoeuvre and tried their best to pursue without endangering any civilians. In less than ten seconds, Rob passed the exit of the hospital he had escaped from. Soon, the guitar solo was blasting but Rob knew he would have to lose his pursuers before they called for reinforcements. Aggressively, he used the Subaru to clip oncoming vehicles just like when he had been trained during selection.

As a result, traffic slowed, almost confused at this mad man in a fast car. He quickly crossed over a third roundabout and saw a pitch in the road which veered off toward the Wolds Way. Rob almost slowed to allow his pursuers to catch up. As he took the junction, Rob slowed to a halt, waiting for the police to be within striking distance. At the same time, the music died to a middle eight, almost a pause. Within the space of a couple of seconds, the blue lights of the police car approached from the bend. Rob knew this was a great opportunity to disable the police car.

Quickly, he put the Subaru in reverse and again, aggressively, put his foot on the accelerator aiming straight for the front of the police car. WPC Emary screamed as she realised what Rob was doing. At the same time, she shouted at her colleague, "For fucks sake slow down!" Within a second, the impact was felt fully by the police vehicle as the Subaru disintegrated the radiator and the rest of the police car, making it impossible for the pursuit to continue. Despite the fact both airbags deployed in the police car, it did not stop both WPC Emary and PC Holland from colliding with the dashboard. Emary suffered a broken nose whilst Holland smashed his teeth against the steering wheel.

As the seconds rolled by, the music came to life again with the singer screaming 'talkin' about my wheels of steel'. Rob quickly put the car in first gear and did not hesitate in making good on his escape whilst driving away in the dusk of a summer evening. Rob was pleased with himself but the fact was, now, he had work to do.

Part Two

Edinburgh

Chapter Forty-nine

The red Corsa pulled up outside the high-rise flats in the notorious Muirhouse estate in Edinburgh. Inside the car was a woman known as Jessica and sat next to her was Amy although Amy's working name was Roxy. Jessica turned to Amy and said in a cockney accent, "You know the score with this job, love, remember once he's paid ya, to get the package. I'll be sat 'ere just going through my Facebook."

Amy replied in a soft Glaswegian accent, "So when are we getting a new driver then, boss? I'm not being funny but I'd feel a lot safer with a driver who wasn't a woman."

Jessica was slightly annoyed and replied, "Look I'm fackin' workin' on it and I don't see you turnin' down the money." Then Jessica changed tack. "You've done this job before loads of times, in fact he asked for you, you know it's an easy gig. Once you get paid, ring me to do the safe and happy, if there's any problems I'll ring the police."

Amy said nothing as she left the vehicle and made her way to the intercom. Quickly, she was buzzed through by the client all the time saying to herself, *'it's just a job'*. However, she wished she had not spent so much on getting her hair done that day in town. As she entered the lift, the smell of stale urine was prominent on the lift floor however, fortunately, no one else was in the steel box. Amy, or Roxy as was her working name, was not your run of the mill escort.

A lot of girls on Jessica's books were hard party girls and drug users. It was only her roommate Sophie who had advised her that this was a quick and easy way to make money. Both Sophie and Amy were at university and Sophie had nearly finished her accountancy degree whereas Amy was just two years into a law degree. It was only when the debts mounted up she considered quitting and going back to Glasgow to be with her six-year-old son who was being looked after by Amy's mother. The debts were mounting and the bills needed paying but this type of work meant that, in theory, she could leave university without any debt and continue on a path as either a barrister or a lawyer.

When Amy first started escorting six months ago, not only was the money good, which meant she could go back to Glasgow to see her son occasionally, but also the job itself was exciting, sexy, a taboo, even if it was dangerous at times. Amy would not have believed what she had done if she had not have seen it through her own eyes. To be fair, most of the jobs were basic, bog standard. They were just single men that wanted a good time but didn't want the hassle of a relationship. These jobs were the norm but then there were other jobs. Sometimes it was couples, other times it was certain fetishes, and by all accounts, the fetishes were weird.

On one job, she was even asked by the client to act like he was a baby and she would literally have to bath and nappy change a forty-year-old man. Other jobs meant working with Sophie if a guy wanted a threesome and although she did not mind this per say, as she had always been bi-curious. However, she would not work with any other of Jessica's girls. Simply because of her own sexual health. It was rumoured that some of the girls had hepatitis C.

As the lift stopped on the fifth floor, Amy became Roxy. She looked at herself in the large metal mirror in the lift, Roxy was by all accounts attractive, although she would never admit it to herself. Twenty-six-years-old, five foot two, size eight, nails polished and dark hair in a neat bob and well dressed in an expensive suit. This particular client was a smackhead through and through. How he got the money to pay for Roxy's services was anyone's guess although it was obvious drugs were involved.

The client's name was Billy and she had to make sure that Billy thoroughly enjoyed himself by making out that Roxy was having the best sex of her young life, all the time surrounded by stains on the walls, empty pizza boxes of takeaways all over the floor and the putrid smell of stale cigarettes. However, Roxy drew the line at kissing. Not necessarily every client but certainly with this one. All the time, Roxy just concentrated on the money and the end game.

Roxy knocked on the door twice and was quickly answered by Billy who came to the door in a pair of jeans and Jesus sandals on his feet and a bare yellowish chest covered in dark blotches. Roxy made a mental note of the time as she was paid for the hour and once she had put the £120 in her purse, she pulled out her mobile phone to ring Jessica. The phone rang twice before Jessica answered with a curt, "Yep."

Roxy just replied, "Safe and happy."

Jessica then continued, "Have you been paid?"

"Yes," replied Roxy.

Then Jessica added, "Have you got the package?"

Roxy then lowered her phone to her chin and said to Billy, "Have you got the package?"

Billy then threw his arms in the air confused and said, "Oh yeah, yeah! I forgot." Billy then disappeared into the spare bedroom and returned within a minute holding a brown envelope.

Roxy then continued on the phone to Jessica, "Yeah, I've got the package now."

"OK, see you in an hour."

Roxy hung up the phone, put the package in her handbag and pulled out some latex condoms then said to Billy, "In here or the bedroom?"

Chapter Fifty

The Sheraton Grand Spa was a 5-star hotel in the middle of Festival Square in Edinburgh. It was a sunny Saturday afternoon and initially the square was packed with the usual tourists from all over the world. The tranquility was soon broken however, when from the corner of the square a group of twenty or so Hearts football hooligans descended onto the square, fueled on alcohol and amphetamine like a pack of wild dogs.

It was derby day at the start of the *'friendly'* football match, and Hearts were due to play Hibs within the next two hours. Before that however, two rival football firms had arranged the usual punch up before the match. This was normally on the outskirts of the city, however the police were getting wise to the normal locations of the fights, so the firms both agreed to meet in Festival Square.

The violence between Hearts and Hibs, although not as brutal as the Glasgow rivals (Celtic and Rangers), was totally fueled by sectarianism.

Almost a civil war between two theologies. The Hearts firm looked at complete contempt at anyone who was in their path, in fact the lucky tourists were the ones who only got death stares, others would be spat at, tables would be turned over at the coffee shops and all the time the police were nowhere to be seen, as they were totally overstretched.

A few metres away from the entrance of the hotel, in a shop doorway, lay a vulnerable tramp obviously down on his luck and sleeping on cardboard with nothing but a blanket and a red sweater to protect him from the elements. Ian, one of the Hearts' hooligans, thought it was a great opportunity to try and impress the lads, he unzipped his fly and began to relieve himself all over the pathetic individual laying in the doorway.

As soon as the tramp knew what was happening, he swore to himself in an English accent, but instead of retaliating, he pathetically picked himself up, tried to get away from his assailant and did his best to prevent his bed from getting any wetter. Ian and the firm thought this was hilarious as the dejected tramp started to retreat from the square.

At the same time Amy was leaving the steps of the Sheraton Hotel, where she had spent the night with a client. It wasn't a bad job in the sense that there was nothing too taxing, however the client was a short, fat, bald, fifty-year-old business man. Even though he had extended twice the night before and wanted to extend further. Amy couldn't be arsed with any more acting, she felt that she had done enough to pay the bills and keep Jessica happy. She made her excuses to leave.

All of a sudden Ian spotted Amy leaving the hotel and he had found a new victim to intimidate. He looked up and pointed at Amy and shouted "Slag" and again he shouted "Slag, slag," as if on cue the rest of the firm joined in on a chorus of "Slag, slag, slag." Soon the crowd of hooligans surrounded Amy and started to belittle and mock her and Ian slapped Amy on the behind. Amy screamed and looked up at the hotel concierge only to see him locking the doors.

Amy was well and truly on her own as the bunch of Neanderthals surrounded her. All Amy could do was lash out and she threw a punch into Ian's face and continued to scream for help. The tramp that was walking away turned around after hearing the woman in distress. Within a second, he had dropped his blanket and started to run towards the crowd like a juggernaut down a clear track.

The tramp in fact was Rob Foster and he pushed into the crowd and threw a punch into Ian's temple, knowing full well it would knock him unconscious. Ian fell to the floor like a disregarded hand towel. One or two of the firm saw what happened to Ian and started to turn their attentions towards Rob. Rob was just up for a fight, even if he knew he could not take on all twenty of them. Amy was still being molested by the rest of the firm, but as if by a twist of fate, across the other side of Festival Square had arrived the Hibs firm.

When the rival firm saw each other they both charged like a force of nature and soon both firms were concentrating solely on knocking the living daylights out of each other. Rob saw his chance he grabbed Amy by the wrist and pulled her away from the chaos. "Wait!" she screamed, and bent over to retrieve her handbag which had fallen to the floor. Rob screamed at her, "Come on for fuck's sake," and then continued to pull her away. Rob was obviously a fit guy as she struggled to keep up with him as he dragged her by the wrist.

Towards the side of the hotel was a side street, Rob pulled Amy for all he was worth, hoping to find a service entrance to the hotel. His luck was in. Halfway down the alley was a fire door which had been left open, Rob quickly pulled Amy inside and slammed the fire door shut leaving the commotion behind. The large room they had entered was a banquet hall however the room was empty apart from a few tables and chairs. "Come on," he said. "He can't stay in here." Soon Rob and Amy were walking together until they found an old store room beneath the bottom of the hotel; it was a large room filled only with tables and chairs. Rob shut the door behind him again and turned on the light. "You okay love?" he asked.

Amy sat down on a chair and began to cry. "Listen, I don't know who you are, but thank you for helping me out"

"That's okay." Rob smiled. "It looked like you were having a bad day."

Amy heard Rob's accent and said, "You're English."

"How'd you guess?" Rob replied sarcastically.

"You must have a lot of bottle to be English sleeping rough in Edinburgh on derby day. Either that or you're completely nuts."

"I'm probably the latter, love," Rob replied.

Amy then began to regain her composure, she looked at Rob's clothes but noticed how athletic his body was, despite the rags he was wearing. "So how long have you been sleeping rough?"

"Just a few days, I've come up here to get myself some work, I'm looking to get some money to get me abroad."

"What sort of work do you do?"

"I was up in the army until recently, but I had some problems so I had to get away for a bit."

Amy thought for a moment and said, "I might be able to help you there, I know someone who is looking for a bodyguard."

"Okay sounds good to me, but in the meantime, I think we better get out of here. Let's go round the back of the hotel and see if we can get a taxi, you can fill me in on what you need."

Rob held out his hand, "My name's Rob," stopping short of giving his last name.

Amy took his hand and said, "Roxy, however my friends call me Amy."

At that moment Rob knew exactly what Amy meant, meaning he knew what work she did. Soon they both were in a taxi as the riot police were dispersing both firms outside the hotel. Being away from the scene of the trouble and leaving the area was a relief to Rob, however he told himself soon he would need his medication if he was to function and ultimately get Charlotte's little girl back. Rob felt Amy could help him.

Chapter Fifty-one

An hour or so later Jessica, Amy and Rob were sat in a pub called Biddy Mulligans in the grass market area of the city. Amy had filled Jessica in on what Rob had done for her that afternoon. As Jessica was looking for a new driver / body guard, initially Jessica thought this was music to her ears. All three parties discussed the role, and although Rob was jittery from the lack of sleep, he was pleased with the progress he was making. Also, the second pint of Tennant's, that Amy had bought him, was going down nicely.

Rob realised that he was talking to a madam that knew her job very well, and by all accounts Jessica enjoyed bragging about when she came up from London twenty years ago and opened the agency. Against all odds the agency had been a success. However, Jessica failed to disclose that she was a heroin addict, albeit a functioning one. At this point another opportunity presented itself to Rob, he turned to Jessica and asked, "Can you get me a passport?"

Jessica looked at him inquisitively. "So what do you need a passport for then, darling?"

Rob had to think fast, despite feeling hazy from the alcohol. "No particular reason just I left Hull so quickly that I forgot to pack my passport and it would be a hassle to have to go back and get it, especially if I'm working for you now."

Jessica took a drag on her cigarette before she answered. "I can sort that out for you, darling, but it may take a week or two, how long are you thinking of working for me?"

"Two or three months," replied Rob. "Just long enough for me to save up some money for me to get to Australia, I have a mate there from the army who has a security firm, he has offered me some work."

Jessica knew instinctively Rob was lying, and as a result of her body language, Rob knew that Jessica has sussed him. To diffuse the situation Rob asked to be excused and made his way to the gents.

As soon as he left ear shot, Amy turned to Jessica and asked, "So what do you think? Is he going to be any good to you?"

Jessica smiled and said, "I think he's facking beautiful I'm going to contact the girls tonight and tell them we have a new minder, however I don't buy this shit about going to Australia, he's on the facking run that one." Then she added "As long as he doesn't get arrested while he's working for me, I don't give a shit!"

A few minutes later and Rob returned, and sat at the table, Jessica said, "Okay, so you start tonight, I have a few jobs booked already and for the time being you can use my car to drive the girls. I take it you haven't got a phone?" Jessica asked.

Again, Rob lied. "Like I said, I left Hull in such a hurry, I left it on charge when I was rushing to catch the train."

Jessica ignored the lie and opened up her handbag, inside were three phones. She handed the cheap looking one to Rob along with a cheaper looking charger. "Right you can use this for now, where you going to be staying?"

"Well I'm not one hundred percent sure yet, but I'll find somewhere."

Jessica turned to Amy and said, "When we leave here take him to the Rock, off Princes Street he can stop there for now." Then Jessica turned to Rob and said, "Book yourself in but don't use your real name, it's a youth hostel so no one will ask many questions anyway, you won't have to pay until the end of the week."

Then Jessica added, "I've got a job booked in at seven with Lexi. It's an easy job. It's just going to The Guards Hotel for an hour."

Then Jessica handed Rob a set of car keys. "I'll make sure the car is outside the hostel at half past six, I will ring you at six with the address for Lexi. Once the job is over, you collect yours and my money and we will take it from there, there's a sat-nav in the car."

Within five minutes all three parties had finished their drinks and left the pub. Amy took Rob in a black cab before dropping him outside the Rock Youth Hostel on Johnston Terrace.

Amy turned to Rob and said, "I'm going to feel a lot safer with you driving us, but watch it, Jessica can't be trusted."

Rob's ears pricked up. "How so?" he replied.

"Just if she can save her own skin she will do," replied Amy. "I've got a job booked in later tonight, hopefully I will see you then, thanks for saving me."

Rob stepped out of the black cab and watched it pull away, before entering the hostel. He gave a false name and made his way up to the ten-bed dorm. On the side he found a plug to charge the phone, then rested on one of the bunk beds. Before he dozed, he had to think where and how he would get his meds. Soon the alcohol and lack of sleep came over him. Within five minutes he was fast asleep.

Chapter Fifty-two

An hour after leaving the pub, Jessica was sat in the office of DCI Steve Johnson, at Edinburgh Central Police Station. Both DCI Johnson and Jessica were on their second line of cocaine as they discussed the matters which were concerning the madam. To say DCI Johnson was a corrupt copper would be putting it lightly. Although he had initially come from a middle-class background, after he left the university with no debt, he joined the Scottish police force.

For the first year or two on probation Johnson kept his nose clean. However, soon in to his promotions he found a way to work both the legal system and the criminal fraternity. Johnson however, was a clever and devious bastard, and rarely did he make mistakes.

When the detective inspector in charge of him realised Johnson was a corrupt copper, it didn't take long for the rumours to spread around the station, and this quickly filtered back to Johnson. The upshot was the DI who started to investigate him was soon blackmailed when the inspector's seventeen-year-old son had ten kilograms of cocaine and a stack of child porn DVDs found in his student digs.

There was more than enough leverage for Johnson to blackmail the DI, who within a month had resigned, only for Johnson to be promoted to DI, and sat in the old detective inspector's chair soon after. Four years later, and Johnson had been promoted to DCI. Recreational drug use was not Johnson's only vice. As well as drugs, money, and power, he also had a taste for more exotic sexual exploits.

Even in his flat, in Stockbridge, in a good area of Edinburgh, he had his own personal dungeon. As a rule, Johnson preferred to be the dominant party, but occasionally he would play the submissive with call girls that Jessica provided. However, it was well known amongst the girls that he liked to be rough, the last time he booked Sophie, she ended in an terrible state. This was the reason Jessica wanted to see Johnson.

"So what the fack did you think you were playing at, last time you booked my girl?" demanded Jessica, as pleasantly as she dared to.

"I don't know what the fuck you're complaining at, Jessica. She got well fucking paid," was Johnson's arrogant reply.

Jessica dabbed her nose, enjoying the buzz of the cocaine. "Yes, I know that, Steve, but she had bruises up and down her body. I had two jobs booked in for her afterwards. She couldn't go on them because she was in that much pain."

As Jessica was speaking, Johnson started to cut another line of cocaine on his desk, with a generous helping for Jessica. Then he replied, "You tell me that she was a girl looking for new experiences, well, I gave her a new fuckin' experience."

Jessica replied, "Fucking hell, Steve, she was off for five days. Just be careful in future. Not all the girls are as open minded, and I've got to look after them, plus, you'll get your cut, so it's in your interest to keep my girls healthy."

Johnson just sniffed, and almost belligerently nodded his head, then shrugged his shoulders. "So anyway," he replied. "Do you have anything new to tell me?"

"Not much. Business is steady, oh, and it looks like I've got a new minder starting today."

Johnson looked at Jessica and said, "Who is he? Another smack-rat off the Muirhouse estate?"

"Not really," said Jessica. "This guy's as hard as facking nails. He rescued one of my girls from a shitload of football hooligans a couple of hours ago."

"Where's he from?" Johnson asked.

'Well he says he's from Hull, and he's definitely got a northern accent. But he could be from facking anywhere. I think he's on the run."

"How so," Johnson asked, the detective in him taking over.

Jessica continued. "Well for a start, he's been sleeping rough in Edinburgh and he claims that he left in such a hurry that he left his phone on charge in his flat. Load of bollocks if you ask me."

"What's his name?" asked Johnson.

"He just said his name was Rob, also he's asked me to get him a passport."

"What's he need a fucking passport for?" replied Johnson.

"He told me he was going to Australia," replied Jessica.

Johnson sniffed. "Tell you what, I'll look into him, see if there's anything on the police computer, if anything comes up, I'll let you know."

Jessica replied, "Yeah but don't do anything that's going to stop him working for me, at least for the time being. He looks like he's going to be a facking good minder."

Johnson replied, mimicking her cockney accent, "Dahn't you facking worry about it, sunshine. Now have another line." Then he added, "So what girls are working tonight then?"

Chapter Fifty-three

News of Rob Foster's daring escape from the medium secure hospital spread like wildfire through the tabloids. Also, the way in which he escaped was sensationalised in order to paint Foster as some sort of mad genius. The police were particularly unhappy, mainly because Foster was in their sight when he escaped but still managed to get away successfully. When the senior police officer was interviewed on live TV, it was almost a bone of contention when the newsreader pressed the officer on Foster's successful evasion. It was becoming apparent that Humberside police were taking it personally.

Another party which took it personally was Simon Grant's family. Not only had they protested that justice had not been served as before, but now the authorities had let this vicious killer escape almost unchallenged from incarceration. Again, Simon Grant's uncle reiterated the words *scum* and *psycho* when referring to Rob.

What made the news story more intriguing was the fact that the Grant family had placed a ten-thousand-pound reward on Rob's head and Simon Grant's uncle had almost implied to the media that Rob was wanted dead or alive, carefully selecting his words.

It was a complete circus, added to the fact that Rob Foster's consultant, Dr Charlotte Beaumont, was also recently in the news because her daughter had been kidnapped in Kenya, and both Rob Foster and Dr Beaumont's pictures were spread all over the news stream as if to imply some sick connection.

The media vultures were constantly parked outside of the secure hospital. It wasn't long before DI Denman contacted her local counterparts in Humberside Police, to find out what was the meat and bones of what was happening in Hull. It was almost as if something didn't add up, but she could not place her finger on it at that stage.

As for DI Denman's case load, the Beaumont case had been given top priority; however, the information coming out of Kenya was sketchy, and nonchalant to say the least. It was almost as if the Kenyan authorities didn't have a clue, or were not particularly bothered, other than securing the tourist money that came in regularly. Therefore, the Kenyan hierarchy continued to play it down, reiterating that events like this were very rare. This made DI Denman's work even more taxing.

It wasn't long before DCI Steve Johnson had also picked up on the story circulating in the media. He quickly realised the connection. Not that he was bothered about Charlotte Beaumont's daughter or Rob Foster being on the run, what he was interested in though was the ten-thousand-pound reward that the Grant family had offered on Facebook. Johnson knew full well not only would he inherit the money if he arrested Rob, but his career prospects would significantly improve. Maybe he would even get a book publishing deal. Johnson could almost count the noughts on the end of his bank balance.

However, he had a problem. The problem was Jessica. He knew full well that Jessica would not be happy if he arrested her new minder within a week of working for her. Suddenly he had a plan. He would ring Jessica directly and tell her he had found out who Rob was. He would also add that there was a reward out on Rob's neck. He would not disclose how much the reward was worth, or maybe even play it down, knowing full well that Jessica would want her cut.

Johnson figured Foster would not be going anywhere soon, so he had time to sit on his hands and devise a plan. Maybe even he could put a scenario in place, a trap for Foster to walk into making Johnson look like a hero instead of the snake he was. Potentially, the reward money would go up. Either way, he enjoyed the idea that soon Foster would make him a lot of money. In the meantime, he would book one of Jessica's girls tonight, and then lean on her for information on Jessica's new minder.

Chapter Fifty-four

Rob settled in quite easily to his new role as a minder for Jessica's agency. Initially, he was nervous on every job. Particularly, as Amy had warned him not to trust Jessica but then Rob realised, part of that was the paranoia he was suffering from. The first job with Lexi at The Guards Hotel took an hour. He had picked Lexi up at the agreed time, making little conversation as he drove her to the job, Lexi in turn had made little conversation as well.

However, when she returned an hour later, she was more open to engaging with Rob. She even discussed some of the activities that had taken place within the hotel room. However, Rob did his best not to pry. Rob collected Jessica's money and his own money and then received another phone call to pick up another girl called Summer and the work went on from there.

At the end of every shift Rob would count all the money and separate Jessica's cut, the rest was his and by the end of the first night he had earnt over

£100. Basically, the job was easy, and most of the time Rob found himself parked outside of some house, flat or hotel reading a magazine or newspaper. Within a week he had saved over £500 just by acting as a bodyguard for the girls.

Rob was also aware that his injection was due soon and once he got his bearings of the city, he quickly sussed out the best places to obtain his medication. He just hoped the places he was going to break into had it in stock. He had recced a doctor's surgery with a pharmacist next door on the Pilton estate.

The pharmacy itself was directly next door to the surgery. However, the security around it, was more vandal proof than burglary proof. The cameras on the side of the building looked like they had not been maintained for years, and it would not take Rob much to get up onto the roof to find if there was an unsecure point of entry. Rob told himself, as soon as he finished his shift that night he would go and do an in depth recce.

Rob also met Amy's roommate Sophie for the first time, although her working name was Layla and although Rob and Amy were becoming quite close, Sophie almost seemed to keep her distance. It wasn't that she was unpleasant or that she was rude, it was just Sophie had a certain coldness to her. Again, Rob had not experienced this world before, and if Sophie did not want to engage in conversation, then it was best all round if he did not push it.

By the same token, Rob and Amy would chat quite openly for hours. Sometimes after the jobs were finished, Rob would drive them to a twenty-four-hour McDonalds. They would both sit in the car park drinking coffee, eating and chatting about life in general. Even though Rob was guarded about what he said to Amy, he felt that if things had been different, then maybe they would have a lifelong friendship.

However, this was never going to be an option given the fact Rob was on the run and again, Rob gave nothing away about who he really was, and what he was really doing in Edinburgh. Rob was intrigued that Amy was on a legal path and that she was hoping to become a barrister or a lawyer. So it came as no surprise to him, when Amy told Rob her roommate Sophie was also on an academic path and would soon finish her degree in accountancy.

Up until this point Rob had always assumed people who went to university had affluent backgrounds and he was quite impressed that at least two of the girls he was working with, were using their spare time in order to improve themselves. It was obvious to Rob that some of the girls Jessica had on her books, although potentially were good looking, were drug users, and once their looks had gone, they would be disregarded, nobody would want to use them. Both Sophie and Amy were using escorting as a way to pay for their education. Rob had to hand it to them, they were both fighters. It reminded him of himself.

In the meantime, Jessica had informed Rob that his passport would be ready in a matter of a few days. However, she gave nothing away, as to where the source of the passport would come from. Also, Jessica knew by now that Rob was on the run. However, she had not been given the full details of Rob. DCI Steve Johnson had timed it just right before he told her.

He waited until he knew Jessica was high on heroin before he made the call. He even failed to tell Jessica that there was a reward on Rob's head, and he also played it down on what Rob was really on the run for. Because Jessica was comatose, she only got part of the information Steve was telling her.

Chapter Fifty-five

Rob parked up about half a mile away from the chemist on the Pilton estate. It was about half past three in the morning and Rob knew he did not have a lot of time before it got light. His last job that night had been with Amy, but he made his excuses and dropped Amy back at her flat, before making his way to Pilton.

Once he killed the engine, he carefully scanned the route for any sign of CCTV. He found none. The estate itself seemed like a ghost town at this hour in the morning. As he made his way towards the doctor's surgery, again he checked for CCTV, and again there was none. The surgery itself was a prefab with a chemist next door, and the graffiti on the surgery was paramount.

The local Neanderthals could not even spell bastard properly from graffiti that they had left on the side of the surgery. There were no shops next to his target, in fact, there was nothing but a park and some waste ground. He knew straight away, there would be no access to the surgery from the front of the building, so carefully he made his way around the back. As if by chance, there was a drainpipe going onto the roof and although it was covered in vandal grease, it was still easily accessible.

He made his way quite comfortably onto the flat roof. Again, Rob would occasionally check to make sure there was nobody in the vicinity. On the roof were two sky lights. Just as Rob had assumed, the steel girders covering the sky lights, would be easily removed with a screwdriver. One even had a couple of screws missing, so Rob decided this would be his point of entry. He toyed with the idea of coming back straight away once he had a screwdriver, but the best laid plans were not rushed. Therefore, he would come back in the next couple of nights. In the meantime, he was sure he could cope with his PTSD condition for the time being.

He lowered himself down via the drain he had come up through, again getting more vandal grease all over his palms. He chose to take a different direction back to the vehicle he had left half a mile away. At every street corner, he pretended to tie his shoes while he checked behind him to see if there was anybody present, his regimental training kicking in. About an hour or so later, he had returned to the Rock, the reception hardly noticed him as he walked in. Soon, he was asleep on his bunk, he would live to fight another day.

Chapter Fifty-six

DI Denman was not happy. The Beaumont case was going nowhere, and even the hierarchy within the Met Police force, whom Denman normally got on well with, were beginning to ask questions. This did not bother DI Denman as much as the fact a seven-year-old girl was missing, and next to nothing was being done by the Kenyan authorities to find her. If there was a body that was one thing; the parents and family could get closure, but there was nothing. It was another reason for her to press on harder, to find the missing little girl.

The sense of hopelessness that bequeathed Denman was with her all day. If it had been her own daughter that was missing, she would be going crazy. She could not believe how Charlotte Beaumont had kept her composure as long as she had, knowing full well she risked never seeing her daughter again. All the options of the investigation were thin, however, Jonathan Beaumont had been given the all clear from the Kenyan hospital, and the British Embassy were making arrangements to fly him home.

Soon Denman would be able to interview Jonathan and find out what he could tell the investigation. Other than this, all Denman could do was to start looking into Charlotte Beaumont's employers. Maybe there would be a connection there that the Met Police had not seen yet.

Within a few days DI Denman had booked an appointment at the hospital where Charlotte Beaumont worked. Denman felt that if she looked, there must be some sort of connection in order to find a successful outcome to the case. However, Denman knew that success meant different things to different people.

"I've got a bad feeling about this job," Sophie said to Rob while driving to the next appointment.

"What do you mean?" Rob asked. "It's a bog-standard job isn't it?"

"Well Jessica says that it's two guys, and they want me for half an hour each but I've just got a bad feeling about it."

It wasn't like Sophie to open up. This in turn almost sent alarm bells ringing in Rob's head. "Well you don't have to do the job if you don't want to. I'll just take you home."

"Oh, yeah, I'm sure Jessica would like that, if I don't turn up to a job that I'm on my way to," replied Sophie.

"Well look, if there's any problems I'll be outside," replied Rob.

"Yeah I know," replied Sophie. "I've got a bad feeling about it, that's all. Can we just drop it?"

As Rob turned on the car radio a slow nineties boy band song came on, and Rob could tell that Sophie was not impressed by what she was hearing.

At the same time Sophie began rummaging through her handbag. "What music are you into? Because this is shit," asked Sophie.

"Classic rock in all honesty. AC/DC, Van Halen, Led Zep, stuff like that," said Rob.

"Just like my little brother," and as she was talking, she pulled a CD case from her bag. "I bought him this today for his birthday." She took the CD out of its cellophane, and placed it into the radio. Soon all that could be heard was a crowd screaming, and then the singer announced, "Oh yeah."

The crowd responded, "Oh yeah!"

Again, the singer shouted, "Oh yeah!"

And again, the crowd responded accordingly.

"Who's this?" Rob asked.

"Judas Priest," replied Sophie. "It's proper music.'"

"You sound like a woman after my own heart," Rob replied.

Sophie almost smiled, as a singer announced to the crowd, "You've got another thing coming!"

Just as the music burst into life, Sophie turned the volume up to full as the heavy Rock 'n' Roll pumped around the car.

Whilst the hard rock blasted on the way to the next job, the streets of Edinburgh almost looked electric, and the heavy rock and roll made the hairs on the back of Rob's neck twitch, the same way he felt when he broke out of the medium secure hospital. Rob was almost enjoying himself again.

It wasn't long before Sophie and Rob reached the next destination. It was a bog-standard house on a bog-standard street. If anything, the house looked rundown. Rob maneuvered the car so he was pointing at the direction he would be leaving once the job was over.

He turned the music down and said to Sophie, "Any problems, I'll be here. I'm not going anywhere."

Sophie then sighed as she opened the car door and walked to her next appointment. Rob watched as the door was answered by a dark-skinned Asian looking guy, who quickly ushered Sophie inside.

Although the sounds of Judas Priest were great, Rob had to stay focused on the job. He killed the radio and picked up the newspaper he had bought that day. It wasn't long before the phone rang. The light green handset told him it was Jessica ringing.

Rob picked up the receiver and said, "Yes, boss, what's up?"

Jessica was on the other end sounding annoyed. She replied, "Rob, something's not facking right with this job."

"Ok," replied Rob. "What's the problem?"

"It's always the same with the facking foreigners. There's supposed to be two guys that wanted one escort for half an hour each, she's just rang me and there's four blokes in there. Go in and get her. Ring me back as soon as you know what the fack's going on."

"Yes, boss," replied Rob, and he hung up.

The nerves in Rob's stomach began to twitch. What was on the other side of this door? Also, were they armed? Gun, knife, hammer, all the scenarios were playing around in Rob's mind. He didn't even bother to lock the car, and as he made his way towards the front door, he tried the door handle. It was locked.

Should he break a window to gain entry? Instead Rob swallowed and raised his fist, and banged as loud as he could on the front door. Through the frosted glass Rob could see Sophie and the Asian guy. However, the Asian guy almost jumped out of his skin when Rob banged even harder on the door for a second time.

He could see through the glass that he was getting closer and Rob psyched himself up for whatever was about to happen. As the door opened, a weedy looking Asian figure stood there, maybe in his mid-twenties or early thirties. Rob looked at Sophie at the bottom of the hall.

"What's going on?" he said to Sophie.

She looked at Rob, annoyed, but without fear in her eyes. "Jessica said there was only two guys. There's fucking four in here and one of them looks about fourteen. I'm not fucking doing it!"

Rob turned his attention to the Asian guy. "So, what the fuck do you think you're playing at?" demanded Rob.

The Asian guy almost smiled and replied in a Bangladeshi accent. "I don't understand," and began shaking his head. Rob could see a door opening behind Sophie.

With authority Rob turned to Sophie and said, "Get in the car now."

The Asian guy suddenly decided that he could speak English. "No, no, you can't do this," just as Sophie made her way past him.

As he spoke, he tried to stop Sophie from leaving. Within a split-second, Rob reacted. He grabbed the guy by the throat and pinned him to the wall. Sophie quickly ushered past, making her way to the car. Rob brought his knee up to the Asian guy's groin and in a matter of seconds he continued to knee the guy as many times as he could.

From the corner of Rob's eye approached another Asian guy from the hall, again in his late twenties or early thirties. He looked like he had an implement in his hand. Rob turned his attention to the second guy, and with his southpaw, punched the second guy in the face as hard as he could.

He wasn't done there, with his right hand he punched and punched into the guy's head. Rob could hear one of his teeth crack. He looked up to see if there were any others, but all he saw was the door closing. The others in the house certainly didn't want to play. Both men fell to the floor and Rob turned to the first assailant. He picked him up and slammed him into the wall. "Right, so we understand each other?" Rob said under his breath. "I need paying."

The guy looked terrified. However, he almost said, "I don't understand," again.

Rob retrieved the wallet from the guy's pocket and removed what must have been about fifty pounds. He then threw the wallet on the floor. "Do you fucking understand now?"

The guy looked defeated and replied, " I sorry. I very, very sorry."

Rob closed up the door behind him as he made his way back to Sophie and the vehicle. He got in the car and wasted no time to get out of the area. It was Sophie who filled Rob in on what had happened. Although she had been booked for two clients, there were four in the house. One of them happened to be a young male, about fourteen-years-old.

They'd all chipped in together for him. When Sophie refused to do a child, who was obviously underage, they began to taunt her, and refused to let Sophie leave. This reassured Rob because it meant he did the right thing. Soon, Sophie was on the phone to Jessica, filling her in on how effective Rob had been on the job.

When Sophie finished the call, she turned to Rob and said, mimicking Jessica, "Jessica says you're facking beautiful!"

Sophie then began texting Amy.

Chapter Fifty-seven

DI Denman arrived at the medium secure unit, and did her best to avoid the flock of journalists that had seemed to have made a permanent residence on the hospital site, like a group of gypsies. Once she had shown the receptionist her credentials she was quickly ushered through the medium secure unit and taken to the senior manager's office. He held out his hand and introduced himself as Lewis.

Lewis Farr was a short fat man in a scruffy looking suit and Denman could smell the cigarettes and assumed he must be a forty a day man. Before she began to question him, they both sat down at a desk. She began to ask Lewis about Dr Beaumont's work history, and although Lewis appeared genuinely concerned about Dr Beaumont's daughter, Denman could tell that he was distracted. Lewis knew what was coming.

"Was there a connection between Dr Beaumont and Rob Foster, the patient who escaped?" She added, "The media seem to assume there is."

Lewis held a hand over his mouth as he began to cough furiously, almost gripping his chest as if he was going to have a heart attack. Once he had finished, he said, "About three times a year, patients run off. No matter how good we are, we cannot foresee this coming at any given time. If we thought they would run off, we would not let them out on leave. If you think I'm happy about it, you would be wrong. I'm not. My bosses are coming down on me already since both the escapes."

DI Denman stopped him there. "Both the escapes?" she questioned. "I thought there was only Rob Foster's escape."

Lewis began to turn red with embarrassment. He had obviously given something away that he did not want out. Then Lewis replied, "A second patient has gone on the run again this week, a particularly dangerous individual called James Crisp. We're hoping to keep it under wraps for as long as possible."

Denman took in the information, and then asked for a file on both of the patients that had gone missing, and then as she was taking notes, she asked, "What can you tell me about both individuals?"

"Well," Lewis replied, "Rob Foster's ex-military. Basically, we know that he's suffering from PTSD. At the same time his wife left him before she had given birth to their son. He's succumbed to psychosis and killed somebody in a park. That's where Dr Beaumont got involved, she became his forensic consultant. By all accounts I think Dr Beaumont and Foster had quite a good relationship, but it did not stop him from tricking her so he could escape."

As DI Denman took notes, she put a question mark next to Rob Foster's name. She would ask Dr Beaumont about this later.

Lewis then continued. "James Crisp is a complete psychopath, almost off the scale. If we hadn't intervened, I'd have no doubt you would have a serial killer on your hands. By all accounts he is an intelligent man. Not only had he got a scholarship to read medicine at York University, but also, he regularly beats grandmasters at chess that come to visit him here. The lads on the ward, though, refer to him as The Surgeon."

"The Surgeon?" Denman said inquisitively.

"That's how he was caught. He began doing surgical procedures on household pets: cats and dogs etc. Classic signs of early psychopathic tendencies. It's well documented that individuals who kill animals early in life will progress onto people at some point."

DI Denman took more notes and then asked if she could interview some of the patients on the wards. Lewis looked at his watch again as if he was in a hurry.

"It's impossible, DI Denman," Lewis protested. "Not only am I short staffed, but I have had to put all the wards on lockdown until this thing blows over. As far as the wards that Foster and Crisp were both on, not only did Foster nearly kill one of the nursing staff that was escorting him on leave, but also the senior manager has gone off sick. That never happens. She's as tough as old boots that one, almost too brash."

Denman closed her notebook, she had enough to be getting on with. Plus, she had been given access to the files on both Foster and Crisp. She had already dismissed Crisp from her enquiries but Foster was someone she wanted to look into. It was as if it was a police woman's instinct that Foster had gone on the run soon after the event.

As Lewis escorted DI Denman back to the reception, she noticed the sweat that was pouring off Lewis. As she went to the airlock, they both continued to exchange pleasantries. Then Denman asked, "You said your senior nurse had gone off sick, and that she was tough as old boots. Why would she need to go off sick?"

Lewis replied, "Sally Cooper, yes, she's hard as nails, but her prize-winning dog's gone missing and that's what she lives for, she's in quite a state."

Denman almost smiled, then she shook Lewis's hand, and made for the exit.

Chapter Fifty-eight

DI Denman felt she was right on the money when it came to James Crisp. There was no connection really between him and Dr Beaumont, she wasn't even his consultant. Rob Foster was a different matter, and if anything, Foster was a smart individual. Although it took up most of her day, Denman dug up on the police computer anything she could regarding Foster.

However, the thing that intrigued her wasn't what was written about his military record, but what wasn't written. The last six months of Foster's service had been deemed as classified. This meant not only could the police not gain access to what was written, which included her bosses, but also the only persons who could gain access would be the top brass in the military, or the Home Secretary.

Also, there was nothing in his medical file to account for his last six months service. The more she thought about Rob Foster, the more intrigued she was to learn. She shut down her computer and picked up the phone, and rang Dr Beaumont.

Understandably so, Charlotte Beaumont was on leave from work. It was almost torture because Charlotte had nothing to do other than watch the news for any signs of her daughter. She had managed little sleep and spoke little to her family. In fact, every time someone rang, Charlotte made her excuse to get off the line. Charlotte knew full well that everyone that was calling, was ringing out of concern. But it was almost as if she could not stand the patronizing tone, even though they had her best wishes at heart. Also, the police officers that were on her front door, were a bone of contention, Charlotte did not want them there. However, it was a lesser of two evils because if they were not present on her doorstep, then she would continue to get hounded by the media.

As Charlotte flicked through the news channels, the phone rang and on the second ring Charlotte replied with anticipation. Was this good news? Was this bad news? Had Amelia been found? Or was there a body?

All she could say was, "Hello, Charlotte speaking."

"Charlotte, It's DI Denman here."

"Ok. Is there any news?"

"There is nothing significant I can tell you at the moment Charlotte," replied Denman. "However, it's my understanding that Jonathan will be landing at Gatwick at four a.m. tomorrow morning. I will need to speak to him as soon as possible and I would like to suggest we both go together to the airport to meet him, as there are a few questions I have to ask you as well."

The fact there was no news, made Charlotte's heart even more heavy. *'How much more of this could she take?'* she asked herself.

But instead, just replied, "Ok. I'll be at my house," Charlotte replied.

Frustratingly for Charlotte, the call ended.

Chapter Fifty-nine

Rob was armed with all he needed to break into the pharmacy. He had even managed to get hold of some surgical gloves, as well as a penknife and a screwdriver. Also, he had acquired a small torch. Rob parked work's vehicle in the same place as the night before and under the cover of darkness, made his way to the pharmacy in the Pilton estate. Again, constantly scanning for any sort of CCTV or people in the area. Luck was on Rob's side. It was just as quiet as the previous night.

Making his way back up the drainpipe, onto the roof, Rob quickly got to work in opening the sky light. Within five minutes, he had managed to gain entry inside the building. At this point he also put on the latex gloves, desperate not to leave any trace. He quickly scanned the area with his torch to find out where the medicine was kept. Soon, he had found the medicine safe, which was held together by locks, at the same time, Rob heard a beeping. *'Shit!'* thought Rob. *A security alarm.*'

It began to count down. Rob realized, he had to work quickly and efficiently. Security alarms usually had between ten seconds and a minute before the siren sounded. He returned to the counter, and looked for a drawer. On the first drawer, he opened it; there was nothing but paperwork. However, on the second drawer, his luck was in, whoever had done the security for the pharmacy was so unprofessional, that they had left the keys for the medicine cupboard, in an open drawer.

As soon as Rob picked up the keys, the alarm sounded. At the same time, the lights within the pharmacy began to flash intermittently. As calm as he could muster, Rob put the key into the lock almost easily opening the safe. All he had to do now was find the correct medication. He opened every box he could find, in no particular order, disregarding the boxes that were no good onto the floor. It was almost as if there was every other medication there, but the one he needed.

Eventually, Rob found his prize, it was Modecate, 24ml, and there were sixteen siphons. At the same time, Rob looked for morphine, the heroin substitute. He wanted the authorities to think that the break-in wasn't for medication, but for the morphine. The stress of the whole exercise was taking a toll on Rob, and he quickly made his way back to his escape route. All the time, the sirens wailing and the lights flashing.

Once on the roof, he did not check to see if the police or the public were outside, he simply threw himself off, onto the ground, in the same fashion as if he was landing from a parachute jump. He quickly made his way through the estate. As soon as he was seven hundred metres away from the pharmacy, Rob hid in a back alley, in order to get his bearings, take a breath, and see what was happening around him.

Fortunately, with the government's cuts to the police, this break in may not be a priority to the local force but he could still not take a chance walking openly in the streets, carrying medication. Rob was wired, and completely wound up. To reassure himself, he had just remembered he had a job to do.

Within an hour Rob was back in the work's vehicle, and taking the longer route back to the hostel. With the paranoia Rob was beginning to suffer from, he thought it was about time that he found different accommodation. If the authorities could trace who had took the medication, it may lead them back to the Rock.

He began to wonder whether Amy would allow him to sleep on her sofa. He had the medication and he also had a little money. Soon he would have his passport to get him out of the country. That was all he needed for the time being. The fact was, Rob was even surprised with himself, to come this far, without appearing on the radar.

He decided not to return to the Rock after all. He would not sleep tonight anyway. and instead he made his way to a drugs' clinic that would open in the morning. There he would be able to get clean needles which he would need to inject himself. He would give a false name, and with the clothes he was wearing and the general sorry state he was looking, Rob doubted the clinic would think twice.

Chapter Sixty

DI Denman and Dr Charlotte Beaumont spoke little at first on their journey down the M1 in the early hours of the morning on route to Gatwick airport, where Jonathan would be landing. It was awkward for both parties. One did not want to talk, the other needed to get information. DI Denman pushed, she had a job to do, and she had to ask about Foster.

As diplomatically as she could, Denman asked, "I had to visit the medium secure where you work, to chat to some of your colleagues."

Charlotte Beaumont felt almost violated. She did not like being checked up on, especially behind her back. "Why did you need to do that?" she asked, with contempt.

"Just routine enquiries," replied Denman. Then she swallowed as she continued. "We do not have a lot to go on at the moment I'm afraid, and so I want to uncover every angle. Believe me, I want to get Amelia back."

"Ok, so what did you want to find out?" asked Charlotte.

"I spoke with Lewis Farr, the hospital manager. He told me you had a good relationship with one of your patients, Rob Foster."

"There was nothing inappropriate if that's what you mean?" was her defensive reply.

"Believe me, I don't think there is. But what can you tell me about him?"

Charlotte sighed. She realised DI Denman was only doing her job. Then she replied, "He's ex-military and by all accounts he's been through a lot of traumatic experiences throughout his service and probably before. Also, his childhood was not as good as it could have been. His mother died several years ago and his father is dying in hospital of cancer. His father was a heavy drinker. I diagnosed Foster with PTSD. However, he's a bit different to your average run of the mill client."

Denman listened intently as Charlotte continued. "For starter's he's got a higher than average IQ. I've no doubt had he not been a soldier he could have quite easily been a lawyer, politician, possibly even a doctor. He was arrested for murder, but it was reduced to manslaughter after I assessed him. Given his previous traumatic history and exposure to intense violence over long periods of time, anyone who's not psychopathic would succumb to PTSD. There were also problems in his marriage, which was exacerbated when he started to drink. He was thrown out of the army. A few months later he killed a jogger in a park. Whatever they taught him in the military he must have learned it very well. The individual he killed must have died within thirty seconds."

As the journey continued, Dr Beaumont and DI Denman continued to discuss Foster further. They talked about the court proceeding, evidence given, the Grant family and the references from Harry Woolen, the publican from the Admiral pub where Rob drank and the Company Sergeant Major, Duncan French. DI Denman felt more of a need to investigate Foster than ever.

Within three hours they had reached arrivals at Gatwick airport, and when Denman parked the car, both individuals made their way through to holding. Within half an hour both were ushered through to a secure area where Jonathan was waiting. They entered a darkened room which held a two-way mirror.

On the other side of the mirror looked a broken man. It was Jonathan. Charlotte gasped as she saw the state of her estranged husband. He looked a pathetic individual, in yellow overalls, his right hand missing, replaced with a bandage on a stump.

Charlotte whispered, *"Look at the state of him,"* and she could feel her heart in her mouth.

Denman turned to Charlotte and said, "You go in first. I'll be here. I'll catch up with both of you in a while."

The police officer then nodded at the guard, who opened the door and hastily Charlotte Beaumont made her way inside the interview room. Tears welled up in her eyes just as Jonathan looked up and saw his wife for the first time in three weeks.

"My god what have they done to you," was Charlotte's greeting to her life partner.

Jonathan fell to his knees, on seeing Charlotte, and began to cry. This was not like Jonathan. In fact, Charlotte could not even remember a time when Jonathan had cried in front of her. Jonathan began to speak. "They took our little girl. I tried to stop them, Charlotte, believe me. I tried to stop them," he replied.

At the same time Jonathan brought his stump and other hand up to his face. Charlotte rushed to her husband. No matter what he had done in the past it was obvious that this was not the same man. As she held him to her chest both parties began to cry. Charlotte knew she had to support Jonathan. It was the only way she knew both of them could get through this. Also, Charlotte knew she needed Jonathan as much as he needed her.

As she held him with tears rolling down her cheeks she said, "We will get through this, Jonathan." At that moment Charlotte knew despite all of Jonathan's faults, her marriage would continue.

From behind the two-way mirror DI Denman saw what she wanted to see. It was apparent Jonathan was not involved directly in Amelia's kidnapping. The trouble was, this meant she had even less to go on. She just hoped the Rob Foster angle could come up with an answer, because something did not sit truly there.

She turned to the guard in the room, and with authority said, "Leave them for a while."

As she left the outer room, she looked back to see Charlotte and Jonathan comforting each other as she closed the door behind her.

Chapter Sixty-one

Rob was the first to be seen at the drug dependency clinic, and it took very little persuasion for Rob to get the clean needles he required. As soon as he left the clinic, he made his way to a Costa Coffee. He ordered a drink and then made his way to the restrooms. Soon he was emptying the siphon into one of the clean syringes. At the same time Rob was trying to remember what he'd been taught during the paramedic phase of selection.

As he undid his trousers, he remembered the rule of administration and injection into the buttock. He had to visualise a cross on one of his buttocks in order to avoid a sensitive artery. Also, he tried to remember the dart technique of administration. This would not have been so bad if he was doing it on a patient, but Rob was doing it on himself. It took several attempts for him to pierce his skin, however on the third attempt it was successful. Soon he was injecting the Modecate into his right buttock and this was a relief in itself as he knew he could cope operationally for the next few weeks, if he could evade capture that long.

Once he had finished, he discarded the needle. He cleaned himself up as best he could, and flushed any evidence down the toilet. Then he took out work's mobile and rang Amy. He explained that he wanted to save some money and he asked if he could sleep on her couch for the time being. Whether she believed him or not he did not know, but she seemed okay with the idea and she did not think Sophie would mind either, however she would have to run it past Jessica.

She agreed to phone him back when she knew what the score was. Rob then left the restroom and made his way to the counter to pick up his coffee. He did not want to hang about, the paranoia still prominent.

Soon he was walking down the high street back to the work's vehicle when the phone rang. It was Jessica ringing. "Yes, boss, what's up?" was Rob's answer.

"Rob, I need to see you straight away."

Rob assumed it was something to do with staying at Amy's, but he did not pursue it. "Okay, boss, I'm on my way."

"Right," replied Jessica. "You know where I live. Just let yourself in."

Within ten minutes Rob was sat in Jessica's living room. It looked just like any other living room or any other house, however, the house was well lived in. It wasn't that it was mucky, but it gave the impression of a woman who had a chaotic lifestyle. Rob had to move some of the clothes in order to sit on the sofa. Also. there were boxes of shoes along with open DVD cases along the floor.

It wasn't as tidy as Rob had expected but it was his boss's home and he had to respect that. Jessica brought Rob a cup of coffee and sat opposite him, moving the papers from the chair as she sat down. It was obvious that Jessica had not been up for long; in fact, she was still in her pyjamas, however the madam was not too bothered about her appearance at this hour in the morning. In a Cockney accent Jessica asked, "So what the fack you been doing in 'ull? And dahn't give me any shit about you left in a hurry."

Rob's mind began to think fast. He realised he couldn't get away with another lie. Having said that, he did not know what Jessica knew, so his best bet was to be as economical with the truth as possible. At the same time trying not to give too much away. Rob just sighed, and replied, "Okay, boss, tell me what you know."

"What I know," Jessica answered curtly, "Is that you're on the run from the police. What the fack have you done? I do not want any of my fucking girls in danger!"

Rob knew the best way to respond was with a question. "How did you know I was on the run?"

"I've got a bent copper on the books called DCI Steve Johnson. He's as bent as a fucking crowbar, but he helps me out now and then. He rang me a couple of nights ago and said you was on the run, but he hasn't told me what for. I've got to make sure, Rob, that you're not some fucking rapist, or worse, some sort of killer who's going to harm my girls." She then added, "If you've robbed a bank or post office, I don't give a shit. If you've kicked the fuck out of someone, I don't give a shit, but what I do give a shit about is the safety of my girls. Also, you've done jobs outside DCI Johnson's flat, and in the last couple of nights he's booked several girls, asking every one of the girl's questions about you. You better tell me what the fack's going on. I want to fucking know now."

All Rob could think of was to stick as close to the truth as possible. "Ok, I'll tell you what I can," Rob replied. "I was in the army up until recently. I was doing SAS selection. I was doing really well," Rob continued. "In fact, I almost made SAS. However, I've got PTSD, post-traumatic-stress-disorder. They kicked me out of the army and locked me up in a funny farm. After a couple of weeks, I managed to break out and that's what I'm on the run for."

Jessica looked at Rob and said, "How do I know you're not going to have a funny turn and harm one of my girls then."

As she spoke Rob ruffled through his pockets and replied, "Look, boss, I'll be okay as long as I can get my medication, and I've got it here." As he spoke, he showed Jessica the siphons and syringes.

"You better be straight with me, Rob, if I'm going to let you continue working for me." And as she spoke, she lit up the cigarette that she'd put into her mouth.

Rob replied, "I'll be honest with you, boss, I'm going to have to make a move shortly. If the police know I'm here in Edinburgh, they'll wanna find me, so I need that passport as quickly as I can. But I'll give you my word, your girls have nothing to fear from me."

Jessica thought for a moment as she exhaled the smoke. She took another sip of her coffee and replaced it on the glass table, just before she stood up, and made her way to the other side of the room, opening a cabinet drawer. She pulled out an envelope and then handed it to Rob. "Ok then, here's your passport. If you let me down, you'll have more than the police to worry about. The other thing, my girls are telling me that DCI Steve Johnson wants to nick ya, and you've got a job at his tomorrow night. I suggest it's your last, if you know what I mean."

"So, you're not going to shop me boss?" Rob asked.

Jessica sat down opposite Rob and picked up her coffee. "DCI Steve Johnson's fleeced me enough over the last few years. He's constantly taken a cut but the thing that pisses me off the most is how he treats my girls. It's about time he got his just desserts. Tomorrow night he's booked Roxy. He's got his own dungeon in his house. Sometimes he likes to be the dominant, sometimes he likes to be the submissive. Tomorrow night he wants to be the sub, I want you to go in there when he's in a compromising position, fuck him over, and then make yourself scarce. When Roxy goes into the address you just fucking ring me, I'll take it from there."

"Okay not a problem, boss, and thank you," replied Rob.

"Don't thank me now. As for staying with Roxy, I don't see what the problem is, if she's happy to put you up. Tonight, I suggest you take the night off and enjoy yourself."

Chapter Sixty-two

The information Dr Beaumont had given DI Denman was enough to keep her going whilst both victims consoled each other downstairs in the interview room. She managed to persuade customs to let them use their computer while Denman did a little digging. It wasn't long before she found what she was looking for. During the conversation with Charlotte, she realised Foster was not the type of person to disregard taking his medication.

The only place he could get this medication would be a hospital or a pharmacy. She logged onto the police computer to find out if any had been hit in the last two weeks. There were three, one in London, one in Liverpool and one in Edinburgh. The one in London looked more like a failed ram raid. It was too impulsive and too messy for Foster, and so she dismissed it. The one in Liverpool, all that was taken was morphine, plus they had people in custody.

However, the one in Edinburgh, there was no sign of identification on whoever had done it. It looked like a very professional job, and although morphine was taken, other medications were taken also. Denman quickly realised that the theft of the morphine was a smokescreen. Foster had to be in Scotland. DI Denman did not know how her superiors would take to this line of enquiry, so for the time being she would go on a gut instinct, more than the correct channels.

She booked in to stay at a Travelodge just outside of Edinburgh the next night, and in the meantime, she would continue to question Jonathan Beaumont to find out what information he could give regarding the missing girl. Also, she needed to speak with the two men who knew Foster the most, the publican Harry Woollen and the Company Sergeant Major, Duncan French.

Rob parked the car outside of Amy and Sophie's flat. He was a little weary from the medication beginning to kick in, but Rob felt calmer about himself. Soon Amy had buzzed him through and he made his way upstairs to the top floor flat. Amy greeted him at the door, and he was surprised at how pleased she was to see him.

"Guess what?" Amy said. "Jessica's given us both the night off, so we're going to order a pizza, watch Netflix, and have a glass a wine or two."

"Ok, cool," replied Rob. "Is that the couch I'm sleeping on?"

Just as he spoke, Sophie entered the living room, with a towel wrapped around her. She looked at Amy and they both smiled at each other. Amy then returned from the open plan kitchen with a bottle of Peroni. "Just chill out and relax for now, soldier." Soon all three were sat in the living room, having feasted themselves on pizza, and watched two films on Netflix. Just before the end of the second film Sophie disappeared into the bedroom, leaving Amy and Rob chatting quite happily on the sofa.

Amy then turned to Rob and said, "Get a shower if you want, there's plenty of hot water."

Rob felt it was more of an order than a request and made his way to the bathroom. As he stood under the hot shower the tension in his shoulders began to ease under the hot water pounding on his back. Once he'd finished, he returned to the living room wearing only a towel. The TV had been turned off and the lampshade was the only dim light in the room. He was just about to lay down on the sofa when he heard Amy call him from the bedroom.

"Rob, can you come here for a minute?"

Rob made his way across the living room floor towards the bedroom. On the large double bed laid Sophie dressed in Agent Provocateur pink silky underwear with white suspenders attached to it. Next to her, on her knees on the end of the bed was Amy wearing a blue Camilla Waspie basque, again, with matching stockings. A nervous twitch went up Rob's spine. At the same time, Amy held out her wrist and invited Rob to step forward.

As Rob approached the bed Amy put her arms around Rob's shoulders and then whispered softly, "We'd both like to show our appreciation for the way you've looked after us."

With that Amy began to passionately kiss Rob. At the same time Sophie removed Rob's towel and then began to take him in her mouth. It wasn't long before Amy and Sophie began kissing each other, soon all three were embraced.

Over the next four hours all three made love to each other constantly, only breaking occasionally for the odd cigarette. The sex was a relief to Rob, almost a tonic to the stress he'd been through over the last six months. It was almost a type of therapy being held in the arms of two beautiful women. It wasn't long before all three were laid naked across the bed together, with Sophie asleep, leaving Rob and Amy holding each other and talking, the way new lovers do.

"Steve Johnson's going to nick you, you know," said Amy.

"Yeah I've heard about it from Jessica, tell me what you know about him."

Amy continued to share with Rob everything she knew about DCI Steve Johnson. The fact he was a bent copper, caught up in the rackets as well as the drugs circuit, also she knew that Johnson had pinned crimes on people that were totally innocent. It was almost as if Johnson used it as a bragging right. Rob continued to hold Amy as they talked into the small hours. However, both began to drift and nod. It wasn't long before all three were asleep. Rob felt he'd had the best night's sleep of his life.

Chapter Sixty-three

DI Denman checked into the Travelodge about five p.m. the next evening. She quickly dumped her bags in the room and then returned to her car in order to make her way to Edinburgh police station. By now the local police knew of her arrival. However, it had not gone through the regular channels, so DI Denman did not know how she would be received when she turned up at Edinburgh Central police station. She didn't think it would be too much of a problem and she just hoped she could make headway on her investigation, even though she doubted herself on this line of enquiry.

She had spoken briefly to Foster's old CSM, Duncan French, and it was almost as if he didn't care to remember anything, he had made his excuses to get off the phone as soon as she mentioned she would be talking to the publican Harry at the Admiral pub too. Either the CSM was a complete bastard or a good liar. As for the publican Harry Woolen the number she'd been given was just an answer machine. She left a message again, and then headed to her car. She questioned herself: Was she doing the right thing by being here?

It was about six p.m. when DI Denman entered the foyer of Edinburgh Central Police Station. Despite the fact that most of the office staff had gone home, she was directed to the chief superintendent's office. As she was escorted, two things raced through her mind. Firstly, had there been a development on the case, and had the superintendent information to share? The other thing that was going through her mind was the fact that she'd not gone through the correct channels and she was just as likely to get a bollocking when she walked through the door. As she entered the office room, the superintendent sat behind his desk in full uniform. However, his tie was loose around his neck. The chief super looked up at Denman, and without even a hello or welcome, directed Denman to sit down.

In a deep Scottish accent, the superintendent said, "I know why you're here. You're investigating a child's disappearance. Also, you think there's a connection between an escaped madman and a child that's missing. The same madman happens to be on my patch at the moment."

Denman stayed quiet. She did not want to give anything away. Her silence was noted by the chief super. Then he continued, "We've had a tipoff from a local madam. Your man's in Edinburgh, all right. He's been working for the last month as a minder for one of the local escort agencies and what I'm about to tell you now, does not leave this room."

DI Denman kept her composure and said, "Understood, sir."

The Super continued, "I get no joy in saying this DI, but one of my officers has known about this information for some time and not only has he not acted upon this information, he's almost been harbouring your fugitive. However, my hands are tied. There've been rumours circulating for some time that my officer is a bent bastard, but there's been nothing in the way of evidence connecting him to anything he's allegedly been involved in. Therefore, I cannot sack him, I cannot arrest him, I cannot prosecute him, and I cannot put him front of the court for trial. I want you to go to his flat now and nick him. You're an officer from a different force, therefore it is not in your jurisdiction. But for the time being I'm going to deputise you to do your job and nick this bastard. Hopefully this will lead you to your man. I have a detective downstairs waiting for you. Also, there will be a patrol standing by. Any questions, DI Denman?"

"No, sir. Nothing."

"Go and earn your pay then, girl," replied the Super.

Denman stood up and left the office.

Chapter Sixty-four

The Admiral pub was light with revellers with it being a week day. Although it wasn't late into the evening, at the end of the bar stood Duncan French. Harry had noticed French arrive but kept busy around the back and out of sight. It was only until later in the evening that Harry came to tend the bar, relieving some of the staff for a cigarette break. Both men noticed each other. Harry walked up to French and asked him what he was drinking. "Low Flier for me," replied French.

Harry picked up a tumbler and fixed a Famous Grouse whisky, leaving it on the bar. As most of the revellers were out of earshot, Duncan French continued, "We've both got a mutual friend, I believe."

Harry was giving nothing away. "Who's that then?"

French was stern in his reply. "Don't give me that shit. We're both too fucking old to bullshit each other."

"Ok," replied Harry. "What's the problem?"

"You've got connections to the Costa Del Sol. A lot of hardcore villains are some of your best friends down there. Our lad's on his way there and he needs a way of getting into Africa through Gibraltar."

Harry stood and looked at French in the eye. "If I got involved with criminal activity, not only would I risk losing my license and my pub, I could go to jail. I don't quite fancy that. Do you understand me? Also, the military have their own connections. Why can't you do something for him?"

French replied, "I'm not high enough up the military food chain to help the lad. Even if I was it would leave a paper trail, and my lad doesn't need to be found."

Harry stood looking at French, almost two wise old lions sussing each other out on the Serengeti. Both men had seen a lot of the world. Both men knew not to make mistakes. However, both men were giving nothing away, like seasoned poker players. Harry looked over the bar to see if anyone was in earshot. He thought for a moment, leaned over the bar and then said, "I wish I could help you, mate, but them days are long behind me now."

At the same time French knocked back his Low Flier and placed it on the bar. Harry picked up the glass and continued, "I wish I could help Rob, but even if I could I wouldn't be able to tell anybody anyway. Do we understand each other?"

French knew exactly what he meant. Harry then added, "Another Low Flier, is it?" French said nothing and just nodded. Harry removed another tumbler from the bar, and raised it up to the optic. He then handed the whisky to French. "Here," said Harry. "It's a double. It's on the house." A mutual understanding had been developed between both men.

Chapter Sixty-five

It was raining as Rob pulled up outside Steve Johnson's flat with Roxy sat next to him. Rob did not know what Roxy knew, other than what Jessica had told him. As she left the vehicle, she said, "Give me ten minutes. I'll get that sick bastard handcuffed to the bed, then I'll give you a call, Rob."

Rob tried not to look nervous as he nodded. He had come so far, he did not want to get caught now, mixed up in a gang feud. It was against all standard operating procedures to go astray from the directive, and his directive at the moment was to keep a low profile. However, he had to block Steve Johnson from nicking him.

He sat there and thought. He wanted to get out of there as quickly as he could. If Johnson had money, he would take that as well. But, again, he felt a certain discontent with the fact that Johnson was a copper, but he was bent. It was against the grain. You had to be either one team or another. The rules were, you didn't play for both sides.

Ten minutes quickly passed and he received a call from Roxy. "He's all tied up and waiting for you, Rob."

Rob left the vehicle and made his way up to the flat. At the same time racing across town was DI Denman along with another detective. Although the sirens were not on, the flashing lights stood out like a paratrooper in a kindergarten. DI Denman certainly knew how to drive, thought her colleague. The brief from the chief had been sparse but to the point. Johnson must have information on Foster. Denman had even checked Johnson's computer before she left the station, and it was obvious that he was involved in something because of the number of hours he'd spent on the Grant's Facebook page where the reward on Foster's neck was posted.

Rob walked in to Johnson's apartment. Rob was still a bit paranoid, almost expecting to be jumped on when he walked in the reception room. Roxy smiled at Rob and said softly, "He's through here."

Straddled across the bed, tied by each arm and leg to a corner post was Johnson with a gimp mask tied to his face. Strewn across the floor were various sex toys of different descriptions. Also, next to the bed were three helpings of cocaine in neat lines.

Johnson was worried, somebody had just entered the room and it wasn't the girl he had paid for. "What the fuck's going on, Roxy?" demanded Johnson.

"It's not Roxy. My name's Rob Foster, and you're in the shit."

On hearing those words Johnson froze. He almost felt sick. Why hadn't he nicked this bastard earlier? He'd left it too long. Rob grabbed Johnson by the top of the gimp mask and removed the eye pieces so Johnson could see him. Johnson knew he was fucked. He had to talk his way out of it.

Before he had a chance to speak, Rob grabbed Johnson by the groin and squeezed. "So, where's your safe? Before I kill you."

The officer knew well that Rob was a killer, and so to buy time he directed Rob to the safe in the wardrobe, slowly giving away the pin number for the safe. Rob opened the metal box, and inside were two large bags of white powder. He assumed they must have been cocaine. Also, there was a wad of money, and next to that was a badge, and an ID in Johnson's name. Rob removed all the contents from the safe. He left the bags of cocaine on the floor of the bedroom. He then stuffed the wads of money into his jean pockets. He began to study the policeman's ID, all the time, Johnsons' mind was racing.

"Listen, pal," Johnson squirmed. "I've been protecting you. I honestly have. That slag Jessica has told you a lot of shit, mate. Pal, I'm being straight with you. If you take the money and just let me go. Take the coke as well if you want."

Rob stood in silence for a minute. Then, he held up the badge. "You see this badge? It means something," Rob said. "It means honour and integrity. It means protecting the weak. It stands for something."

Johnson looked almost bemused. He did not know what this madman was on about. Rob continued. "You fucked up when you came after me. I've worn a badge similar to this, and it meant something to me, it should mean something to you. You're a disgrace to your uniform, but I'm not gonna kill you. Instead, I'm gonna turn you in."

As he spoke, he flicked the ID at the policeman. Johnson began to get scared. "Look, pal, please," he replied.

Rob picked up the phone and rang Jessica. She answered with a curt "Yep."

"I've got him," said Rob, "I've got his money. I'm gonna get out of here soon."

"Just fucking hold on. I'm on my way."

Without replying, Rob ended the call. He then looked around the flat and found an A4 pad and a pen, and began to write. Soon he began to hear Jessica approaching from outside, coming up the stairs. As she entered the room Rob was sellotaping the piece of paper he'd written on to Johnson's chest.

Jessica saw the cocaine on the floor and picked up a bag, handing it to Roxy.

"Take this and wait in the car," she ordered. She then looked at Johnson. "You've took the piss for fucking long enough, sunshine, and I think it's about time you get what's coming."

"Look Jessica. Come on be reasonable. Don't let those bastards catch me, they'll fucking kill me in prison." Johnson then began to shout. "For fuck's sake, Jessica."

As he was shouting, both Rob and Jessica left the room, closing the door behind them. "You better get going then, cowboy," Jessica said to Rob.

"Look after yourself, boss. What are you going to do?"

"I'm going to wait here for the police to arrive. I rang them earlier. They won't nick me, not when I can hand them a bent copper who happens to be a rapist. You better get off."

Rob shook Jessica by the hand as a mark of respect, then left.

Chapter Sixty-six

DI Denman began to approach Johnson's flat at speed with the detective beside her. Rob saw the police car's flashing lights and realised he had to make hay. As he passed work's vehicle, he saw Amy probably for the last time. He quickly bent down and opened the door. "I've got to go now, love. I don't know when I'll be back but take good care of yourself, sweetheart."

Amy quickly grabbed Rob and kissed him hard on the lips, and as she let go of her embrace she whispered, "Take care of yourself, soldier."

Soon Rob was running down the street, determined to get away, and putting as much distance between himself and his pursuers just as DI Denman and her colleague reached the foot of the flat. Denman recognised Rob from his photo. His physique and clothes were typical of an off-duty squaddie. Even if she could catch him, he would put up a fight. Also, there were other issues, not least the little girl. She decided not to follow him.

The detective with Denman asked if he should follow Rob. Denman looked at him. "Let him go," was Denman's curt reply and then she made her way up to the flat.

Inside the flat she saw Jessica, the madam, sat in one of the leather chairs, holding a cup of coffee. As Denman and the detective entered, Jessica just said, "Johnson's in the bedroom."

The DI asked, "Is he dead?"

"No," was Jessica's short answer.

Denman turned to the detective and said, "Wait here."

She entered the bedroom and almost laughed when she saw the sight before her. She quickly realised what Rob had done. Denman read the note taped to Johnson's chest, explaining about the bent cop and included where the evidence would be. She quickly discovered the cocaine lines at the side of the bed, and the bag on the floor.

Johnson just stared at her. Denman said, "Detective Chief Inspector Johnson, my name is DI Denman of the London Metropolitan Police Force, and I'm arresting you for possession of a Class A substance, withholding information on a police investigation, and bringing the police force into disrepute. You do not have to say anything, but it may harm your defense if you do not mention when questioned something which you may later rely on in court Anything you do say may be given in evidence. Do you understand?"

Johnson just spat. "Fuck you, you fucking bitch."

Within an hour the police had raided Johnson's flat and discovered more evidence of drug paraphernalia and a stash of indecent images of children. Jessica had been questioned and released without charge, however she would have to appear at the police station later to give evidence. In the meantime, Johnson was bundled into the back of a waiting police van. Amy, or Roxy as she was known, had the good sense to get out of the area. When Jessica rang her, both arranged to meet straight away at Buddy Milligan's pub. Soon, Amy handed Jessica the other bag of cocaine. Then Amy asked, "Do you think Rob will get away?"

"Yeah I should think so. He's not a fucking daft lad."

Amy thought for a moment, then said, "He enjoyed himself last night."

Jessica took a drag on her cigarette, and replied, "Yeah I thought he facking would do, he looked like he needed it, men are a lot happier after they cum. I'll square you both up tomorrow."

Amy just shrugged. "Both Sophie and I are not that bothered, to be honest."

"Well that's up to you, darlin," replied Jessica.

Amy sighed. "He was a good driver wasn't he, boss?"

Jessica took another drag and replied, "Yeah, he was facking beautiful."

Edinburgh Central Police Station was a hive of activity after Steve Johnson's arrest. It was almost a relief to some of the junior officers, and there was an excitement and a buzz around the station. Most of his colleagues agreed that Johnson had had it coming for a long time. DI Denman was sat in the charge room writing up her report. The detective with her was also writing up his report. He turned to Denman and asked "When we had the chance to nick Foster, why did you stop me from arresting him?"

Without hesitation Denman replied, "Because Foster's the only chance of getting the girl back." Then she added, "That's off the record."

All the staff at the Admiral pub were closing down for the night. Then Harry turned to his head barman, Elliot, and said, "Get my phone book from upstairs, then get yourself off. I'll close up tonight."

As soon as Harry had his phone book, he took some loose change out of the till and made his way across to the phone box outside the pub. He entered some coins and dialed a number. The phone rang three or four times, when it was answered by a Liverpudlian accent. "Terry, it's Harry. Listen, I need a favour."

Chapter Sixty-seven

The Home Secretary, Elizabeth Price Jones, was not happy as she entered her office at Whitehall in the evening. The Bullimore enquiry had not gone as well as planned. In fact, the panel caught the Home Secretary off guard on a number of points, leaving her open to more questions. She had no doubt she would be called back later to give more evidence. This was the last thing she needed right now.

As she entered her office she made for the decanter of whisky on the table near the window, which showed one of the best views of London. As she poured herself a generous helping of Bushmill's she raised the glass to her lips and looked out of the window at the view. Although the government were in the lead in the polls, the Opposition had been gaining momentum recently, not least because of how the trouble with both the Fire Brigade and Nursing Unions had been going. Both were beginning to receive public support. It was almost as if the UK electorate just did not get it.

Other factors which had swayed the polls towards the Opposition was the news that a back bencher had recently been photographed while coming out of a brothel. This wouldn't have been so bad had the said minister's wife not been eight months pregnant. It was almost as if these men, who had the best of educations, thought constantly with their dicks and even the Prime Minister had an illegitimate child outside of his marriage. It was only a matter of time before the world's press found out. It would be at that point that Elizabeth Price Jones would put herself forward to the party for the top job.

As she looked out of the window her eye caught the photograph of her and her father in a time long since passed. The photograph showed a loving and warm man who had just given his ten-year-old daughter her first horse, Shadow. The photo betrayed what her father was really like, he was a bully through and through. Although he paid for Elizabeth to have one of the best educations in the world, in the best private school in the country, Elizabeth hated the school holidays where she would have to return home to her abusive father and nonchalant mother.

Even her brother, Giles, had feared her father, however Giles had more in the way of favouritism from both of her parents. Not long after the photograph was taken, her father had died of a massive heart attack. Attending the funeral, all the good and great of the business world turned out to show their respects. However, in hindsight, most of them had no real loyalty to her father or her family. In fact, once the money had gone there was very few friends around. Fortunately, her father had paid for her education upfront and she continued with her studies, trying to win back favour on the family name. At the same time, Giles had blown all of his inheritance, and last she heard, he was living in America.

The whole thing made her bitter, bitter against how her father had bullied her and her mother, bitter at the fact her father had died, bitter at the fact her mother had fallen apart soon after the funeral. She was consumed with anger, and this made her more determined than ever to change the world in which she was brought up. Ultimately this left her on a path of politics. Her job was now the UK Home Secretary.

On her desk was a file on Rob Foster. It was a top-secret file as it included not only his medical history but also all details of all his military service. It had been wildly publicised in the news about Foster's escape. The news stories became even more sensationalised when it transpired Foster had been living in Edinburgh working as a minder for an escort agency. At the same time as he was on the run, Foster had handed the Edinburgh police a corrupt policeman. The policeman himself was caught up in drugs, prostitution, perjury. It was a tabloid's dream.

The more the Home Secretary read about Foster, the more she could not help but warm to him, even in her position. However, the fact was, this escapee was her department, as she was responsible for what went on in the Home Office. Again, thinking tactically, this may even affect the polls even further if this situation was not contained. She toyed with the idea that it may be best all around, if Foster was eliminated, but she quickly dismissed this, not least because Rob Foster could be used as an asset. She picked up her phone on the desk and said, "Put me through to the SAS at Hereford. I want to speak to Sergeant Knott immediately."

Chapter Sixty-eight

It was raining as Dr Beaumont entered the reception at Hull Royal Infirmary. She made her way to the Casualty Department and asked the reception where Ricky Foster was being treated. The receptionist looked on her computer and pointed Dr Beaumont to the overnight ward behind the casualty department. It was a Friday night and it was full of the usual drunks, hypochondriacs and overzealous security. As she approached the admissions ward, she introduced herself to one of the doctors behind the desk.

"Good evening, my name's Dr Beaumont. I'm here in an unofficial capacity, as I would like to have a word with one of your patients, Ricky Foster."

The doctor behind the desk smiled and she held out her hand, which Charlotte received. "Hi, I'm Dr Patridge. We spoke on the phone, I believe."

Charlotte was reassured, and both doctors made light conversation as they made their way towards Ricky Foster's bed. Dr Patridge explained that she didn't think Ricky had long, in fact, he had already contracted pneumonia.

The attending doctor pulled back the curtain on Ricky Foster's cubicle, and she quickly glanced over her patient, before saying to Ricky, "Ricky, you've got a visitor here."

Ricky looked up from his death bed to see Charlotte Beaumont, and in almost a whisper he said, "Come in. Sit down."

Both doctors looked at each other and nodded as Dr Patridge left the cubicle and headed back towards her desk, leaving Dr Beaumont alone with Ricky. Dr Beaumont had worked with the dying before during her medical training, however this was a different set of circumstances. It was something she wasn't trained for.

"Mr Foster, my name's Dr Beaumont. I'd like a quick word with you, if I may."

Ricky almost smiled and said, "I know who you are, love. I can still read the papers you know, I'm not that dead." Then he added, "Pull up a chair, love, sit yourself down."

Charlotte did as she was told, and the plastic chair scraped harshly on the tiled floor as she sat down. Then she asked, "Has Rob been to see you, Ricky?"

Ricky looked disappointed and sighed. "I can't help you, love. I've not seen him."

"It's really important. I need to find him. My little girl has gone missing in Africa and the police think he's gone there to look for her. I just don't know what to do with myself." As Charlotte spoke those words, she realised the complexity of the situation.

Ricky replied, "He's stubborn, my son. Once he's got his sights set on something, he won't change his mind. Just like his mother. She was a determined one too. You could say the whole family is bloody minded. My other son did what he wanted to do, damn the consequences."

Charlotte's ears pricked up. "I didn't realise Rob had a brother."

Ricky replied, "Yeah, our Peter. He's a Hell's Angel or biker or something. Last I heard he was working in Liverpool or Glasgow, or somewhere."

Charlotte was surprised. There was nothing in Rob's file about his brother. Then she asked, "Rob never spoke about him, why was that?"

"They had a fallout some years ago, we all did, before my wife died. It was nothing spectacular, just some dolly bird both my sons got caught up with. Our Rob and Peter spent the whole night fighting in the back garden. My wife tried to stop them but I held her back. I told her to just let them get on with it. But it even surprised me how long the fight went on."

"Who won the fight in the end?" Charlotte asked.

"Neither did. I went outside with a pickaxe handle and belted them both. Soon after that Peter left."

Charlotte thought for a minute and then asked, "Would Peter know where Rob is?"

Ricky then started to cough furiously. At the same time spots of blood flew out of his mouth. Charlotte put her arm on Ricky's shoulder.

Ricky then continued, "I doubt very much our Peter would know where Rob is. They both took different paths. Ricky thought for a moment and added, "I can tell you this, if our Rob has gone looking for your little girl, if there's any iota of a chance of finding her and bringing her back, our Rob'll do it. He'll keep just going and going and going, leaving no stone unturned. Nothing will faze my son. Like I said, he'll just keep going and going, completely bloody minded."

It was almost comforting to her what she heard, in fact it was her first time since Amelia had gone missing that she felt reassured in some way or another. Charlotte was about to leave, realising Ricky did not have long, as she stood up, she said, "I'm sorry to bother you with this, Mr Foster. I'll leave you alone with your thoughts."

Ricky looked up and said, "I've not got long left now, love. I can feel it pulling me under." As he spoke, he wearily held up his left hand. "I don't wanna die alone. I reckon I've got a half hour, tops. Will you stay with me until I go?"

Instinctively Dr Beaumont took Ricky's hand and sat down again. Neither patient nor doctor said a word, but Charlotte continued to hold Ricky Foster's hand, his grip getting weaker and weaker by the minute. Within ten minutes Ricky Foster's eyes were closed, his hand had gone limp. Within five more minutes Ricky Foster breathed in for the last time and then gently passed away. All the time Charlotte Beaumont holding his hand.

Charlotte stayed with Ricky for another half hour, at which point she felt it was an appropriate time to leave. As she made her way through the hospital, she thought about what Ricky had told her on his death bed. Walking through the exit, she stopped and took a breath.

Stood at the exit were various patients, some in wheelchairs, some attached to drips, all smoking. She ignored it and looked up into the night sky. Then she whispered, "If there's a God, please help Rob Foster bring my little girl home."

Part Three

Kenya

Chapter Sixty-nine

Rob wasted little time in getting out of Edinburgh. Within half an hour of fleeing the scene he had hotwired a car and made his way down the A1 towards Newcastle. He had nothing in the way of luggage, not that the staff at Newcastle airport were particularly bothered. He did however have over ten thousand pounds in cash, most of which he managed to change into US dollars at the departure lounge at Newcastle airport. The passport which Jessica had provided him with was more than adequate against the unprying eyes of a bored and uninterested border patrol officer who simply stamped his passport and waved him through.

Luck was also on Rob's side as they did not even bother to check him, making sure he could escape the country with his medication. While Rob was at the airport, he purchased several newspapers, gathering what information he could on the missing girl. One even had a picture of Charlotte Beaumont and Amelia together, with Amelia holding a lion teddy bear. Rob still had two hours to kill before departure, so he went to the internet cafe in the departure lounge and researched as much as he could in the way of information that he could get off the net.

Within three hours Rob was on his way to Malaga, the nearest airport to the Costa Del Sol. He felt sure he could get some sort of passage into Africa from there, possibly through Gibraltar. However, Rob did not have a contact so he would have to make it up as he went along. At the same time Rob knew, now he'd left the UK, he was well and truly on his own.

Unbeknown to Rob, within six hours Terry Galagher had men waiting for him. Once Rob was out of the airport and in a taxi, the red BMW followed Rob on his journey to the Costa Del Sol. It wasn't until Rob was nearing the beach that he noticed the BMW deliberately following him. Soon, the taxi was on the strip next to the beach along with all the bars and nightclubs adjacent to the strip. As Rob looked out of the taxi window he started to wonder if the taxi driver was in on whoever was following him. Rob quickly dismissed this but again asked himself why he was being followed, after all, nobody knew he was here.

He asked the taxi to stop just as it was nearing dusk, and tried not to notice as the BMW behind pulled in. Rob started to walk towards the beach, hoping to lose his pursuers. There was two of them, both sporting Everton football shirts with their haircuts to match. Rob crossed the road and in between the bars he found an alley. He quickly ducked down the alley and hid behind a skip. Both men followed. Rob quickly jumped from behind the skip, punching the first one in the face. As he turned his attention to the second assailant, the scouser pulled out a gun. It was a Browning revolver. Then in a soft Liverpool accent he said, "Calm down, our lad. You've just broke my man's nose, you've got nowt to worry about. Our gaffer just wants a quick word."

Within half an hour Rob was sat in a private cubicle in a nightclub called Romeo's along with his two pursuers and Terry Galagher.

Chapter Seventy

Terry Galagher was a villain through and through. His shiny bald head and lines on his face were telltale signs of a man that had a lot to worry about. He sat there smoking a cigar, and drinking champagne, not even considering the no smoking signs in the club. Gallagher didn't care. He would do what he wanted in his own club, and when Harry asked him for a favour, he would deliver. After all, Harry knew a lot more about his past than even his third wife. Too many drunken nights bragging, but to be fair, Harry had never asked him for anything before.

As Rob sat down, Terry looked at one of his henchmen, blood all the way down his shirt. Terry soon realised that Rob was a fighter. He turned to one of his men and said, "Go and get yourself cleaned up."

With that, both men made for the exit, and Rob noticed Terry nod to the second henchman who had the gun. Terry then turned his attention to Rob. "So, you're the lad who's going looking for the missing girl, are you?"

Rob's mind raced. How did this villain even know he was here, let alone what he was up to? He played it down. Rob said nothing. Terry noted.

"I know, lad," replied Terry. "Resistance to interrogation, eh? They teach it in the SAS. I've read Andy McNab," he paused, "I've got a plane taking off. He's picking up a load of blood diamonds. It can drop you off in Kenya, if you want to take it. The choice is yours, lad. It's either that, or you spend the night sleeping on the beach where the local Guardia police will kick the fuck out of you at some point."

For the first time Rob spoke. "Yeah it sounds like a better option."

Terry nodded and finished his cigar, then replied, "Okay then, lad, follow me up to my office."

Terry made his way through the club, as Rob followed. Some of the customers didn't know who he was, others looked on in awe. Everyone made a beeline. Soon, Rob and Terry were in his office along with the two henchmen who had followed Rob from the airport. Terry sat in his leather chair behind his desk and offered Rob a seat. Then he turned his attention to his heavies. "Get this man a Jack and coke and get me one while you're at it."

As Rob tasted the alcohol, it felt good and warm and for a second Rob started to wind down as Terry was talking. Rob did not notice the henchman behind him with the cloth in his hand covered in chloroform. Soon the heavy with the gun had covered Rob's mouth and nose, and within a second Rob was unconscious. He would not wake until several hours later.

Chapter Seventy-one

Elizabeth Price Jones had met with Sergeant Knott of the SAS and was quite happy with the way the Foster investigation was going. A woman in her position had little difficulty in tracking Foster using all at her disposal, including MI6 and GCHQ. She even had an agent on the ground when Rob was picked up by two heavies in the Costa Del Sol. Sergeant Knott explained how he was just about to pass Rob for SAS when he fell apart at the last hurdle. Other than this, Rob was a fully trained SAS operative. Again, this was political music to Elizabeth Price Jones's ears.

Fortunately, there was a meeting with the prime minister at Chequers this weekend. Most of the cabinet would be there, but it was an ideal opportunity to corner the PM, and explain how Rob Foster's breakout and evasion from capture with the view to retrieving the lost little girl, would be an ideal news headline. It could even be covered up under the guise of an SAS operation. Sometimes the mere mention of the SAS were good ratings figures for whichever government was in power.

As Sergeant Knott was also aware of what Rob Foster was up to by this stage, he explained that once he found the girl the best way back to the UK would be across the Mediterranean. The Home Secretary took this on board and knew full well that HMS Iron Duke was in the area, captained by Jack Middleton. If things went according to plan it could be a good outcome all round. Then she questioned herself, what would be done about Foster on his return?

Rob felt like he was in a large coffin when he awoke. Both his legs and his arms were shackled together with plastic seals, plus he had a dry mouth. Soon however, he realised he wasn't in a coffin, but was in a light aircraft. The aircraft was bare, with the exception of the two pilots in front. Rob noticed that one was a woman and the other pilot manning the controls was broad and stocky. It was the woman who noticed Rob staring at first. Soon she was pointing a pistol at him. In a South African accent she said, "This is a tranquiliser pistol. If you try anything, this'll knock you out for another six hours, so just behave until we get where we're going."

The other pilot looked over his shoulder at Rob but said nothing and returned to flying the plane. As Rob looked out of the window in the light aircraft, beneath him he saw what looked like a mixture of sand, shrubbery, and occasionally the odd wild animal. The pilot was obviously flying low to avoid radar. At the same time Rob knew he was flying south by south-west, because of where the sun was in the sky. Rob turned to the woman and asked, "Where we going?"

She looked at him, still with the weapon in her hand, then replied, "We're not going anywhere. You're getting dropped at Mandera Airport in Kenya. Should be another three or four hours depending on weather."

Then for the first time the male pilot spoke, again with a deep South African accent. "Just sit tight and keep your mouth shut. We won't ask you any questions so don't ask us any. Maybe we'll let you live, eh?"

Chapter Seventy-two

Mandera Airport looked just as Rob had imagined as the pilot taxied the runway. It was sparse, basic and obviously did very little in the way of security. As the male pilot went to check in at arrivals, the female undid Rob's restraints. Rob managed to check his pockets, he still had three vials of his medication and it looked like he still had all his money in US dollars.

The South African woman just looked at him and then said, "Off you go." Rob doubted there would be CCTV in the airport and so covertly as he could he made for the fence. Once out of the vicinity, Rob needed to find where Amelia and her father were staying. There may be signs or evidence as to where they had been taken. After doing his research at Newcastle Airport, Rob knew the name of the farm where both were housed. He climbed in a taxi, and went straight to that destination.

It was getting near dark when Rob arrived, and there was almost a chill in the African air. Rob asked the taxi driver questions on the way to the farm and he soon discovered the farm was regularly rented out via a contact at Mandera Airport. "That was worth knowing," thought Rob to himself, the chances are that the contact must have been in on it.

Whilst at the farm, Rob sat and waited until it was fully dark. He quickly scaled the fence and it was obvious which hut Amelia and her father had been placed in as there was a police line over the door. However, nobody was guarding it. Rob ducked under the police tape, entered the shack and closed the door behind him.

Once inside, he felt for a light switch, the welcoming click lit up the room. The furniture was on its side and there were obvious signs of a struggle. Rob then checked the other rooms, and noticed the back door was also unlocked. It was obviously planned. Rob then returned to the living room. On the floor, matted into the carpet, was a large stain of dried blood. Rob quickly realised they had severed Jonathan's arm in this room. He'd seen enough.

Rob made one last inspection of the room. As he removed the cushions from the sofas, he found something that made his blood turn cold. It was a lion teddy bear, and Rob remembered the photograph he'd seen of Amelia with her favourite toy. He picked it up and put it in his pocket. As covertly as he could, he turned off the light switch and made his way back towards Mandera. The next thing was to find a room for the night. Once he'd done that, he'd return to Mandera Airport and look for the travel agent.

Chapter Seventy-three

Rob had found a cheap and nasty room for the night in a basic hotel near the airport. He'd checked in using a false name. Not that anyone at the African Castle Hotel was interested. Rob was up early the next day, had a quick breakfast of cereal and was at Mandera Airport for seven a.m.

Rob bought a British newspaper and then sat in a corner and waited. Most of the kiosks began to open at nine a.m., but the kiosk Rob was most interested in, with the word 'Safari' above it, did not open until half past nine. Rob spotted the African opening the shutters and just from his body language alone Rob knew from instinct that this man was involved. He did not want to move too soon, so instead he carried on with his newspaper and watched.

During the course of the morning several people approached the kiosk. Rob noted as sums of money were handed over, and at the same time, the African from behind the counter would direct them personally to the taxi rank. Rob saw a pattern emerge, the fourth person who the African directed to the taxi rank, Rob decided to follow. From a distance, he could see the host packing them into a taxi, then the agent walked around the corner. Rob saw him get into a yellow Fiat. This type of vehicle was common in Africa. The African sat in the car smoking whilst on the phone. Rob saw his chance.

Rob circled the vehicle from a distance. He then began to approach from behind, but out of view of the mirrors. Just as the African had finished his call, Rob opened the car door. Before the guy had time to react, Rob was in the seat next to him, and with his right hand, punched hard into the man's temple, knocking him out cold. Rob felt for a pulse. He wasn't dead. Rob knew he did not have a lot of time. He looked around to see if anyone else was in the staff car park, there was no one. He took the keys from the culprit's pocket and then as quickly as he could, opened the boot.

The guy was thrown in the back along with the spare tyre, the jack and other travel items. Soon, Rob was driving away from the airport to interrogate his prisoner. No one in Mandera Airport would notice a thing.

Chapter Seventy-four

Rob found what he was looking for within ten miles of leaving Mandera Airport. It was a discrete location. In fact, the last town must have been five miles away. Rob parked a kilometre away from the main road on an old dirt track, surrounded by a handful of trees. He opened the boot, the guy was awake but weary. Rob grabbed him by his shirt and pulled him out of the vehicle. To get his attention he kneed him in the groin. "What's your name?" Rob asked.

"Abass," he replied wearily. "What have I done, sir?" he continued.

"What happened to the little girl, Abass, that was taken with her father."

Abass's eyes turned to the right as if to think of an excuse, it was a giveaway sign to Rob knowing full well that whatever was going to come out of Abass's mouth now would be a lie.

"I know nothing, sir, honestly, I know nothing! Ask police! Ask police! I know nothing!"

Abass was still weary and was no way capable of stopping Rob. Rob took Abass's arm and twisted it and with his left arm punched the shoulder, breaking Abass's arm straight away. Abass screamed out in pain.

"Okay, hurt me no more, hurt me no more," screamed Abass.

Rob remained calm throughout. "Okay, tell me what you know."

"I sold the Englishman the holiday to Safari. I put them in the car. I do not know more than that, sir! I think they were taken by the East Side crew!"

Again, Rob knew from instinct that Abass was lying. Rob began to squeeze where the arm was broken. At the same time, Abass howled again in pain.

"Okay, okay, I know, I know. The leader of the East Side crew is Mousa. He asked me to get him white girls. He pays me good money if I tip him off."

"Well done, Abass," replied Rob. "What else can you tell me about him?"

"He lives in Somalia, he is a powerful warlord, I think he will have taken the girl to be traded on the market."

"Do you know whereabouts in Somalia that Mousa lives?" demanded Rob.

"I can't say, I can't say, he'll kill me!"

Rob squeezed Abass's arm harder.

"Okay, okay, Baidoa, I take you there!"

"How long does it take to drive to Baidoa?" Rob asked

"Eight or nine hours!"

Rob punched Abass again. This time he grabbed him by the hair and forced him back towards the rear of the Fiat. Rob checked Abass's pockets for his mobile phone, and when he retrieved it, slung Abass back into the boot. Rob now had a clear idea of where his target was. He slammed the boot door down on Abass, and climbed back inside the vehicle.

He checked the fuel gauge. There was just over half a tank. Hopefully there would be a filling station on the way. Rob put the car into first gear and started towards Baidoa. Rob's objective was now clear. Hopefully he would find the girl. Rob also hoped he would get the chance to kill Mousa.

Chapter Seventy-five

The road to Somalia was long, hot and dry. After he had left Mandera boundary, the road almost became a dirt track. Occasionally Rob would see the odd people carrier or truck. Rob consciously made a point of checking the mirrors to see if he was being followed, but there were no obvious signs of a tail. All the time, the odd blast of wind would come on the road scattering red dust across his path. After two hours, Rob had found a filling station. Rob knew full well he would be able to pay in US Dollars.

Once he had filled the car and paid the attendant, he selected a few cold drinks from the fridge. The food in the same fridge did not look like it was safe. The last thing Rob wanted was to have the trots all night. Returning to the Fiat, Rob took out Abass's phone. He googled the address for Mousa. At this stage, Rob did not know if it was in a built-up area or a discrete location. When Rob clicked onto Google Earth, it was a mixture of both. The houses looked old and run down, almost like a shanty town. However, there was a certain distance between each individual letting. Rob doubted very much if any of the neighbours would come out if they heard a commotion. This was all in Rob's favour.

Rob looked at the clock. It was two p.m. With any luck, he should reach Mousa's house by nightfall. Rob just hoped Amelia was still there. He put the Fiat in first gear and rejoined the dirt road, never once bothering to check on the culprit involved in the boot.

Chapter Seventy-six

As Rob drove on and on towards Somalia, the road became more worn. However, the vegetation started to change. As opposed to dust roads, there was more in the way of greenery. Rob did not know where Kenya ended and Somalia began but he was sure it must be close if he had not crossed it already. The further east he went, Rob made a point of checking for road signs. Also, Rob had to plan what to do if there was a checkpoint. In this part of the world, it was doubtful that there would be one, but there was always a chance.

Soon, Rob saw a sign for Badoia and estimated it was about an hour away from his objective. The closer he got, the more stressed Rob became. Every scenario that he could think of, ran through Rob's mind. Just as it was getting dark, in the distance Rob saw various lights. Rob figured some must be street lights, others must be for the local Seven Elevens. He took out Abass's phone, and typed in Mousa's address on the SatNav, in theory, this should take Rob straight there.

With Rob's heart beating with anticipation, soon his palms felt sticky with sweat against the steering wheel. Rob turned off what was left of the highway and made his way through what appeared to be some sort of industrial area. Following the directions for another ten minutes, Rob appeared to be in some sort of plantation, with houses on either side of the road. When they were built, Rob reckoned they must have been worth quite a bit of money, however, now they looked run down, almost a ghetto. Rob noticed there was a couple that were empty and looked like they had been set on fire.

The phone beeped telling Rob he had reached his destination. He saw the house in front of him, there were three vehicles parked outside. He carried on and drove straight past slowly, taking in as much detail of the location as possible. He saw a corner and turned right and hid in the side street. "This is where everything came into play," thought Rob to himself.

Once he had parked the vehicle and killed the lights, he took a few more sips of water and sat and thought for no more than five minutes. Rob looked up into the night sky and noticed the moon. It was almost blood red and part of him remembered what he had done to that poor bastard in the park. He had to shut it out of his mind and carry on with his objective. He opened the side door, climbed out of the vehicle and opened the boot. Abass was clearly weakened by the long drive and extremely dehydrated. Rob pulled Abass out of the boot and handed him a bottle of water. Abass quickly ripped open the cap and hurriedly gasped in between mouthfuls, almost finishing the bottle within two seconds.

Once Abass had recovered, although he was weary, Rob spoke softly. "Now you're going to help me!"

"Yes, sir, yes, sir, I will!"

"I want you to ring Mousa and tell him to send his men to Mandera straight away. Tell him another shipment of Westerners has arrived. However, they're only staying for twenty-four hours. Tell Mousa there's four women, three girls under seven and two men. If you do that, I'll let you go."

Abass was beaten. He could not even contemplate reasoning with Rob. Rob handed over the phone and Abass was more than happy to oblige. Rob listened intensely to every word Abass said to Mousa. When he was finished, Rob took the phone from Abass.

"I can go now, sir, you said, we had a deal."

Rob thought for a second: "We do have a deal, Abass, but for the time being I need you to get back in the boot."

"No, please, sir, I help you, we have deal."

"Just get back in the boot, and everything will be okay, Abass."

Begrudgingly, Abass did as he was told. Just before the defeated Abass returned to his cage, Rob noticed a hosepipe in the boot next to the jack. He quickly retrieved it and then shut the boot down on this man responsible for pedalling in children.

Rob returned to the front of the car. He looked in the glove box, but there was nothing. Instead he looked on the back seat. Again, there was nothing he was looking for. Then he saw in the passenger footwell, on the floor, was an old dusty set of mats. Rob removed it, then exited the vehicle. Tactically, Abass could give Rob away at any point.

Rob knew there was no way Abass could be trusted all the time he was alive. Rob began to secure the hose to the exhaust pipe. At the same time, he ripped in half the mat from the footwell and placed it round the rest of the exhaust. He then ran the pipe to the back window. He would down the window slightly in order to feed the hose into the vehicle. Once he was satisfied that everything was secure, Rob turned the ignition and carefully shut the driver's door. Covertly as he could, Rob just walked away, leaving Abass to his fate.

Chapter Seventy-seven

Rob walked into the night back in the direction of Mousa's house. It was dark and there was little in the way of street lighting, however the moon lit up the objective. Everything was in Rob's favour. However, was Amelia there? Would he have to go further into Somalia to find her? Not to mention, what type of mental state would the little girl be in? Rob felt in his pocket, and he still had the lion cub teddy bear, it was almost a comfort to him as what it would have been to the little girl.

Adjacent to Mousa's property was an empty house. Rob took cover near the porch so he could watch Mousa's men. The less men guarding the girl, the easier it would be to deal with. All the time, Rob noticed his breathing, but at the same time, a peaceful calm had come across him, almost as if this was his life's work. The fact was, all Rob had ever known since leaving school was how to kill people. He had learned these lessons well and effectively, and even Rob would admit to himself, at this stage of the game, he was a ruthless killer.

Rob's calm was suddenly broken when he heard the sound of a squawk overhead. Rob recognised it instantly. It was the sound of a guillemot. Within a second of its defiant cry, the bird landed on the roof of the objective. How it had got this far inland, was anyone's guess, but it was here. In fact, it was almost a spiritual guide telling Rob he was in the right place. Rob carried on watching as the bird sat staring on the roof of Mousa's house straight in Rob's direction. Occasionally, the bird would shout one or two squawks, almost as if they were aimed at Rob, but definitely defiant.

Within half an hour, four men had appeared at the front of Mousa's house. All four climbed into two of the vehicles that were parked outside, leaving just one vehicle. At the door, Rob saw the silhouette of a tall African. Rob assumed, this must be his target. However, he still did not know where Amelia was. Within two minutes, the vehicles had driven off into the night, and the whole neighbourhood was quiet again, with the exception of the guillemot who was in no way fazed by the sight of four killers leaving the house. Covertly as he could, Rob made his way across the street. As he approached Mousa's house, he looked around for points of entry.

As he made his way around the back, there was nothing but rubbish in the back yard, and a pitiful looking fence. Carefully, Rob climbed over the fence, and from a distance looked in the windows. The first room was empty, despite the light being on. Covertly, Rob made his way to the left of the house, and again looked through the windows. This time, Rob saw his target. There was a sofa, an old box TV in the corner and what appeared to be a half-naked stoned woman passed out on the floor. At the same time, Rob watched as Mousa smoked what appeared to be a crack pipe. At this stage of the game, Rob did not think there was anyone else in the house. However, to make sure, Rob peered through every other window. Again, he saw nothing.

Carefully, he made his way to the front door. If need be, Rob would kill the woman too, but for the time being, he would deal with Mousa accordingly. In theory, someone high on crack would be immune to any pain, but it also meant their reflexes were slow. The wooden panels on the porchway creaked as Rob made his way to the front door. Placing his hand on the handle, Rob gently twisted and soon the door became open.

Chapter Seventy-eight

The first thing Rob noticed as he entered what appeared to be the hallway, was the noise blasting from the TV set in the living room. Rob looked around for signs of a weapon. Initially, he saw nothing, but moving further into the house Rob found the kitchen. Still conscious of his surroundings, Rob looked for a knife, and quickly found what he was looking for. Then there was the dilemma. Should he kill Mousa first and then look for the girl? Or, look for the girl and then deal with Mousa? Once Mousa was dead and, if the girl was not in the house, Rob would have no idea how to get to Amelia.

Carefully, Rob left the kitchen, the blade still tight in his fist. As he made his way gently towards the stairs, he saw the living room to his left. Carefully making his way towards the stairs he peered in and saw both its occupants almost passed out. The woman was obviously a prostitute of some kind, and at the same time Mousa didn't seem to take his eyes off the TV screen. He would deal with them both later.

As lightly as he could, Rob began to climb the stairs, carefully taking one step at a time. Were there other people in the house still? How would he deal with them if they were? Rob began to kick himself. He needed longer to do the recce, but he was here now, therefore he would have to adjust and overcome. With each tread on the stairs, there was a slight creak. The house was obviously showing its age. Slowly, he reached the top of the stairwell.

The upstairs looked just as much of a slum as the downstairs. Carpets were worn. The walls were dirty. However, there was little in the way of furniture. At the top of the stairs there were three doors to the right. Rob carefully opened the handle on the first door. Inside was a bathroom, again, the filth was evident. As quietly as he could, Rob closed the door. He moved along the corridor, all the time conscious of his footsteps.

Opening the second door, the room was bare, with the exception of a bed with a dirty mattress. There wasn't even a carpet in this room. However, Rob noticed dirty syringes on the floor. Again, Rob closed the door and made his way towards the third room.

Slowly turning the handle, the door opened. Amelia was here. The little girl's arm was secured to the bed by a makeshift chain. She was curled up in a ball, but it was obvious that this was Charlotte Beaumont's daughter. She had a bruise on her right eye, and several cuts and bruises on her legs. Rob knelt down beside her. She looked at Rob with fear, and it was obvious to Rob that the little girl was traumatised. With his left hand he held his fingers to his lips and whispered softly, "Amelia, I am a friend of your mummy's, I've come to pick you up and take you home. First of all, I need you to do something for me. I need you to be quiet, just for a few minutes until I come back."

The little girl said nothing. It was almost as if there was a distance in her eyes. At that moment, Rob could hear footsteps coming up the stairs. Although the steps were not light, Rob did not think they belonged to Mousa. As the steps were getting closer, Rob braced himself to thrust the knife into whoever it was. At that moment, he heard the bathroom door open. Rob saw his chance and quickly stepped out onto the landing. Just glancing as the little girl looked up at him. Rob could hear the trickle of someone urinating. Then the toilet flushed. Rob quietly placed the knife on the floor.

From out of the bathroom appeared the stoned prostitute. As she saw Rob, her eyes widened, and she was just about to scream when Rob covered his hand over her mouth and pulled her towards him.

The prostitute began to fight. Rob secured a holding around her head. Then, just as he had been taught, he yanked her head upwards and twisted to the right, breaking her neck and severing her windpipe. The body stopped moving instantly and the neck was obviously broken. As delicately as he could, he laid the lifeless woman on the floor. "One down!" thought Rob. Now he had to deal with Mousa.

He picked up the knife from the floor and went back to check on Amelia. Again, Rob held his finger to his lips and quietly whispered, "Just stay here, I'll be back in a minute." All of a sudden, Rob felt a sharp pain across his back, and he fell to the floor. He looked up and saw Mousa standing there.

Chapter Seventy-nine

"You killed my woman, white man! You're gonna die very soon." Rob ignored the comment and tried to pick himself up off the floor, at the same time as trying to reach for the knife. Mousa launched at Rob, almost winding him as he fell back to the floor. Rob could hear Amelia begin to cry, and at the same time punched Mousa several times in the face. Mousa was now on top of Rob. The iron bar which Mousa was holding was now squeezing against Rob's neck. Mousa then began to shout. "I am the Warlord of Somalia, I am a general of all I command. You are the oppressor, for that you must die, white man!"

Rob looked into Mousa's eyes, the retinas were almost yellow, but Rob could see Mousa was off his face and high on whatever he had been smoking, but Mousa was strong. Rob punched Mousa again and this time connected with his jaw. The force was so strong, Rob saw two of Mousa's gold teeth spit out onto the floor. At the same time, Mousa's mouth began to bleed profusely. Rob felt for the blade on the floor and grabbed the handle. With all his might, Rob thrust the blade into Mousa's right leg. For the first couple of seconds, Mousa felt nothing. Then all of a sudden, he let out a howling cry. Rob twisted the handle of the knife. Mousa stepped back off Rob, dropping the iron bar.

The knife still hanging out of his thigh. Rob saw his chance. He grabbed the iron bar and with as much force as he could, swung towards Mousa's temple, knocking Mousa out cold. Mousa then fell to the floor. Rob was still not sure if he'd killed him.

Rob looked at Amelia, the little girl had stopped screaming but was obviously in shock. Rob unchained Amelia from the bed. The little girl almost appeared frightened of Rob and almost fought against him picking her up.

"Try not to worry, Amelia, I'm trying to get you home safe. I'm a friend of your mummy's, do you understand me?"

Wearily, the little girl just replied, "Okay."

Rob continued. "I need you to do something for me now, Amelia. We're gonna go outside, but I need you to close your eyes just whilst I carry you downstairs. I want you to close your eyes and think of your mummy and daddy." It took no longer than a second for the little girl to comply, and Rob wasted no time in carrying Amelia across both bodies and down the stairs into the hallway and outside to where the last vehicle was. The door was open, and Rob placed the weary little girl in the passenger seat.

He checked the back of the Jeep and found what he was looking for. It was a petrol can. It clinked as he removed it from the boot. Then Rob quickly glanced at Amelia. He didn't know if she would run away, and then he remembered the teddy he had in his pocket. As he handed it to the little girl, he whispered, "I need you to be really good for me, Amelia, will you wait here until I come back, and then we can go and see your mum."

Again, the only reply was, "Okay."

Rob continued, "Can you promise me you'll wait here?"

And as she held her teddy bear, she looked at Rob and replied, "I promise."

Rob returned to the house with the petrol can, and wasted no time in returning to where Mousa fell. He quickly doused Mousa in petrol, and at same time Mousa began to groan as he came around. Rob did not want Mousa getting away. With what was left of the chain attached to the bed which held Amelia, Rob secured Mousa. Hopefully, the chain would hold until Mousa had burnt to death. Mousa began to plead. "White man, don't do this."

Rob just ignored him. Rob then removed the blade from Mousa's thigh and carried on dousing petrol around the room. Then, he grabbed Mousa's hand and held it up to the wall. Mousa looked at

Rob, wondering what was coming next. Within a second, Rob thrust the knife into Mousa's hand, the force was such that the blade stuck into the wall, with Mousa's hand attached. With a howling scream, Mousa cried.

Rob closed the door behind him leaving Mousa doused in petrol chained to the bed and pinned to the wall. Rob began to slowly make his way down the stairs, running petrol throughout the house. In the living room, Rob found the lighter. Also, a set of keys for the Jeep. Rob torched the petrol at the foot of the stairs and the flames wasted no time in reaching their objective. Soon, Rob could hear Mousa's screams in agony as the flames burnt into his body. Rob felt nothing as the fire did its work.

Rob quickly made his way to the vehicle and saw Amelia cuddling the teddy bear. Rob wasted no time in getting inside the Jeep, however, once inside he quickly looked to the top of the house. The guillemot was still there, however it was getting ready to fly off. Almost in a goodbye, it squawked one more time at Rob, then it flapped its wings and flew off into the night.

Rob put the car in reverse. For a second, he stopped and continued to listen to the screams, and then as he turned the car, he put it in first and put his foot on the gas. Part one of his objective was complete. Now it was time for part two. But how the hell was he gonna get Amelia safely out of Africa?

Chapter Eighty

It didn't take long for the boffins at GCHQ to track Rob's location. Abass had been under suspicion for some time, given his connection to the missing girl. As such, his phone was being tracked, along with his phone calls. As soon as it became apparent Abass's phone was heading towards Somalia, GCHQ tracked it and it didn't take them long to realise the connection to Rob.

Twelve hours after Rob had seized the girl, satellite images over Somalia picked up the damage Rob had done. It showed the extent of the severity of the fire done at Mousa's hideout. They continued to track the phone and it was obvious Rob was heading north. Just as Sergeant Nott had suspected.

This was all music to Elizabeth Price Jones's ears. Not only had the child been rescued, but politically it could be a great coup for the government, as long as it was handled correctly. In the meantime, the Home Secretary contacted the PM to keep him abreast of what was going on, on the ground.

All Rob had to do now was make his way to the Mediterranean without any problems. It was obvious to all concerned, that a man of Rob's skills should easily be able to make his way to the Med with their being few obstacles in his way. All the Home Secretary had to do now was wait. However, she knew full well it was not a done deal.

Chapter Eighty-one

As Amelia and Rob headed north, the little girl said nothing, which was hardly surprising given what she'd been through at such a young age. However, Rob did not know how to be with children generally, so all he could do was to not engage with her for the time being. She needed time to process what she had been through. Also, she had to know that Rob was not her enemy. Ultimately, Amelia had to trust Rob.

Eight hours into the journey, the little girl had not slept, but tiredness was beginning to catch up with Rob. Initially, after he had freed the little girl, he was completely wired, as if he'd had too many cups of coffee. However, now, several hours into the journey, Rob struggled to keep his eyes open. It was another two days drive north west to Sudan. The main thing for Rob, was to cross the border into Ethiopia. He still had his passport and his medication, but most importantly of all, he still had the US dollars that he had stolen from the bent copper's house and changed at Newcastle Airport. It was these US dollars that were going to get them both home. Rob looked across at Amelia. She'd fallen asleep. That was good, it meant she could rest.

It wasn't long before Rob reached the Ethiopian border. He wasn't sure what checks would be done here. By all accounts, it was a poor part of the world. Rob took a $100 bill out of his wallet and as he approached the checkpoint, prepared to pay handsomely to be let in to Ethiopia, leaving Somalia behind. He doubted very much, in this part of the world, that the border would have an ethical conscience.

Just as he suspected, the border guard was more than happy to take the $100 bill and almost rushed Rob into the country. Soon, Rob had found a cheap and nasty hotel. He pulled into the basic car park, then picked up the sleepy little girl. He looked around him to see if anyone saw him, then he made his way up to the room. Placing the little girl into the single bed, Rob then laid on the floor. Absolutely shattered, Rob fell asleep within a minute.

Chapter Eighty-two

Rob woke with a start. It was daylight outside and his mouth was dry. Although he had slept, it still took him a minute or two to realise where he was and what he was doing. He looked across to the bed, but Amelia was gone. Then, within a second, he heard the toilet flush in the bathroom and the door opened and Amelia came in. Rob was relieved beyond words.

The little girl looked up to him and smiled. "You snore! You woke me up! My daddy doesn't snore as much as you do!"

Rob smiled and said, "I'm sorry, Amelia, I was very tired last night. Now just sit on the bed because I need to tell you something."

Amelia did as she was told immediately, at the same time, she picked up her teddy bear and listened to what Rob had to say. Rob did not want to remind her of what she had been through so got straight to the point. "Amelia, it's very important, you listen to what I tell you, and it's really, really important that you do what I tell you to do, because I don't want any bad things to happen to us."

"Okay," replied the little girl.

"Also, we've got a very long way to go before we get home. It may take us a lot of days, and it might be a bit scary now and again, but if you do as I tell you, you'll be back home with your mummy and daddy before you know it."

"Will Mummy be coming to meet us?"

"I have to get you back into Britain first, and then I'll get you to your mummy as quick as I can, but I want you to promise me, like you promised me at the house, that you will not walk off or go anywhere without me."

"What, even to the bathroom?"

"No, you can go to the bathroom, but I'll have to be very close by when you do, but you must promise me that you will not go anywhere or walk off without me."

"Okay, I promise."

"Okay then, Amelia, give me a few minutes, and then we'll get going."

Rob quickly freshened up in the bathroom. With all the stress he'd been through, he did not know whether to take more of his medication early. He checked the box and only two of the syphons had not broken. That would last him about six to eight weeks. Again, Rob toyed with the idea of giving himself another injection, but in truth, he did not know how long it would take him to get out of Africa and into the Med. So for the time being, the medication could wait.

The sun was baking hot as Rob and Amelia left the hotel. Rob looked at Abass's phone. The nearest city to their location was Raaso. Rob would make his way there and see if he could bribe a pilot to take him to either Egypt or Libya.

Chapter Eighty-three

DI Denman had received little in the way of commendation for her actions in Edinburgh, in fact, after ten years in the police force, it was the biggest bollocking she cared to remember. Not even during police training had she received such chastising. The way her superior talked to her, she assumed it would not be long before she was taken off the Beaumont case. This made her want to continue even more. The hierarchy of the police could kick her out of the force if they wanted, but she needed to get this last case closed. She had dealt with many cases in her career, some were horrific, however this case in particular stuck in her throat, because it was not resolved.

The hierarchy were more concerned because Denman had not followed protocol, but the way the DI saw it, she had a gut feeling and more than this, she knew she was right. In the cop movies, they called it a hunch, but this was more than a hunch. She did what she had to do, and she would do it again given the circumstances. Damn the consequences.

As she sat at her desk, she noticed how some of her colleagues refused to engage with her, almost giving her the cold shoulder. She had no doubt the gossip would be all over the office floor when her back was turned. 'Fuck the lot of them,' she thought to herself. 'I did the right thing'. Just then, the phone rang. It was a relief from the disassociation from her colleagues.

"DI Denman, Met Police."

"This is Margaret Bernard, the Chief Constable's Secretary, can you come up to my office right away, the Chief Constable wants to see you immediately."

The DI replaced the receiver, picked up her handbag and headed to the door for what she thought was her execution. As she was summoned, all she could assume, was that she had been sacked from the force. As she took the lift to the top floor, every scenario was going through her mind, should she tell the Chief Constable to shove his job up his arse, and that he was a jumped-up, stuck-up, pompous little bastard anyway. In honesty, that's how she felt. Diplomatically, should she take another route? Should she beg to be kept on, at least until the case was resolved. How would she word that without losing her dignity?

A mixture of emotions ran through Denman's body as she knocked on the secretary's door. A polite, "Come in," was the response, and she turned the handle to see Margaret Bernard, the Chief Constable's secretary. Almost smiling, Bernard simply said, "DI Denman, go straight in, he's waiting for you."

Chapter Eighty-four

Denman did as she was told, lightly knocking on the door before she entered the room. It was a similar set up with the Chief Constable in Edinburgh. The usual memorabilia were scattered across the office. Pictures of the chief shaking hands with royalty, the usual pictures of the 2.4 children obvious on the shelves. However, on this occasion, the chief had another visitor, he was a tall man in a dark suit, probably early fifties.

The chief looked at Denman and almost smiled. "DI Denman, take a seat, and before we begin, I need you to sign this document."

This took her aback. "What is it I'm signing, sir?"

It was the third man in the room who answered. "It's an updated version of the Official Secrets Act. What you're about to be told cannot leave this room," there was a pause, and then he reiterated, "Ever."

"I don't mean to be rude, sir, but who are you?"

The Chief replied, "Denman, you're in enough shit as it is, sign the document, and sit down." The Chief's tack had definitely changed.

Denman signed the document and then handed it to the Chief Constable. Just at that moment, the third man picked up the document, shook the Chief Constable's hand, and headed for the door.

"We'll catch up soon, Walter," were his parting words, and then he took Denman by the hand. His grip was firm, but cold. "DI Denman, good luck with the rest of your career." The third man then closed the door behind him, and was gone.

"His name's Campbell," said the Chief Constable. "He's a senior officer in Five."

"Five?" questioned Denman. "As in, MI5?"

"I've gotta be honest with you DI, you were right on the money to let Foster go, and as it happens, it's not only helped a situation develop, this could also forward your career."

"Has Foster found the girl, sir?"

"He's done more than that. Not only has he freed the girl, but he also killed the people that took her. The intelligence we've received indicates Foster and the Beaumont girl are out of Somalia where she was taken to, and are heading north. Had you not let Foster go, there's a good chance the little girl would have been trafficked as a sex slave. Well done, DI. You went with your gut and the result is positive.

However, I cannot reiterate to you enough that nobody knows about this information. The Home Secretary rang me personally today to make sure you understand, also, if all goes to plan, you'll be having a meeting with the Home Secretary to discuss further options."

"Where's Foster now, sir?"

"This is why nobody can know, we do not have a fixed location. What we do know, is the Beaumont girl is with Foster and we're assuming they're heading north. All Foster has to do now is get her into a safe country. Interpol will take it from there, and at the same time, we'll issue an arrest warrant for Foster."

"With respect, sir, Charlotte Beaumont will have a nervous breakdown if I don't fill her in on developments."

"This is a direct order, DI Denman. Nobody is to know anything. This includes Charlotte Beaumont, Johnathon Beaumont, any of your colleagues, and if you do not follow this order, you will be punished to the limit of the law. I do not need to remind you, that breaching the Official Secrets Act, can result in a lifetime in prison. Do you understand me, DI?"

"I understand, sir, but what should I say should Charlotte Beaumont call me?"

The Chief began to get annoyed. "Either don't take the calls, or tell her we're investigating."

"Is that all, sir?"

"For now, as soon as there's any change, I'll let you know."

"Yes, sir," and the DI stood up, and headed for the door.

As she entered the outer office, and closed the door on the Chief Constable's office, she whispered the word, "Bastard" under her breath. Then she looked to see Margaret Bernard had overheard her.

Margaret smiled again and said, "He's like that sometimes when he's not had a coffee in the morning."

Chapter Eighty-five

Rob scanned the horizon of the Mediterranean taking in its beauty for all it was worth. He was on the coast of Egypt, a country which was at war with itself. He was less than fifty miles away from Libya. How he had managed to get here, surprised even Rob, but fortunately he and Amelia were still together and by all accounts Amelia was holding up very well. It was about five a.m. as he scanned the horizon and the sun was well and truly up and burning into the golden sands of the coast. Also, the sun beat down on all the other refugees which surrounded Rob and Amelia. There must have been fifty in total, mostly men, with about ten women and children.

Rob stood out like a dot on a domino, as he was the only white person there. Fortunately, whilst in Raaso, Rob had managed to buy Amelia a burkha. She was tall for her age, and the burkha covered up the fact that she was white. To be fair to the little girl, other than saying a handful of times that she was really hot and thirsty, the Arab clothing had not bothered her in the slightest. Rob almost suggested to Amelia if she put the burkha on, it would make her invisible. Generally, the cover story worked, however this was a different set of circumstances.

The gangsters Rob had paid to join the refugees in dangerous boats to cross the Mediterranean were ruthless, almost bloodthirsty, but by no means were they stupid. Nothing was said regarding Amelia, but looking in the eyes of one or two, it was obvious they wanted to see who was hiding under the veil.

From a distance Rob could hear motor engines and it wasn't long before three shoddy looking motor vessels were approaching the shore. Rob doubted himself. He'd come so far, bribing a pilot to bring him and Amelia to the north of Egypt. In theory, he should have had enough US dollars to get him and Amelia home, but the pirates had taken the lot. Rob knew the score. Most of the time these gangsters would bribe refugees, promising a future in the west, only for them to be working as sex slaves in brothels across Europe, or the men used as drug runners, mainly for the Russian cartels. That was, of course, if they survived the journey across the Med.

Rob looked at the sea. It looked dangerously calm, and the red sky above indicated that a storm was due soon. With no money and no alternative, Rob had zero option but to smuggle himself along with the rest of the refugees. Rob quietly cursed himself and under his breath said, "Fuckin' hell, I've come so far. Don't let it fuck up now. Amelia is counting on me."

Just then, Rob heard the cocking of rifles. He held Amelia's hand and turned around. Every rifle was a Kalashnikov and five of the gangsters were aiming them straight at the refugees. This included Rob and Amelia.

Chapter Eighty-six

The leader of the gangsters began to shout in Arabic to all the refugees. Rob could not understand what he was saying, but it was obviously an order to get into the floating death traps that were approaching the shore. Slowly, everyone started to walk into the sea with the exception of one young Arab. He stopped and began walking up to the leader to protest. The leader said nothing, an iciness in his eyes, then nodded to his henchman on his right.

Within a second, the Kalashnikov burst into life and at the same moment, all the crowd began running towards the boats. Nobody bothered to look behind to see the protester. His lifeless body at the end of its journey. Rob picked up Amelia and headed for the raft which looked to have the most stability. There wasn't much choice but at least this raft had spare fuel, or at least it had two fuel cans. There was no cover in the raft. There was nothing in the way of food or shelter. Rob hated to admit it, but he was starting to feel afraid that he and Amelia would be lost at sea.

Soon, all three rafts were heading out towards the north. Rob did not know if his next destination would be Turkey, Malta or possibly even Italy, or whether or not his next destination would be a white shark's stomach. The further out to sea the raft travelled, the larger the swell. As the Mediterranean rose and fell like a fun park ride, Rob held Amelia. The raft was packed and it was not designed for fifteen people. More like three or four at the most. Rob whispered some insurance to Amelia. "Are you okay? Just a short trip across the sea and we'll be home."

"Was there not enough room on the boat for the man that got shot?"

Rob did not know the answer he should give, so instead he just responded, "Try not to worry about that now, it won't be long before we're back home, I promise."

Amelia looked at him through the gap in her burkha. Her eyes were definitely like her mother's. It reminded Rob of why he was here. After all Charlotte Beaumont had done for Rob, he had to fulfil and complete this last mission. He knew full well, he could not live with himself if Amelia died. His own death didn't bother him, it was the business he was in. Just as he looked away from the little girl's glazing eyes, he noticed water beginning to seep in, albeit slowly, through the panels. Rob said nothing, but held the little girl that bit tighter.

As he looked to the horizon, he noticed the waves getting bigger and bigger. It wasn't long before the storm came.

Chapter Eighty-seven

Captain Jack Middleton left Gibraltar two days earlier. The orders were to pick up a refugee boat, identify one of the refugees as Rob Foster, then as soon as the other refugees were dropped in Sicily, to make full speed back to Portsmouth. Jack Middleton was a confident but calm sailor. He never went along with the crowd, not that it was important, but it made him stand out as an officer.

Middleton had the respect of all the sailors underneath him and he enjoyed his role as Captain of HMS Iron Duke. As he sat on the bridge, Middleton read the orders once more. They had a fixed location on Foster's position. However, the mobile phone signal was all they had to go on, and even that was getting weak. Foster was about one hundred miles north of Egypt, however, given the wind direction, the position seemed to be sliding north west. Foster was in international waters now.

Middleton took his first officer aside and explained to him the scenario. Everything was top secret, but in honesty, that's how Jack Middleton liked it. The less people that knew, the less questions were asked later. All the crew were told it was a routine humanitarian mission to look for refugees. They would then be taken to a safe zone and await further instructions. Middleton could feel a smoke break coming on. Fifty-seven years of age, and it was the one vice that he enjoyed when at work.

Jack was the captain of the Iron Duke, no one was going to tell him off for having a smoke. As he left the bridge, he headed for the outer deck, lit a cigarette and looked out at the sea. She was his mistress. He estimated it would take two days to reach Foster. He thought to himself, 'This should be an easy job,' as he took another drag on his Benson and Hedges.

Chapter Eighty-eight

Rob had no idea how they had survived the storm. Every wave that crashed against the makeshift raft sent a shiver down Rob's spine. It was made worse due to the fact it was night. It would not have been so bad had the raft been seaworthy, but the fact was, it was only good for firewood. By now the storm had passed and Rob held Amelia for all she was worth.

During the storm, the two other rafts had become separated and Rob was sure he could hear screams in the dead of night only a few hundred yards from his location. As to the whereabouts of the other raft, Rob had no idea. Everyone was scared, even the pilot looked like he was ready to get off as soon as he could. In reality, he was just as much a victim as the circumstances his masters had put him under.

Rob took out Abass's phone from his pocket. Turning it on he could see the signal was weak, however he looked for an app which would tell him how far he was away from land.

Just then, Amelia shouted, "Look, dolphins!"

Rob looked to the right to see fins sticking out of the clear blue waters. There were two of them. Rob knew straight away they were not dolphins. It was two sharks that were circling the vessel. They must have been drawn to the craft from the scent of urine in the water. It drew them quicker than a moth to the flame. Rob played along with Amelia, pretending that they were dolphins. Rob and Amelia must have been at sea for eighteen hours now. Both of them were hungry, wet and tired, however, given the circumstances, Amelia seemed to be quite chirpy. This in itself was a great comfort to Rob.

In the distance, just beyond the horizon, a flare shot up into the sky. The pilot was startled and revved the engine away from the flare, almost directing the floating coffin back towards Libya. Rob looked again and there was a second flare. In the distance two crafts were approaching. "Thank God," Rob said under his breath, "We're saved."

It took the Royal Navy less than a minute to catch up with the craft in their highly efficient motor craft. At the helm of the first craft, was obviously a Royal Marine. Behind him were three of his colleagues armed with SA80 assault rifles aimed right into the refugees' direction. It was the same with the second motor boat. In less than a minute, the Navy had attached a rope to the bow of the craft. A third raiding craft approached and soon all four vessels were making their way towards a warship in the distance.

Although the Navy had given everyone on Rob's craft an orange life vest, none were allowed to leave the vessel. There was one raider pulling the craft, one behind on the stern and one starboard side with Royal Marines aimed toward the refugees. As all the craft began to approach the vessel, Rob could easily recognise it as a type 23 frigate. It was HMS Iron Duke.

Chapter Eighty-nine

Rob and Amelia were the first to be taken to the mess deck and given medical treatment. The Royal Navy had wasted no time in removing everyone from the floating death trap. Within an hour of every party being back on board HMS Iron Duke, the marines had left explosives in the refugee raft and sunk her to the bottom of the Med. One less raft for the smugglers to use. Amelia looked to be fine, although she was tired and a bit weary, however she was impressed and felt important to be on such a special ship, as Rob had told her.

Rob gave his medication to the nurse and it was quickly administered. Rob and Amelia were then escorted by two marines to a bunk and a female rating was left with Amelia. Rob was then taken to see the captain. On seeing Rob enter the bridge, Captain Middleton's first words were, "You're a sorry looking sea dog."

Rob was tired and weary but just responded, "How did you know where to find me, sir?"

Middleton acknowledged the address of 'sir', it meant a certain mark of respect, in fact, it had scored Rob a few brownie points. "We tracked the phone you had from Somalia. It seemed obvious to someone in Whitehall that you'd be coming via the Med. My orders now are to place you under arrest and hand you over at Portsmouth after we drop the rest of the refugees at Sicily."

"What happens to the girl?"

"Again, she'll be handed over to the Navy police at Portsmouth and then taken back to her parents." Jack thought for a second as he looked at Foster. "You've done a hell of a lot to help that family, I don't suppose you'll get many thanks once you get home, but well done, it's a good result."

"Thank you, sir," replied Rob. "If it's okay, I'd like to be kept with the girl until we reach Pompey."

"There'll be a wren attached to your quarters for the duration of your journey, if you need anything, ask her, she's under orders to report directly to me. Also, I have Royal Marines on standby, I'm assuming I will not need them. I take it you understand me."

"Absolutely, sir," replied Rob.

"Okay, go get yourself cleaned up, the galley will sort you out a meal. Well done again, Foster."

With that, Rob left the bridge and made his way back to the sleeping quarters. He checked in on Amelia, then got a quick shower. The wren saw to

Amelia's needs, helping her shower and dressing her in a clean navy shirt. Portsmouth was three days sail away. Rob slept for most of it.

Chapter Ninety

DI Denman had been summoned by Elizabeth Price Jones to Whitehall. Also, she was under orders to pick up Charlotte Beaumont from the Union Jack Club in Waterloo. MI5 had ushered her down there in the night. Denman pulled up at the hotel and parked on the double yellow lines adjacent to the Waterloo Pub. Security soon let the DI in once she showed her credentials and Charlotte Beaumont was in the lobby, looking absolutely shattered.

As soon as Charlotte saw Denman, she questioned, "What's happened?"

Denman could not stand to lie to this woman in her darkest hour. 'Fuck the Chief' Denman thought to herself, 'I'm telling her'.

"There's been a development, Charlotte, we think we've found Amelia. That's all I can tell you for now."

Soon, both doctor and police officer were making their way across Central London to

Whitehall. It would not be long before both were sat in the Home Secretary's office.

Elizabeth Price Jones was pleased. More than pleased. It was just the story the government needed to remain ahead in the polls. Not only had the little girl been found, but also, she was alive and, by all accounts, well. There were, however, a few loose ends to tie up. The fact was that the DI policewoman, with her instinct, had saved Amelia's life. However, being a politician, and a Home Secretary at that, it was best not to acknowledge it to her.

As for Charlotte Beaumont, as far as she was concerned, the government had just saved her little girl. It would be very easy for her to sign the documents that needed a signature on. Once that was wrapped up, there would be the usual photographs for the tabloids, but the question still remained: What must she do with Rob Foster?

Charlotte Beaumont and DI Denman were quickly ushered through at security. The senior politician even came to greet them at the office door, putting on her best empathetic and public smile. Denman could see right through it. A copper of ten years more experience, it wasn't surprising, but Charlotte was just numb. All three ladies sat in comfortable chairs next to a fireplace as Price Jones's secretary brought them all a coffee. The Home

Secretary then announced, "The SAS have found your little girl, Mrs Beaumont. She's alive and well and will be arriving in Portsmouth very soon."

Charlotte took in the information, almost dropping her coffee cup and began to cry profusely. The Home Secretary saw her chance, and quickly put her hand on Charlotte's. It was a skilled orchestrated manoeuvre, in order to win over her compassion. Although not completely unwarranted, after all, Elizabeth Price Jones was human, but she also had her eyes set on the PM's office.

Denman was the first to speak. "Are you saying Rob Foster is SAS?"

The Home Secretary started to blush, holding her tongue.

At that point, Charlotte Beaumont rolled her eyes and said, "Yeah, it figures."

The Home Secretary saw her chance. "DI Denman, thank you so much for your assistance on this case, you will be pleased to hear that you will be put forward for commendation. However, I would like to speak with Mrs Beaumont personally, if you would not mind, could you give us this room?"

The DI stood up, knowing full well that the Home Secretary was after something, however the Beaumont case had gone far better than anyone had expected. What was the point in rocking the boat now?

Politely as she could, the DI said, "Yes, ma'am," and headed for the door.

Charlotte looked up. By now the tears had gone. "We will catch up soon."

Denman looked at the Home Secretary and Charlotte Beaumont for one last time, and she closed the door. It was a good result.

Chapter Ninety-one

It was about eight a.m. when HMS Iron Duke docked in Portsmouth Harbour. Both Amelia and Rob enjoyed the view of coming in from the Solent. In the distance, Rob could make out a submarine in the dry dock. He pointed it out to Amelia "That's HMS Alliance, it's an old submarine they used to use many years ago."

"What's a submarine?" Amelia asked.

"It's a special boat that sails underwater without being seen."

"Does that mean it can see dolphins?"

Rob smiled for the first time in a long time. "Yeah, I suspect it can see dolphins." Rob looked around him, there was only Amelia and Rob on the deck. Rob did not want Amelia to see him handcuffed by the Navy police, who he had no doubt were already in the dock waiting. Rob then said, "Amelia, I bet I can get you off this ship without anybody noticing."

"How do you mean?" replied Amelia.

"Well I'll make a bet with you that I can hide you and get you on the other side of the water without anybody noticing."

"I bet you can't!"

"Do you want to try it?"

Amelia thought for a second. "Yeah, okay."

Rob took the little girl by the hand and said, "Come with me then."

Walking through the ship, it wasn't long before Rob had found what he was looking for. It was an old sailor's kitbag, a handle on the side and a twisted rope at the top. Also, he found a Royal Marine's uniform with a green beret to match. Soon he was walking down the gangway with Amelia hidden in the Navy holdall and, without being noticed, quickly walked past the Navy Police towards the exit.

Captain Jack Middleton was informed within an hour that Rob and Amelia had gone missing. Middleton was neither concerned or bothered in the slightest. He simply stood on the bridge, a strong, hot tea in his hand and a cigarette between his fingers.

"How could he have got away, sir?" said the junior rating.

"It's what he's trained to do, sailor."

"You don't seem concerned, sir."

"I don't think I am, to be honest. I'm thinking about my retirement."

In the distance, Jack Middleton could make out the Gosport Ferry. On the top of the ferry Jack could easily see the uniform of a Royal Marine with what looked like a seven-year-old girl next to them. Jack then turned to the sailor and said, "Yes, I think I'm going to retire."

Chapter Ninety-two

After disembarking at Gosport Terminal, Rob and Amelia held hands as they walked down the high street. Rob knew this area well, as he had done some diver training here with the Royal Navy during selection, not much, but enough to get his bearings. It wasn't long before they both reached South Cross Street Police Station. Rob looked down at the little girl. The mission was done and he hated having to leave her. He knelt down and held the little girl. "If you go in here and tell the policeman who you are it won't be long before you see your mummy, I promise."

"Are you going to come and see me again?"

Rob felt his heart in his mouth, however, he still could not cry. It was almost as if that was behind him now. "Maybe one day our paths will cross again, but in the meantime, tell your mummy I said hi and that our paths will cross again soon."

Rob then held open the door for the little girl, for what he felt would be the last time. As the door began to close, Rob was about to walk off when Amelia shouted, "Wait!" Rob stopped in his tracks as the little girl ran towards him. In her hands she pulled out her teddy bear. "Will you look after Bo Bo for me?"

Rob felt a frog in his throat. "I promise," replied Rob.

The little girl then headed back into the police station. The sergeant behind the desk wasted no time in looking for Rob Foster. The little girl had not even been in the station for fifteen minutes when every officer in the area was looking for him. They could not find him. He had disappeared.

Part Four

Hull

Chapter Ninety-three

Callum Squire was on his fourth sambuca shot in the ex-serviceman's club in Hessle. As he was banned from the Admiral pub, which in turn meant he was banned from everywhere except from the Ex's. The amphetamine that he had took earlier that night was starting to wear thin, however, he still had two wraps in his coat pocket and was hoping to persuade Rachel to come back to his like he had done the week before.

The fact was, Rachel did not know what she was taking and just as she had fallen asleep on Callum's sofa, she woke to find the animal on top of her. She wanted nothing to do with Callum. As Callum approached her, Rachel made for the door. Rachel stepped into the night, with Callum in pursuit. As she crossed the road, Callum followed, calling after his prey. In the spur of the moment, Rachel turned to Callum and said, "Not tonight, Cal, time of the month I'm afraid, maybe next week!" As Rachel walked off, Callum was going to try his luck with other victims in the club. Just as a tall Asian guy approached him from behind. In a polite Indian accent, the Asian guy addressed Callum. "Excuse me, is it Callum? Can I have a word?" he said.

Callum replied, "Yeah, what do you want, Paki?"

Within a second, the Asian guy pulled a cloth out of his pocket and covered it over Callum's face. The rohypnol only took a matter of seconds before Callum was incapacitated. No one saw as the Asian guy bundled Callum in to the back of the Ford Transit van. Callum would be out for some time yet. The Transit then drove off into the night.

Callum did not know where he was when he woke up. It seemed to be some sort of metal container or box. He could hear a person behind the curtain, and there was a big light at the foot of what appeared to be some sort of bed that he was strapped to.

"What the fuck's going on?" shouted Callum.

With that, the curtain drew back and Callum could make out a figure wearing surgical clothes. Callum began to feel afraid, especially as he could not move.

"You're awake," proclaimed the dark-skinned figure in doctor's overalls. "That's good!"

On a tray at the foot of the bed appeared to be several surgical implements. Callum turned to his tormentor. "Look, mate, what the fuck's going on? I think you've got the wrong guy, mate. And besides, I'm well connected, do you know what I mean?"

The Asian guy said nothing as Callum continued to squirm sentences together. Then Callum asked, "Look, mate, who are you?"

The guy pulled down his mask revealing his full face and he looked at Callum in the eye. "I'm a friend of Rob Foster, my name's Jimmy Crisp, however, some people call me The Surgeon."

On hearing Rob's name, Callum began to look frightened and began to wet himself. The Surgeon noticed Callum leak all over the floor. Then he continued, "I'm going to remove your spleen, however, I have not done it before so you'll have to bear with me. However, I'm sure I can successfully remove it without affecting your intestines. After that, if I have time, I'm going to do some work on your pre-frontal cortex it's a part of your brain you won't be needing."

Nobody could hear Callum's screams from within the container that was dumped in a farmer's field two miles from the nearest living soul. The surgical drip that the surgeon had placed in Callum's arm meant that Callum felt every slice of the surgeon's knife without passing out. Callum underwent the most horrific torture for the next five hours. The end result was that The Surgeon was pleased with his work.

Chapter Ninety-four

THREE WEEKS LATER

Westbourne Cemetary in Hull was quiet. It was nine a.m. and it was raining. Rob looked wearily at Simon Grant's grave. Rob did not know why he came, but felt he had to. Reading the headstone, it gave Simon Grant's date of birth, the epitaph underneath read: 'Taken too soon, missed forever.' The headstone was obviously new. It could have not been put there more than a couple of days ago.

Rob just closed his eyes and tried to pray. The scars from that night almost a year ago were still vivid. Rob would always be a marked man by the Grant family, however there was nothing Rob could to do to rectify anything that had happened. Rob began to question himself again. Had he not killed Simon Grant, would Amelia be dead? It was a question that went on forever.

Rob pulled out a mobile phone from his pocket and rang his solicitor Laura Allison. "Laura, it's Rob Foster. Can you talk or are you busy?"

"I can talk, Rob, but you need to hand yourself in."

"Can you come and get me?"

"What do you think, Rob."

"Yeah, I know, we're all Hannibal Lecters."

"It's not that, Rob, I can meet you at the police station, but I can't pick you up. It may be misconstrued and I could get disbarred for aiding and abetting. Where are you anyway?"

"I'm in Hull."

"Rob, the best advice I can give you is to hand yourself in straight away."

"I'm going to, Laura, believe me. Will you still represent me?"

"Of course, I will, but I can't help you until you hand yourself in. If you want, I can ring the police and they can come and get you."

Rob looked down at the grave, all the time still on the phone to his lawyer. "Okay, I'm gonna hand myself in, I'm gonna go for a pint first."

Rob hung up the phone, took one last look at Simon Grant's grave before he said the words, "Sorry, mate."

Then he walked away.

Chapter Ninety-five

Harry was reading the newspaper at about eleven a.m. in the Admiral. The headline read *'SAS Elite rescues British Child'*. The doors had just opened, and Rob walked in. Harry held up the paper and said, "This owt to do with you?"

Rob smiled and shrugged. Harry continued, "Take it you want a pint."

"Like you wouldn't believe, mate, feels like my throat's been cut."

As if on cue, Harry began to pour Rob a Guinness, then Harry said, "I can't help you any more, Rob. You're gonna have to go round the back, also, I've not seen you."

"I know, mate, I just wanted to have a couple of pints, I don't think I'm gonna have the chance to have another one for a while. I'm gonna ring the hospital from here, they'll come and pick me up."

"Yeah, okay, Rob, but remember: I've not seen you."

Rob held the pint to his mouth and it felt refreshing, almost touching every nerve in his tongue. He almost downed half the glass before leaving the bar and making his way towards the back room. There were the usual bar flies in the pub, the seasoned alcoholics whom Harry could set his clocks by. Also, there were Joss and Gary, both long haired rockers, in early to get drunk and play pool.

Rob took a seat in the corner and pulled out a mobile phone. Rob then rang Charlotte Beaumont.

"Charlotte, it's Rob, I'm gonna hand myself in."

Charlotte almost took a deep breath as she heard Rob's voice for the first time since their last meet at the hospital. "Where are you, Rob?"

"I'm having a pint in the pub."

"Is it the Admiral?" Charlotte questioned.

"Yeah"

"Wait there, I'm on my way."

Within half an hour, Charlotte had walked into the Admiral. She looked at Harry, but he pretended not to see her and went round the back. Charlotte saw Rob for the first time in eleven months. He looked well, considering. However, keeping her composure, she looked at Rob and said, "Give me two minutes." She then returned to the bar and ordered a pint of Guinness. Sitting down next to Rob, she said, "I think I owe you this."

"How's Amelia doing?" Rob asked.

"Remarkably well, from a psychiatrist's point of view. From a mother's point of view, I'm never gonna let her out of my sight ever again."

"I think you better give her this," and then Rob pulled out the lion teddy bear from his pocket. "I've washed it, but I think it's best she has it."

Charlotte smiled as she placed it in her handbag. "I'll make sure she gets it, Rob." Charlotte then said, "Rob, I want you to know, I was with your father when he died. His last words were of you, and he went peacefully."

Rob took another sip of his Guinness. "It was probably best that way. He wouldn't have wanted to see me, on his death bed, handcuffed, with two guards." Rob put his pint back on the table, and asked, "Is the husband okay?"

"We're both doing fine. I don't wanna talk about that anyway."

"So what happens now, do I go to Rampton? Will they ever let me out?" replied Rob.

"Rob, I want you to know I can never repay you for what you did and I know full well you put yourself in the firing line by going after Amelia, but also, there's something I need to show you."

Rob drained the rest of his glass and picked up his fresh pint, at the same time, Charlotte removed a large envelope from her handbag. Rob could not help but notice that the envelope said 'Operation

Turngate' with the words 'Top Secret' in red. "The Home Secretary has asked me to give you this, but there's certain conditions. You're to be badged as an unofficial member of the SAS, E Squadron I think she said, Deniable Operations. Also, I'm to be your handler. As your psychiatrist, I know if things are going wrong or not, and I'm to make sure you get your medication."

Rob replied, "Does that mean you're my new boss?"

"Yeah, basically, it does. I had to sign an official secrets act and I'm to tell you, you've got two choices. You either join the SAS or you go back to hospital. So what you gonna do, Rob? What do you want to do?"

Rob smiled, "I'm gonna finish that pint."

Joss and Gary had finished their game of poo[?] not noticing Charlotte or Rob and certainly [?] knowing why they were there. Joss approache[?] jukebox just as Gary shouted to his mate "P[?] 23-a on. It's Iron Maiden." With his long r[?] covered in a vampiress tattoo, Joss push[?] buttons. Soon, the quiet in the pub wa[?] the scream of, "Can I play with madne[?]